loving cee cee johnson

loving cee cee johnson

LINDA LEIGH HARGROVE

MOODY PUBLISHERS
CHICAGO

© 2008 by
LINDA LEIGH HARGROVE

Most Scripture quotations are taken from the King James Version.

Other Scripture reference: the *Holy Bible, New International Version*®. NIV®. Copyright © 1973, 1978, 1984 by International Bible Society. Used by permission of Zondervan. All rights reserved.

Editor: Kathryn Hall
Interior Design: Ragont Design
Cover Design: Linda Leigh Hargrove
Cover Images: www.photos.com < http://www.photos.com >
Author Photograph: Kendra Cleavenger

Library of Congress Cataloging-in-Publication Data

Hargrove, Linda Leigh.
    Loving Cee Cee Johnson / Linda Leigh Hargrove.
      p. cm.
    ISBN-13: 978-0-8024-6270-1
    ISBN-10: 0-8024-6270-7
    1. Women television journalists—Fiction. 2. African Americans—Fiction. I. Title.

PS3608.A735L68 2008
813'.6—dc22

                                                        2008015175

1 3 5 7 9 10 8 6 4 2

Printed in the United States of America

to my husband

Prologue

BROTHER WAS SCREAMING. He had come from the front of our trailer, running faster than the time that black snake chased him down the lane. He hid behind some of the bushes at the edge of the woods next to Fat Anne's double-wide.

I could see his little body shaking from where I sat with my older sister, Tabby, on our back step. He was a fast little rabbit for a six-year-old but he wasn't very smart. Daddy was sure to find his little tail hiding right there at the edge. He had run and hid in the bushes before and it was always because a beating was coming.

Tabby wiped the back of her hand across her smile, filled with satisfaction. Even in the shade, I could see the red marks from the cherry-flavored punch on her dark skin. They curled like single cherry quotation marks on either side of her mouth. She had already finished two jars full. The greedy alligator!

Tabby leaned forward and wagged her finger at the dusty boy in the brush. "He gonna get it this time. We need to teach him how to hide better."

I giggled. The rumble of the sound mixed with the tinkle of ice in my half-empty punch jar. I was drinking slowly, savoring every moment, letting the frosty droplets that covered the bottom of the jar drop on my bare knees.

"Brother, come back here," Mama yelled through an open window. She called him Brother. Well, we all did. Not Junior. Not Quincy Jr. Just Brother. I thought that was funny.

I was smiling about her calling him Brother when the music started. It was suddenlike and way too loud. Daddy's music. Some slow, sensual tune. One of the 45s he'd bought from the records Miss Emily sold in the back of her grocery store downtown. *Sade, Barry White, Earth Wind and Fire.*

Mama yelled again. "Oh no! No, Quincy!"

Then there were sounds of crashing, breaking. And then a shriek.

I closed my eyes but it didn't stop my mind from replaying the bloody memories from the last time Daddy beat her.

"Tabby, Cee Cee!" she yelled to us through a window. "Girls! Find Brother. Run. Hide!"

Hide! My mind raced but I didn't, couldn't move. *Hide?* Tabby yanked me up.

"My jar! What about my jar?" It was my favorite, an old familiar canning jar from Grandmamma. I looked at Tabby's, a broken shell on the bottom step.

Tabby gritted her teeth and barked at me, "Come on!" She yanked harder on my arm. I let my glass slip from my fingers. Tabby was big for twelve and, it seemed, at least twelve times as strong as me.

Brother was already running when we reached him; Tabby grabbed his arm anyway. The movement snapped his little round head back.

"Tree house," Tabby panted.

I wrenched myself free. "We gotta tell somebody."

"No!" Tabby reached for me again.

"Miss Dusty. I'll tell her and meet y'all at the tree house."

"No!" shouted Tabby.

"But, Mama . . ." I tried to reason with her.

"I'll go to the grader for Mr. Abraham after I get y'all to the tree house. Now come on," Tabby said with all the authority of an older sister.

The cucumber grader was on the other side of Thirty Foot Road. That was too far away. Anything could happen to Mama by the time Tabby got back with the big white man.

"No!" I screamed back over my shoulder.

Miss Dusty was a better bet. I could see Miss Dusty's old Ford pickup in back of her trailer halfway down the dirt lane that ran along the edge of the woods.

"I'll meet you there." I looked back to see Tabby crouched with Brother behind a big pine. She was breathing hard. Hate in her eyes.

"Cee Cee, you better come straight to the tree house. You hear me!"

Miss Dusty was my classmate Violet's mama. The mother of five was always working. In fact, I was surprised, but grateful, to see her truck that day. She was forever willing to help Mama and us when we needed it. Though Mama only took her help grudgingly, saying the word *trash* under her breath.

Violet met me at the door. The sun slanted in across her bright yellow hair and her light blue eyes. She looked like a fairy princess; except, that is, for the black eye. It wasn't fresh; just a puffy, yellow half-moon under her left eye, but I still winced when I saw it.

"Mama's not here," she said, anticipating my question.

I looked at the truck and saw for the first time that one of the rear tires was gone. The metal parts of the wheel were sitting up on cinder blocks.

Broke down as usual, I thought.

The TV was blaring behind her but I could hear her daddy snoring; kids were yelling and throwing mess around. "Y'all's phone working?" I asked.

She stepped out onto their cinder-block steps and closed the door carefully behind her. I couldn't see why since half the screen hung from the frame.

"Naw. Why? What you need it for?"

I didn't respond. Suddenly I was embarrassed or maybe just not certain what she could do to help Mama. My mother's screams made me jump.

I took off running for home. Violet followed. She stumbled into me when I stopped. I was beyond words at the sight of my father making a fire in the trash barrel behind our trailer. Mama sat on the bottom back step. By the way she was crying, I could tell Daddy wasn't just taking out the trash.

He reached into a cardboard box at his feet, pulled out a large brown envelope, and tossed it in the fire.

Mama's book.

Tears filled my eyes. My mother had been typing on it almost every night for months. "Grown folks business," she would tell me whenever I asked to read it. Now it was gone.

"Good God A'mighty," Violet whispered and covered her mouth.

"What?" I followed her gaze.

Violet had seen what I didn't at first. Daddy had a gun. As he turned the evil thing, barely bigger than his hand, it glinted like fresh tar in the sun. He pointed it toward Mama and pulled something else from the box on the ground.

My Jesus statue.

I had recited the Twenty-third Psalm flawlessly for the vacation Bible school lady and received all nine inches of that sanctified plastic at the First Baptist Vacation Bible School on Freeman Street. That meddling white-Negro church, as Daddy called it.

More things from VBS went into the fire. Tabby's drawings of Noah's ark and Brother's replica of David's slingshot. Then three tiny New Testament books. All consumed by the flames.

I didn't hear Tabby and Brother coming through the bushes. Neither did I notice when Violet left. I used my sleeve to wipe at my tears, choking on the smells from the trash barrel. Thick smoke climbed into the air. Nearby pine trees had begun to drop their needles from the heat of the fire. What else had Daddy put in that fire?

"Where'd Violet go?"

"Cee Cee," Tabby hissed, shaking me like she did when it was time to get up for school.

"He's burning it all, Tabby."

"Come on, I gotta get y'all to the tree house."

I followed numbly, thinking of Mama's bare feet among the broken pieces of Grandmamma's canning jar and Jesus in the fire, along with Mama's novel and all our VBS treasures.

Chapter 1
Twenty years later

⚭

MY DADDY was no good. But it wasn't until recently when I realized that it was my father, a dark figure in my early childhood, who had influenced my belief in Christ.

Sometimes it's hard to remember things from my youth. Like when and how I stopped sucking my thumb . . . when I got my first cycle . . . when I learned to whistle. It's not that I'm that old, I kid myself. I've just had a full life of words and sounds and smells in all my crazy adventures, traveling around the state on assignments.

In the quiet moments—the few I have these days—I try to remember the unstable times of the late eighties. Those times when my "occasional" father would show up and show out.

Those times when my mother would try to be sane and strong—like she thought a black woman should—for her three children and the man who had drained her beauty away. But I've found that when I attempt to collect the sights and sounds again, either the memories don't come or they come back to me all jumbled.

In any event, it's always a smell that triggers the memories for me. And you know how smells can be. They catch you so unawares. And then the memories flood back, strong and plentiful, like tears that suddenly begin to flow for loved ones who have long since passed away.

The memories of that day—that day I proudly held the image of Christ in my little brown hands—were set off by the smell of burning plastic that was all around me.

It all came back to me as I stood on the streets of downtown Raleigh, primping for the camera. I motioned to my cameraman, Bob, to give me five minutes to myself. The sanitation engineers would just have to wait for me to immortalize them with my journalistic genius.

I am so my father's child, even though I cringed at the very thought of it. Demanding, everything had to be my way. But capturing these memories was too important for me. I was certain they would still be burning trash on the front steps of City Hall five minutes from now. But the words, the tears, the joy and anger inside me at this very moment were sure to be gone.

So I sat down on dusty concrete in my dark blue pants and made notes about that fire-darkened Jesus figurine that had caused me to look hard for the true Christ during my college years.

Bob turned his ball cap around and hoisted the camera to his shoulder. "You're crazy, Celine."

He was a good kid. One of the few guys at the station whom I could tolerate. Fresh out of some West Coast film school, he had a good eye and could swing a half-decent camera. But most importantly, he wasn't a tattletale. We'd had a few tangles since he came on six months ago but I'd seen worse rookies.

"Just a couple more minutes." I turned a page in my journal.

"Like last time." His sarcasm was pretty obvious.

"Don't let the Man dictate your genius, Bob," I shot back.

He chuckled and turned on the camera. "You are too crazy. Don't make me look bad."

Bob had dated my housemate for a brief time, a focused little Asian-American named Ming. He'd hung out at my house and eaten my food. I guess that made him feel like he knew me, like he could talk to me as though we were buddies or something.

I flashed him a frown and returned him the favor. "I'll make you shine, white boy."

Later, with the last of the late-evening sun glinting through the thick magnolias across Glenwood Avenue, I sat listening to the radio and thumbing through my journal.

I'd taken a shower after work and changed into sweats. My hand had brushed the lump in my breast as I pulled the tank top on. It seemed larger. I hadn't touched it really—not since that first time I saw it two days ago poking out like an egg under my skin.

Call your doctor.

There was that little pesky voice again. I left my journal beside my cold chicken dinner and went out onto the tiny porch. Across the street, a scruffy musician played his harmonica in front of Lilly's Pizza.

Water bubbled over fake stones in the small fountain in the corner of the porch. The thing had been Ming's idea of ambiance. Cicadas screeched from the trees overhead. The bustle of rush-hour traffic was nowhere close to fading.

Call the doctor.

I closed my eyes against the tears and let the sounds and smells of other people's lives cover me, trying to push the fears of death away.

When I tried to pray again, three words came to my heart like water washing over stones: Listen, Learn, Love. They were words that had haunted me since my childhood.

Dear God, make Yourself plain. Please help me live and not die.

Chapter 2

"YOU REMEMBER John Manning, don't you?"

It was my mother. *Ten o'clock on a Friday night and she wants to call me and be chatty*, I thought. This just wasn't a good time for me. It had been a long and trying week and all I wanted to do was get some much needed rest.

"No, Mama."

"Yes, you do. He was in your grade. No, wait a minute. That was his brother, James. Well, actually James was his half brother. Sort of."

"Mama, I'm tired."

She continued on as though she hadn't heard what I'd said. "John Manning was a couple years ahead of you. I need to pull out the yearbook."

Not right this minute, Mama.

"What about John Manning?" I asked.

"What's wrong, Cee Cee? You sound tired."

"Did he die or something?" She was always calling me when someone died. Like I needed proof that the population of Pettigrew was shrinking.

"Who?" she asked.

I sighed and braced myself for all the details about how

he died in a farm accident or got burnt to death while fighting underground peat fires. In her mind these were the things I should be reporting.

"John Manning, Mama. Did he die?"

"Oh no. He ain't dead. He's written a play."

"That's nice." I yawned. Bob and I needed to be in the mountains by nine in the morning to do a little piece on the annual flower show held in Ashe County. I needed sleep, not the latest dirt on some small-town wannabe playwright.

"It's about you and your daddy. And that burnt-up Jesus you used to have. And that day . . ."

Her voice trailed off, like someone had a hand around her throat. Words failed me. I sat up and fought the urge to hold my breath.

"Celine?"

Why did the world need to know about that day? The day my father tried to burn Jesus out of our family and had ended up burning down half the trailer park, with Violet's father trapped in his living room.

I never understood my father. Never dared get close enough to him to ask him what drove him to do it. He died of lung cancer in Central Prison. There was a grave in Pettigrew not three months old.

Truth be told, there were things I didn't fully comprehend about that day. But I had no desire to know the whole story. No one else needed to know it all either. His was a story that didn't need to be out in the world for everyone to be reminded of. No one needed to relive that dreadful day.

And who was this John Manning? Why did he feel so passionate about exposing that dark day? What did he hope to gain? Maybe it was heat from some skinheads or some Black Panthers behind this. Daddy had made enemies on both sides. Bringing my father's dealings to light would ruffle those feathers again but that wouldn't lead to a trail of money or fame.

"Most town folk don't want it put onstage. But I do." She paused. Was there pleasure in her voice? "I want you to read it. I could get him to e-mail it to you."

"I don't want to read it, Mama. And I don't want anyone else to read it either. Don't be giving out my e-mail to strange folk, Mama."

❉ ❉ ❉

My mother was a hardheaded woman. That's what I decided as I opened her e-mail on Sunday afternoon. She'd sent it minutes after our conversation Friday night but I'd been out all day on Saturday in pursuit of the perfect story. And then on Sunday morning I'd been running behind six crazed three-year-olds in children's church. That major event was followed by a Web site coaching session with the church's secretary for the umpteenth time.

Opening my mother's e-mail had been the last thing on my weekend to-do list. But there it was—a forwarded message from the playwright himself.

A file was attached. I clicked the link to download it. I would glance at it, I decided, and e-mail her back to tell her how unsuitable it was.

John Manning?

As I sat waiting for the virus scan to finish, I puzzled over the name. I vaguely remembered James Manning. He was a grade below me. He had an annoying laugh and a big head and had moved away when I was in tenth grade. Somewhere like New York. James was hard to forget.

But *John* Manning? I couldn't place John.

The phone beside my computer rang. I picked it up without checking caller ID.

"Hey, Cee Cee? Did I wake you up?"

"No, Mama."

"Got company?"

She always seemed to think I napped too much and didn't have enough friends. The virus scan had finished and I double clicked to open the file.

I sighed. It was only a matter of time before she asked me about the e-mail attachment. "No, Mama, but I'm expecting a return call from an escort service any minute now."

"Well, I won't be holding you long."

My humor was wasted on my mother. I glanced at my computer screen. The file had finished opening. The first page read: *Black Jesus: The Quincy Johnson Sr. Story* by John Carter Manning.

I froze.

John Carter. I knew a John Carter; or rather, I knew of someone named John Carter. The John Carter I remember was a boy three or four years older than me who had big white teeth and dark hair down his back. It seemed like he never failed to have a blonde girl on his arm. He was the big, silent type.

I felt so stupid. Was Carter his middle name and Manning his last? I was about to ask my mother but she cut me short.

"I forgot to tell you to RSVP to the Pettigrew Homecoming."

"You're gonna have to tell me what that is, Mama." I glanced at my watch. Almost 4 p.m. Bob was due to come by in half an hour with some Asheboro Zoo footage on a story we'd inherited from a reporter on maternity leave.

I glanced around at the stacks of papers and books in my tiny office. I'd need to hide a few things before he arrived.

"The Pettigrew Homecoming. I told you about it."

I rolled my eyes and wedged the cordless under my chin so I could get two hands under the stack of manila folders on my scanner.

"Tell me again." I blew air and waddled to the hall closet.

"It's the reunion thing up at the state park," she explained.

Folks had family reunions at Finleigh State Park all the time. There was nothing special about that.

Her voice had taken on an airy quality like she was describing how nice her new drapes looked.

She continued. "Children of slaves and slave owners coming together to celebrate."

Was she reading this from somewhere? "Uh huh." I grunted against the weight of the box of old books I'd just pulled from under my desk.

"What are you doing, Celine? All that huffing and puffing."

"Celebrate what, Mama? What's there to celebrate at a plantation? Who's behind this thing? Like, who's funding it? Coordinating it?"

"Why are you asking me all these questions, girl? Just check out the Web site."

"What—"

She cut me off again, saying she needed to get back to babysitting Tabby's twin girls. I asked for the Web address and she huffed like I was a telemarketer asking for her social security number.

"Check the e-mail I sent you." And she hung up.

"I love you too, Mother."

I pushed a few more stacks and boxes into the closet and

ran a damp paper towel over the dusty monitor just as someone knocked on the back door. I cringed and rushed through
the kitchen, wishing I'd thrown those empty tuna cans out.

"Yes?"

"It's me, Celine."

I opened the door and let my cameraman in. He was smiling as he handed me a stack of DVDs labeled "Zoo." I stared
at him a bit. Something was different.

"No parking out front. All those Lilly's Pizza hippies and
junk parked everywhere along Glenwood. How can you take
it?"

"Can you see me, Bob?"

His grin widened. "The new me."

"Lasik?" I asked.

"Nope. Finally got contacts." He glanced toward the narrow hallway that led to the rest of the house. "Ming around?"

"Not tonight. She's preparing to defend her dissertation
soon, you know?"

He nodded. I imagined their breakup had to do with how
grad school completely consumed her life. "You hungry? I'm
hungry," he asked.

I shrugged. *Where'd that come from?*

"Not really hungry, Bob. But if you'd like, I could fix you
a tuna sandwich before we get down to work."

"No thanks. How 'bout coffee? Do you want coffee?" He
was blinking a lot and touching the bridge of his nose like he
needed something to push up.

"Are you asking me out for a cup of coffee?"

"Well, yeah. Yes, I am." He made a funny face with his
lips screwed to one side. "How's Third Place?"

"Fine, I guess."

When I was in the mood for some fresh, expensive coffee early on Saturday mornings, I often wandered over to Third Place. It helped that it was next to Lilly's Pizza. Both places had WiFi and wonderful smells. The people watching was hard to beat.

"Just give me a minute to grab my laptop."

"Well, Celine . . ." He made that face again.

"This is a social thing, isn't it?"

"Yeah. Is that okay?"

Chapter 3

WE SAT near the back. He had a cappuccino. I had a hot white chocolate. An oil painting of a blue dog leaning against an orange tree hung over his head. I smiled at it.

$1,200? Costs more than all my furniture combined.

"I like your hair that way." Bob interrupted my thoughts.

I'd French braided it that morning and used the curling iron to do a couple of loose corkscrews on either side of my face.

Actually, it was nappy and dry; I needed a perm. But he didn't need to know that. I simply patted my hair and thanked him.

"Kept it out of harm's way during children's church this morning."

"You go to church and junk? Didn't know that."

I nodded. It seemed like Ming didn't talk about me nearly as much as I thought. She never told me Bob was so boring.

"I go to Hayes Barton Memorial sometimes," he said.

I tried to imagine him among the high-bred types at that big ornate edifice up the street from my house. But it was a vision that didn't quite come into focus.

He tapped the table with his right thumb and studied the

far wall. It had been a while since I'd been on a date, but I couldn't help thinking that this felt too much like an awkward one.

I'm on a date with a younger man. A younger man of another color, I pondered.

Could he see that little flash of panic on my face that rose up from my stomach? I snatched up my cup, drained my lukewarm drink, and swallowed hard.

I glanced around at the handful of people nearby. No one had been staring at us. Of course, what was I thinking? We were in Five Points, after all. A mecca of trysts and all manner of furtive behavior. All roads led to Five Points, it seemed, bringing desperate singles from across the entire Triangle area.

"Maybe we should get to work on that zoo piece," I suggested.

"That can wait," Bob responded.

"Wait a minute! What about the flower show piece? We still have to wrap that up."

"Coulton's given that to Sharon's crew. We got Erika's zoo piece instead, which is almost finished. And we picked up—" Bob was back in full work mode. He fished his notepad from his back pocket. "We picked up . . . um . . . Pettigrew Homecoming. You're from Finleigh, right? That's near Pettigrew."

I stared at him. "How'd this 'reunion thing' get past me?" After all, it's not like I'd been inaccessible or anything. On the contrary, my nose had been to the grindstone as usual. My boss, Coulton, should have filled me in on the assignment himself. That way I could have talked him out of it on the spot. Or, at least I would have tried to.

Bob went on. "Coulton figured you'd have an inside track. Cut through the stranger phobia mess we usually have to deal with. You look shocked."

Shocked didn't come close to the dread that roiled within me. Bob was green but honest—a virtue that carried a lot of weight in broadcasting. That went without saying.

He would never have understood me telling everyone I had come from Finleigh instead of Pettigrew. So there was no use in trying to explain it to him.

But, on the other hand, I had Coulton in my back pocket. He would understand. He was a seasoned TV man. He knew what a body needed to do sometimes to get in the business. And what was required to stay in the business.

Now the lies I'd told about my background were about to come out of the closet. I prayed it wasn't too late to cut off the damage at the pass. A talk with my boss would surely clear things up. He'd see things my way and reassign me.

I wiped the look of utter distress from my face and cleared my throat.

"Well, Bob, this is the first I've heard of these changes. Coulton usually calls or e-mails me first."

"Sudden death in the family this morning. Sister in Canada, I think Sharon said. Don't know when he'll be back," he explained.

"Sharon's in charge?" My mouth dropped open again.

He nodded. "The crews are pretty thin so I don't think we can switch things around. She wants us to wrap up the zoo thing tomorrow and be in Pettigrew day after tomorrow. There's a meeting with some bigwig farmer with deep pockets —Abraham Benson. That's Tuesday late afternoon. And then a writer character named John Carter Manning, after that. About a controversial play he wrote. And—"

"Tuesday? Preliminary stuff, of course. Meetings. Initial contact. Key players." I was mumbling to myself. Trying to steady my breathing and stop my head from spinning.

John Carter Manning. There's that name again.

"And a woman in Pettigrew named Melissa Johnson. Any relation?"

Mama! So that was it. I can't believe she had set me up!

"We're supposed to meet with Ms. Johnson for dinner and stuff."

"What!" That was about all I could take.

"You okay, Celine?"

I stood up, bumping the table so hard that my cup toppled. Bob righted it and used a paper napkin to mop up the little white puddle that spilled out.

"I'll walk you home," Bob offered.

On the pavement leading up to my steps, I fumbled with my keys and dropped them. Bob picked them up for me and bounded up the steps to my porch.

"Thanks for going to Third Place with me." He unlocked my door and gave me the keys.

"No problem," I replied.

"I kinda wanted to thank you for not trying to ditch me all these months. I saw the look on your face when Coulton paired us up back then. The new kid from California. Funny talking Bob Hollywood."

"I never said you talked funny."

He flashed a smile. "But you call me Hollywood."

I grimaced. "Only when I'm annoyed with you. And never out loud."

"I'm from Baja. Not Hollywood."

"I knew that." I'd helped hire him. "Listen, you want to come in for that tuna sandwich?"

"Naw. I'd better get going. See you in the morning. Tell Ming I said hi."

I walked him to the edge of the porch. My keys slipped

again. I stooped for them and so did he. His longer fingers reached them first.

"Clumsy me."

I extended my hand but when he didn't release the keys into my waiting palm, I lifted my head. He touched my chin and pulled my face closer to his. The warm breath from his parted lips was heavy with the smell of coffee.

He closed his eyes and wet his lips.

"Bob!" I fell backward with the force of air from my lungs.

Shaking his head, he dropped my keys and stood up. "I'd better go."

I didn't watch him go. My keys lay on the front porch for the better part of an hour while I sat in my kitchen with my head in my hands.

A coworker had almost kissed me. And not just any co-worker but one who looked half my age. What was he thinking?

In less than thirty-six hours I'd be back in a town that I hadn't visited in years, working on a story that I didn't want, with a man who had just tried to kiss me. All the old Pettigrew memories were washing over me like hot wax. I couldn't stop them—and they hurt so much.

No more, Lord.

Chapter 4

WHEN I ARRIVED at the office the next morning I was desperately hoping to speak with Sharon right away. I had to get out of this assignment. Maybe telling her about my cancer scare would make her change her mind. But instead I walked into a state of confusion and bickering. No one was making any sense to me.

Maybe it was the heat. Whatever benefits I could have reaped from the open window were being canceled by all the hot, agitated bodies crammed into my office. The air-conditioning had been out since Friday morning. That didn't help much to keep the crazies from coming out first thing Monday morning.

I could hear my grandmother's words: What kind of mess was going on here?

The old Donna Summer song coming from the CD player on my desk soured my mood even more. I stepped into the small crowd and held up my hands.

The noise subsided a bit. I spoke up. "Okay, how about y'all just take this into the conference room and—"

"No way, Celine. You started this," Sharon protested.

I looked my temporary station manager in the eye. "Sharon,

no one in their right mind would have started this craziness."
From what I could finally gather, everybody was in an uproar
about some T-shirts. "Besides, I did not order these shirts."

I sat down and glanced at the shirts; they were the last
thing on my mind. I wanted to talk to her about putting me
on another story, not about these stupid shirts.

"Clue in, Celine." She snapped her fingers in my face like
she was breaking me from a hypnotic trance. "Man, it feels
like an inferno in here. Who called the heating and air guy?
Never mind. Nobody said you ordered the shirts, Celine. You
suggested the name. Remember? You said, name the team
Hot Stuff." She turned to a pale guy with a beak of a nose
standing next to her. "That's what Kevin told me."

All heads turned toward him. He smirked, up to his elbows in a box of T-shirts labeled "The Hot Stuffers." Kevin
withdrew his pasty arms from the box and shrugged his thin
shoulders.

"We were gonna miss our deadline for the discount on
these babies." He held up an extra large across his body and
grimaced. "I assumed everybody had voted."

The room erupted into a mixture of protests and cheers.
Someone cranked up "Hot Stuff" louder and started singing
along with the song.

"Sharon," I said in a loud whisper. "I want to be on something closer to Raleigh. I'm concerned that I might have cancer so I need to schedule some tests." I pulled out the big
guns, not caring who overheard.

She leaned into me, bobbing her head a little to the
music. "You look fine. You're going to Pettigrew. No Plan B
here. See you when you get back." Sharon left the room sig-
naling the discussion was over. The crowd finally began to
disperse from my office like so many scattered mice.

I fell back in my chair and rubbed my hands across my face. And I thought Coulton could be difficult.

Bob pulled out his footage on the zoo piece that we needed to wrap up. He leaned over to shut off the music. "Gives March Madness a new meaning, doesn't it? I'll take the music box with me when I leave."

As we tied up the loose ends to the story, he winced and rolled his shoulders then looked up at me for a second before averting his eyes. I looked down to see him arranging some equipment in his camera bag in the corner. "You need anything? Coffee?"

It was his week to man the coffeepot. But I was in no mood for coffee, T-shirts, or any of this craziness. It was a wonder that we had managed to squeeze in a little work once all the turmoil had subsided.

I shifted my weight forward and answered him without looking directly at him again. "No, I'm fine. I've gotta make a few phone calls before we head out early in the a.m."

"Well, you know where to find me." He cleared his throat and stood up, hoisting his equipment bag to his shoulder. He grabbed the music box with his free hand and left.

I was almost alone, except for one more person to contend with—the thin guy in a T-shirt two sizes too big. Even though I'd been ignoring him, he had been lingering around in the background.

"Kevin." I closed my eyes. "Your fans are waiting."

"You gotta be kidding me. They'll eat me alive. I'm not leaving this room without you." He pulled at the tail of the T-shirt that flowed around him like a kid's nightshirt. "You did tell me to order these. I don't do basketball. Look at me!" He gestured to his narrow face and large nose. "I do *Jeopardy* and *Wheel of Fortune*."

I chuckled and turned to the window. It had started to drizzle. A light breeze was blowing small dots of water onto the tripods stacked under my window.

"Bye, Kevin. See you when I get back from Pettigrew."

I listened to him leave but I didn't turn around. I didn't make a move to gather up my stuff or call my mother either. Now that everything had settled down, the only thing that was left to do was for me to stall. So I just sat there watching the rain.

It had been lightning for some time. Suddenly, clean sharp flashes coming from the east turned the sky as black as night. Thunder rumbled in the distance. I sank deeper into the brown leather of my chair and listened to the sounds, trying to find the words of an old familiar psalm in my memory. Something to do with courage. I desperately needed courage to face my dilemma.

Just a little encouragement, Lord.

Outside, the wet sidewalks were empty except for a shaky old man on a bicycle half a block away. He wobbled and fell over. But there, like a vision from the mist, came a woman with an umbrella helping him up.

I closed my eyes against the sudden tears, inhaled the dank smells of wet pavement outside my window, and let my mind go. It immediately flashed back to a memory of my first kiss and the first day my daddy slapped me.

✳ ✳ ✳

Dale was about to break the door down. I was three months shy of being seventeen and he thought he owned me for the six hours I worked weekends at his hole-in-the-wall coffee shop.

"Cee Cee, tell me this. How are we gonna have a show tonight if the first act is in the bathroom crying?"

It was my debut. Open mic in downtown Finleigh, the only town in the county with stoplights. Civilization in the sticks: traffic lights, a library, and a coffee shop with a PA system. My turn up at the mic and all I could do was cry.

Truth was I had been crying nearly all day. I'd gone to work at my Saturday morning job and typed and cried my way through five hours of line edits at the county weekly, *The Finleigh Record.* The senior editor, Mazie Giordano, normally a mean-spirited verbose ex-housewife, had slid me a box of tissues and kept her distance.

All the hate and fear and confusion that I'd held for so long, too long, was coming out. It just kept coming like it had no end. But it had to end. My daddy wasn't going to win this one.

I hated my mama. I hated Tabby. I hated Brother. But most of all, I hated Quincy Johnson. He'd slapped me—hard, on the face—and accused me of being loose. He'd been out of prison, after serving a seven-year sentence for manslaughter, all of three months. Maybe his own anger was still stewing. I don't know. Didn't matter. It was wrong and he knew it. They all knew it. That slap and what he did afterward—I didn't deserve that.

My mama and my siblings had sat there and watched him slap me. Then without a word or a flinch, they'd turned their faces to the TV and finished their stale cornflakes.

Dale pounded the bathroom door some more. "Cee Cee!"

"I'm not crying."

In my mind, I could just see that man swelling up like an overinflated balloon.

"All right then. Whimpering. Sniffling. Whining. Call it

whatever you like, Cee Cee. Just come outta this daggone bathroom." He jiggled the knob.

"It ain't every night I let the hired help up on my stage. Just bring your stubborn self out here, girl."

"Don't call me girl!" It was my turn to swell up and show out. Dale was helping me put a little money away for college but that didn't mean he could get ugly.

That little hole-in-the-wall on east River Street was his pride and joy. Dale was from Raleigh and he knew some things about entertainment, or at least he made us think he did. The establishment was more than a coffee shop, juice bar, wireless book nook, spoken word nightspot. It was a haven of new Southern culture, perched like a shiny half-dollar on the curb, a quirky little magnet that was a safe place for white and black kids to mingle. No one looked sideways at you if you were with a white boy; not even if you kissed one.

That's where I met Steven.

Dale kept yapping. "Let me get this straight, *woman*, you think you can come in here late, dressed like you're doing a night at the Apollo and then hole up in the bathroom. Oh no-o-o." He drew out the no for several seconds.

I heard him marching away, muttering about how he wasn't paying me for crying in the bathroom unless I had a mop and pail. I reached for the doorknob and strained to hear over the Four Tops music drifting in through the speaker over my head. Someone tapped on the door. I jumped back.

I heard someone whisper my name. "Celine, it's me."

Steven. I slumped back against the wall. Tears welled up in my eyes again. I wouldn't let him touch me or kiss me or even see me. Never again.

Just leave me alone.

"I just wanna help you, baby."

"Go away. Please."

"Just open the door, okay?"

I rolled my eyes and reached for the roll of toilet paper on the edge of the sink in front of me. "No."

I tore off a wad of paper and wiped my nose. The doorknob jiggled again. "I'm sorry, baby. I don't know what got into me. I really care a lot for you, Cee Cee. Please open the door. I just wanna talk."

With my face in my hands, I tried to press out the sensation of his hand up my blouse and his mouth on mine. My father's slap still stung and accusations burned straight to my heart.

"No, Steven. Good-bye."

I refused to open the door that day. Steven had left me forever. Dale had fired me for refusing to work. Worst of all, Quincy Johnson Sr. had spread lies, telling everyone that his daughter was loose.

I guess in his mind I had asked for it. Going on a date with a white boy. In a sense, my father had saved my virginity that night he discovered Steven on top of me in my room. For the humiliation I gained in return, I wished he hadn't.

❋ ❋ ❋

Around noon I knew that it was definitely time to move on and prepare for the coming events of the next day. The rain was hitting the tripods under my office window harder now, making tinkling sounds against the metal that brought me back to the present. I slapped my leg and pushed myself out of the warmth of the leather chair.

I closed the window and grabbed my laptop case. *Time to*

face the music. Pettigrew was like a huge animal looming over me. It wouldn't go away all by itself.

For all the folks around the state who gushed over my very shadow, there were plenty of folks in Pettigrew who would roast me alive. And I wouldn't blame them. My big-city-girl charade was finally going to catch up with me.

And then there was Bob. I knew facing amorous Hollywood was inevitable but I was going to put it off as long as possible. He'd lost the coin toss, meaning he had to do the driving. An answered prayer, for sure. I planned to feign sleep for the three-hour trip.

Chapter 5

SNUGGLED IN the passenger seat, I heard Bob draw a big breath. "Celine, we've got to talk."

My stomach lurched and I opened one eye. I stretched and pretended to be pulling myself from some deep state of satisfied slumber. "What'd you say, Bob?"

My phone rang.

"Hello, Mama."

"Y'all coming up today?"

"In the van right now. A couple more folks are coming up Thursday."

"Y'all staying here?"

"No, Mama. We're not staying with you."

I spoke with my mother two or three times a week. Maybe more if she'd seen some flaws in one of my reports. Encouraging me to do better, she called it.

The last time I saw my mama face-to-face, she had slammed the door on my fingers and said, "Don't come back here until you have some children."

That was ten years ago. I haven't darkened her threshold since that day. I moved to Raleigh to attend NC State and stayed in Raleigh. My sister had given her twin grandbabies.

No husband in sight but she'd produced some babies. And Mama was happy. For a little while.

"Why come y'all ain't staying with me? You know you're welcome anytime. Your cameraman. What's his name? Bill?"

"Bob."

Bob glanced my way. "Yes?"

I covered the phone. "My mom calls you Bill. I was correcting . . . No, Mama. I'll be in and out all hours. You know how I live when I'm on the road. I don't want to put you out."

"Child. Why don't you stop putting on?" She grunted. She was the one who was putting on. "You grown, I guess. Call me when you get in town."

I said good-bye, put the phone away, and closed my eyes again.

"I'm sorry for trying to kiss you Sunday night," Bob continued.

Bob's words had come out smooth and strong. I had to open my eyes and look at the man. There was clarity in his voice that I'd never heard. When had Hollywood grown up? He was in control and I had turned into a sixteen-year-old girl cringing under her daddy's glare.

I nodded my acceptance of Bob's apology and turned to face my window. *Should I say something?* I wondered.

Bob's tone had loosened a little. "I was out of line; my actions were totally off. I respect you and your work. I've learned so much from you, professionally speaking and stuff. And I don't want to ruin our professional relationship in an attempt to satisfy my personal longings."

Longings? Longings!

Oh, good Lord. Who knew Bob Hollywood had longings?

"Am I making sense?"

"Yes, you are. You certainly are." I glanced at him. His face was stoplight red. His knuckles were white.

"I'm not gonna try anything like that again. It'll be strictly business from here on out. You can trust me."

"Yes, Bob, I know I can."

He'd opened up his heart and made it all clear to me. I prayed I could trust him. I'd need all the help I could get in Pettigrew, professionally and otherwise.

Chapter 6

I LOOKED OUT at Abraham Benson's house and shoved another breath mint into my mouth. It was the tenth one in as many seconds. My mouth was on fire and I was sweating bullets.

Focus, girl. Don't you dare cry.

"Those things are gonna kill you, Celine." Bob turned off the engine and opened his door. "That's a monster of a house. Is the guy from Texas or something?" Bob laughed.

"Get back in," I directed.

"Huh?" Bob was puzzled.

"Let's go check into our B&B first."

Bob just sat there staring at me, one hand on the steering wheel and one eye on the house. "You remember this house, don't you? Something bad happen here?"

I nodded. I remembered the house from my growing-up days in this small farming village. But it wasn't the sight of the large white clapboard farmhouse that was giving me pause. It was memories of one Abraham Benson, the man who had refused to come the day my daddy burned my Jesus.

"Let it burn," he had said when we told him our trailer might catch on fire.

As a result most of the trailer park had burnt to the ground and my friend Violet's dad had been killed. In my mind, Abraham Benson's apathy had killed just as much as my daddy's anger. But the rich white man had gone free.

"Whatcha wanna do, Celine?"

Bob's words brought me back to reality. I blinked the tears away.

"We'll call after dinner. He's not expecting us until later anyway."

I directed Bob through the sleepy streets of Pettigrew. Funny how very little had changed. It had been ten years since I set foot on these dusty streets. Ten long, eventful years.

On Main Street, there was Miss Emily's next to the beat-down Soda Shop. A couple of rusty pickups were parked out front. Two men in overalls sat outside sipping sodas.

The sun was high in the sky, shining like a bare bulb behind a blanket. I rolled down the window and smiled. The air was sticky, heavy with the smell of rain.

"Turn here," I told Bob.

Heady scents of Miss Mae's gardenia bushes filled the van. It was a welcomed aroma. This felt like home should.

Bob pulled into the driveway opposite Miss Mae's, killed the engine, and got out.

Miss Mae had been a sweet little black woman who had let us trailer-tramp kids, as we were called to our faces, play with her kids.

Hide-and-seek. Freeze tag. Tea parties with mud pies. We'd play it all until the sun would sink low behind her cedar trees. Smelling those gardenias. Sampling my pies when no one was looking. Wishing like anything that I lived in a house in town.

I started at the sound of Bob's door slamming. "Here we go again. I'll check in." He jabbed his thumb at the two-story yellow house next to the van. A black-and-white shingle hung on a pole in the front yard. Pettigrew House, it read.

"Don't you smell that?" I got out and took a deep breath.

"Mmm. Nice." He walked away, shaking his head as he went.

"Bob, wait a minute."

He turned, a smirk playing across his face. "I know, I know. You need to write some stuff down in your diary."

"It's not a diary." I fingered the worn edge of the journal that I held behind my back. "I'm gonna need your help here."

He frowned. "Here?"

"Yes. Here."

I sighed and hung my head. What a sad black woman I was. Not a soul to trust in my hometown but a white kid with feelings for me.

I was desperate for some guidance. But asking for help would mean telling the truth. I'd lied about my hometown. I'd lied about my family. Not just to a few people—it was in print in numerous places. Engraved in a few trophies even.

Celine Johnson. Fatherless. Finleigh native. I was a sham and it was going to come out and come out ugly.

"I need you to keep me grounded. Focused."

"You're not making sense, Celine. Focused on what?"

"On the story, for goodness' sake." I blinked at the tears and took a breath. "I'm sorry for snapping at you."

His face softened, reminding me of the way he looked that evening on my porch. I gulped. No sense encouraging any feelings I couldn't return. He stepped toward me. I held up a hand to stop him.

"You know what. I think I'm gonna be okay."

He screwed his lips to one side and shrugged. "If you say so. I'll give you a moment alone to *focus* with your diary."

I gave him a weak smile and let him enter the house. Then I just stood there with my eyes closed, inhaling the thick sweetness of the gardenia blossoms and crying. Writing could wait. At that moment, I had to let some emotions out.

Regrets. Fear. Anger. Even happiness. They had been jumping around inside me for too long. So I let the tears fall, hoping that if I did, they wouldn't come knocking later. I had to collect myself, whichever self that was: the country girl or the polished professional. My "selves" kept flip-flopping like two Muses.

I shook my mixed feelings off, dried my face, and walked up the steps. Time to face the music.

The unwelcome smell of burnt food overtook me as I stepped into the house. I stood on the Oriental runner and gagged. White smoke clung to the ceiling; my eyes watered.

A blonde woman wearing an apron rushed toward me. She smiled and took my hands in hers.

"You must be Ms. Johnson. I'm Summer Courtland, owner of Pettigrew House. I'm so glad to have you with us." She was pumping my hand hard. I put on a happy face.

"Please forgive the smell. Burnt scones. So sorry. Those congressional hearings started yesterday morning. They've been distracting me to no end."

I'd read about the hearings but that was as close to politics as I wanted to get, particularly politics that involved Abraham Benson. Perky Ms. Courtland finally released my hand and waved toward the back of the house. Her platform sandals thudded along the thick rug that ran the length of the house.

"Please, come this way."

I held my hand over my nose and followed her into a little alcove off the breakfast room. My hostess's blue eyes flashed as she apologized again and slipped a card in my hand. A few steps away I saw Bob nose deep in a plate of eggs, barely paying attention to the talking head on the small TV suspended above the breakfast nook.

BREAKING NEWS: Investigation of Hate Crimes Legislation, the banner across the screen read. Had that investigation started already? My mind went to Abraham Benson again. I vaguely recalled hearing the tail end of a conversation at one of my networking groups back in Raleigh. His name and that of his son, twenty-three-year-old, Isaac Hunt, had been mentioned again and again.

"You only need to fill in the top part, Ms. Johnson," Ms. Courtland said, breaking into my thoughts. "I started a new batch—of scones, I mean. You'll have some. Please do. Your cameraman is already chowing down on some breakfast."

She whirled around on her platform sandals and pushed through the saloon-style doors into the kitchen. I started writing on the card with the pen she offered. Fans buzzed on full blast in both windows of the breakfast nook, drowning out the reporter on the TV.

The sky-blue eyes of Abraham Benson staring out from the screen made me catch my breath. His lips were moving but I couldn't hear his words.

"Bob, turn the sound up."

He surfaced long enough from his mound of food to grunt and hunch his shoulders. I scanned the two other small tables in the nook. No remote.

"Wow. That's what's his name," Bob mumbled. "That Benson guy." He stood and started looking under tables. "I thought I saw the remote around here somewhere."

47

I pushed past him and jabbed the volume button until I could hear above the noise of the fans.

"Well, Tom," said the woman reporter, "it's my understanding that Abraham Benson was part of the problem, so to speak, for many years."

People bustled around in the hallway behind her. A congressional seal gleamed on the wall to one side.

She continued, "And as you pointed out, Mr. Benson was a major player in the underground racial hate group, the United Front. His family's corn farming operation in the small town of Pettigrew has been financing the Front's efforts for decades. It's astonishing—the things he's confessed."

The man in the studio made a few noises of agreement and astonishment as they cut to the videotape. Benson's testimony on the Hill had been recorded yesterday, containing sound bites I'd heard on NPR the night before. This was my first chance to see it. I couldn't help but stand there and tremble inside.

Abraham's face loomed over me again. His deep voice filled the room.

"I am not proud of what I have done with my life, Mr. Chairman. I have tortured and maimed several African-Americans. All of it was done in the name of faith and my dedication to my family. I am ashamed and I am sorry."

The camera switched to a man seated behind a long shiny desk. Sheaths of papers were strewn before him. He laid a hand on one of the stacks and frowned as he spoke. "Well, Mr. Benson, I appreciate your remorse. As I'm sure your state's legislators are appreciative of your help with their prosecution of long-standing hate crime perpetrators in North Carolina."

The subcommittee chairman, Senator Fenton Barstow

from South Carolina, was known for his verbosity. He was a pasty old guy with a thick lower lip that seemed to stretch from ear to ear. In my book, he had a big mouth and just liked to hear himself talk.

He leaned forward and continued.

"I assure you we are all grateful, as I've mentioned before, for your willingness to testify in this congressional investigation that will effect changes in federal hate crimes legislation. You have been most helpful to your fine legislators and lawmen in North Carolina as they continue to conduct the United Front trial that we've all been watching closely for over a year. But before we go any further, sir, I must confess my own curiosity as to the veracity of your statements. What has prompted your willingness to divulge all this information, implicating yourself in the process?"

I frowned and stepped closer to the TV. That had been my question as well. Did the man have a death wish?

Abraham cleared his throat and spoke. "I can only repeat what I said yesterday. 'I once was blind but now I see.' As a young man, I was indeed blinded by loyalty to family and what I thought was faith in God. What I was taught from a young age clouded my judgment. It was all that I knew."

"Mr. Benson," Fenton interrupted as his wide bottom lip moistened, "I remember your testimony from yesterday. I'm not trying to ascertain your culpability here, sir. You had these damning documents for decades. Why did you come forward with them at this time? It is my understanding that the FBI has been courting you, as it were, for years. Why now—"

"Mr. Chairman, if you'll excuse me." He paused and drew a breath. "I can only say that it was fear. I've been motivated by fear all my life. Fear of what others would do to me and what my family represented kept me silent for so many years. Fear of what society wanted kept me from the woman I loved. But I was only out to protect myself until the day when I saw my son Isaac as a grown man being pursued by the monster I helped create. That's when I knew it had to die. It had to end. And if it meant that my life ended with it, so be it."

He stopped talking. Tears trembled in his eyes. The camera cut to a wide-eyed Fenton and back to Abraham, who licked his lips and continued. "I am not an eloquent man. I'm nobody's hero. I just want to do the right thing for the first time in my life. That is all, sir.

"A little while ago I watched a black man die in prison. He was in there for killing a man that I wanted dead. All the same, a decade ago I would have called him an enemy. But that day as I stood beside his wife and held his hand, Quincy called me brother. We had made our peace with God and our peace with each other.

"He made me promise that I would do whatever I could to stop the hate. I aim to keep that promise."

A single tear ran down the man's cheek. The camera lingered on his solid features, his cool blue eyes, before cutting to the woman reporter again.

Quincy? As in my father?

What hadn't my mother told me? My mind was reeling. I shook my head to clear the confusion.

Chapter 7

BOB'S VOICE made me jump. "Wow. This Abraham guy, he's a character. That was quite a speech—and on TV and stuff."

"They've been talking about this all day long," Ms. Courtland said. The B&B mistress had been leaning against a table behind me. "That was the first I've seen it all. Yes, quite a speech indeed. I wonder if anyone in this town is getting anything done today."

I shook myself. Realizing that I was near tears again, I turned to leave.

"Do you wanna go over to his house right now?" Bob asked.

"No, not yet. I'll call his number again. After two days in DC, I wouldn't be surprised if he would like to reschedule our interview. You go take a rest." I spoke over my shoulder as I stood facing the note card I had yet to finish filling out. I scribbled my information down without much thought. "I'm going to go out for a quick walk."

The cloud cover was thicker as I stepped outside. The air was clammy and warm, a perfect summer afternoon for enjoying a grilled hot dog from Miss Emily's.

Miss Mae's gardenias held me in a little familiar cocoon for several minutes. But, try as I might to replace my sour mood with memories of hide-and-seek and hot dogs, I couldn't.

Abraham Benson was on my mind.

If it meant that my life ended with it, so be it. I recalled his words.

Not the evil white man I remembered. What would cause a man of his station and rank to change so drastically? Who was this grown son named Isaac? This was the first I'd heard of him. I knew Abraham was a widower. According to my mother, his wife, Olivia Ross Benson, had died a couple years back. Mama had sent me a program from the funeral, like Abraham's loss was meaningful to me.

Olivia was movie-star pretty, reminiscent of Ava Gardner. The kind of woman I could imagine on Abraham Benson's arm. They had been married several years. She had bore him one child—now a school-aged boy.

There was only one way ole Abraham had a twenty-something son. So where was Isaac's mother now? Thinking about that poor black woman and what she must have gone through made me sick. Steven Kepler's face loomed before me. How could Abraham Benson say he loved that woman? What Steven had tried to do to me hadn't been motivated by love.

I was playing a little game of diversion with myself. Puzzling over all the questions surrounding Abraham's testimony helped me keep my emotions at bay and focused on the story Coulton wanted. I yawned. Fatigue was gnawing at my limbs but I now knew what I had to do.

Bob Hollywood was snoring by the time I tapped on his partially open door. He was stretched out on the bed, asleep on the covers with his boots on.

Poor kid, I thought. I've been working him too hard. I

would just slip out for a bit. He needed the rest. We'd been in the field so much lately. I guess it was taking its toll. He looked like a little boy, stretched out with a corner of the bedspread flung over his unbuttoned shirt.

The van keys were on the nightstand. I scribbled him a note on the pad beside the phone and tiptoed out.

A light rain was starting when I backed out of the Pettigrew House's driveway. By the time I tugged at the collar of my shirtdress and dashed across the Benson lawn with a plastic shopping bag over my store-bought hair, it had turned into a steady rain.

No one answered my first knock but I could hear voices. Really happy sounding voices, in fact. I checked my watch—3:16 p.m. I probably should have called first.

Never visit on a whim, Celine.

My van was the only vehicle parked out front but I spied the rear ends of a white truck and black sedan through the open door of a red barn in the distance.

The laughter grew louder inside the house. I sighed and faced the door again. No use standing here.

I didn't like this indecisive mood I was in. Unsettled and off balance. I had to reclaim my old confident self. But how? On the TV screen Abraham Benson had portrayed a different man than I was used to. But so help me, I felt like a poor little black girl standing on his porch begging for bread.

I whispered a prayer, "Lord, just a little help. Please." I squeezed the handle of my handbag, like that would make God answer quicker, and waited.

Nothing.

Opening my eyes, I fluffed my wig and knocked on the door again. It opened to a big, dark-suited black man in shiny shoes. His gold earrings glinted in the light of the chandelier shining overhead.

Listen. Learn. Love.

The three words were like heaven's shouts to my soul. Shaken to the core, I stared at the man across the threshold and searched for words, but nothing would come.

God, You need to work on that timing thing.

"Yes?" the black man said.

I cleared my throat and finally spoke. "I'm Celine Johnson with WCNC-TV."

"Special Agent Buxton with the FBI. We were expecting you later."

I frowned at the badge he flashed. We shook hands. *FBI. Protection, of course.*

"I see. Yes. I should have called first."

He was no longer shaking my hand; just holding my fingers lightly. His dark brown eyes were narrowed. A small smile played across his lips. Was he hitting on me or preparing to frisk me? He cut a nice manly figure in that dark blue suit, but I didn't like the prospects of entertaining romantic advances or being patted down. I glanced at our hands and gave a little please-release-me smile.

He apologized and let go of me. "Please come in out of the rain."

I stepped forward. We turned at the sound of footsteps on the polished tiles that covered the expanse of the entryway. A young man approached us, wiping lipstick from his lower lip with a tissue; he had his head down. He stuffed the tissue in his pocket and extended a tanned hand to me.

He had blond hair and very, very fair skin. But without a doubt, I would have called him a black man even on a dark night. He smiled like a man who had just won a lot of money.

And I couldn't help but smile back. But seeing the blue eyes and square Euro-American jawline on someone who moved like a man of my own race, I fought the urge to frown.

"Hello, Ms. Johnson, I'm Isaac Hunt."

The infamous Isaac Hunt.

He stood an inch or two taller than the FBI guy. His shoulders were somewhat squarer and judging by the loose fit of his crisp lime oxford, he carried less weight on his frame.

"I'm sorry for showing up early. From the sounds of revelry inside, it's obvious this isn't a good time."

"It's okay, Ms. Johnson. My fiancée—"

The FBI agent interrupted Isaac with a slap on the back. "Congrats, man."

"Thanks, Gerome." He turned back to me, his eyes twinkling. "I just proposed."

"And she said yes?" I smiled back, forcing down a pang of envy. A woman's laugh rang out again, followed by a man's hearty chuckle. The noises came from upstairs. I let my eye follow the polished wood of the winding stairs and swallowed the sour taste that threatened to rise from my stomach.

"I'll bet Dad just showed her the dress."

Isaac laughed and nodded to Gerome before leading me with the sweep of his hand up the stairs. "Dad's expecting you. But I'd like you to meet my Catty too. If you don't mind, she's so eager to meet you. Watches you every Saturday night."

I smiled and shrugged. Why not kill me with two birds?

Don't you dare throw up.

Chapter 8

"BE PREPARED to give a couple autographs," Isaac said as he tapped on a set of double doors at the top of the landing.

When the doors opened, a very dark-skinned woman sprang forward and wrapped her arms around Isaac's neck. She pulled him down into a kiss. A large Afro puff crowned her head and a sizable diamond glittered on her finger.

The scene caught me by surprise. I wondered what had brought this son of privilege together with this particular young woman? She could possibly be a domestic. At least that was my guess. I assumed she was a hired servant, but I couldn't be sure; neither could I make sense of it all.

What did the so-called reformed racist think of it all? In my mind, I worked a new angle for the story. So lost was I in my thoughts that I didn't see the big man at first.

He pressed past the couple kissing in the doorway and extended a large hand toward me.

"Hello, Ms. Johnson. So good to see you again after all these years."

"Why yes, sir. Yes, it is," I stammered in the voice of a little girl.

"Call me Abraham, please." His manner was smooth and

measured, much more relaxed than I had seen on television. But there was something else about him. I fought the urge, though, to be put at ease by his smooth drawl or rugged tanned face.

I would play the game, sure, but I had an interview to conduct. He could be all butter and cream; that was fine with me. But he was still going to tell me the truth. Or my name wasn't Celine "Cee Cee" Johnson.

I smiled and took a breath. "Call me Celine."

"Welcome to Benson Ridge Farms, Celine."

I nodded my gratitude. He had opened the door a little wider, revealing more of the vast bedroom beyond. Hanging over the fireplace, the life-sized portrait of a white woman in a pink satin gown caught my eye. *Olivia Benson.*

A million questions formed in my mind at that moment. My interview was taking on a new tack. New butterflies swarmed in my stomach—the happy, excited reporter kind.

The couple broke from their kiss. Isaac, his lips reddened once again, tipped his head toward me and then toward his beloved.

"Catty Wright, Ms. Johnson."

The young woman turned the sweetest almond-shaped eyes on me and squealed. She wrapped her arms around me.

"Oh, my goodness. Celine Johnson. It is so good to meet you."

"Catherine, let her go," Abraham said, "she can't talk."

The little woman had the limbs of a child but she could sure squeeze like a vine. She let me go. I sucked in a big breath and offered my hand.

"Hello, Ms. Wright."

She took both my hands and smiled. "Call me Catty."

"Congratulations."

"Thank you." Her white blouse cast a glow on her neck and chin. She was radiant. "It's so good to meet you, Ms. Johnson."

"Celine."

She gushed. "Celine. Can I get you something? Coffee? Tea?"

Isaac moved closer and whispered something in her ear. She nodded.

"Please tell me you'll stay for dinner."

The big white man looming behind her turned away to answer the phone that buzzed on his hip. I felt myself relax even more.

"Thank you so much, but I can't stay long." This was supposed to be a quick interview. Not a social visit. I'd do my bit and send Bob to get some footage tonight or tomorrow without me. "My cameraman wasn't feeling well. He'll come by later."

"I see," Catty said. "I think Mr. Abraham wanted to do the interview in the office. Follow me."

I followed Isaac and Catty downstairs and into a paneled room off the entryway. A fire flickered in a large fireplace at one end. Full bookshelves lined two walls. Special Agent Buxton stood with his arms crossed at the open door until Abraham arrived.

"Sorry to make you wait." He settled in a burgundy leather chair opposite mine.

"No problem. A person who shows up early and unannounced should be prepared to wait."

He smiled.

"Are you thirsty? Catty can get you a little refreshment. Coffee? Warm cider?" He motioned to the FBI agent straddling the threshold of the open office door. Buxton shifted forward with raised eyebrows.

"No, thank you."

The agent settled back into a statue pose.

"Where should we start?"

"Well, before we start talking about the Pettigrew Home-coming, I have to ask you something. Satisfy my curiosity. Catty. Why does she call you Mr. Abraham? She works for you?"

I was buying time, trying to create an amiable mood and form a new angle in my mind. Rain beat on the double French doors behind us. I longed for a blanket and a book. Abraham's jaw tightened and he sat upright. So much for a relaxed conversation.

"Yes. I've known her since she was a little girl. Her father was my mechanic for many years. He died about three years ago. She's worked here for about two years as a domestic. She's like a daughter to me. I treat her like family. Don't know why she still calls me Mr. Abraham."

He paused and watched me rummage in my bag. I pulled out my tape recorder and slipped a cassette tape inside.

"Is this okay?"

He nodded like a robot. Might as well go for the jugular.

"What was your relationship with my father?"

Abraham smiled and fingered the metal brads on the arm of his chair.

"At one time, Quincy Johnson was my best enemy. That's what I used to call him. He was worse than a cocklebur in your boot on a cold day."

He looked off into the fire and chuckled.

"There were many days that I wanted to wring his brown neck."

There was no humor in that statement. I looked at him with what I hoped was professional detachment. He glanced at me and cleared his throat.

"I'm sorry. He saved my life once—from a bear. Black bear around here are more afraid of you than houseflies, but there was one that decided he wanted me for breakfast one morning.

"I was setting bear traps around one of our cornfields near Lake Finleigh. Around six o'clock in the morning. Summer of the year I turned nineteen. Your daddy, he was a couple years younger than me. Out hunting squirrel, so he said, when he saw a white man being chased by a bear. He nipped that bear in the nose from more than fifty yards away. He was a good shot. Didn't kill him, just scared him away.

"'If I'd known that bear was chasing you,' he told me, 'I would have saved my gun for the squirrels.'"

Abraham chuckled again. "No way he had been out hunting squirrel with a handgun."

Agent Buxton let out a soft snort. I'd forgotten about the protector at the door.

"You were there when he died." It wasn't a question, but I wanted a response. I placed the tape recorder in my lap and leaned forward.

He nodded. "I gave the eulogy. I guess your mama didn't tell you."

I sat there quietly until tears burned my throat. My professional detachment had melted away and my guard had dropped. I didn't know how to prop it up again. Abraham Benson. Intimately involved in the life of my family? Why?

My father had told me not to visit him in prison. We'd argued a few weeks before he died. Even on his deathbed, he held anger toward me. I was mad so I didn't go to the funeral. Sitting there at that moment with Abraham watching me fumble with the recorder, I couldn't, for the life of me, remember what my father and I had argued about.

"Mama's still mad at me for not attending the funeral,

I'm afraid." The cassette slipped from my trembling fingers and the tape fell to the floor.

Abraham picked it up and glanced at Buxton. "Do you mind, Gerome? I'll behave myself."

The FBI agent smiled and left the room, closing the door behind him. Abraham cleared his throat and rose from his chair.

I rubbed my sweaty palms across my lap.

"Your daddy was a runner for the United Front for many years. That's what kept him alive. Lord knows he would have been laid in an early grave otherwise. He was an ornery fellow —with all of his radical, black militant talk."

My mouth fell open. A runner? Guns? Drugs? My mind raced.

"But he was a valuable asset. He helped the Front on many occasions. Running information about guns, training camps, secret meetings. He was a major player in that information network. Very loyal and thorough. No one suspected him.

"We paid him well. I'm not sure what he did with the money. It's obvious y'all never benefited from it. I was his contact here in The Blacklands. From the Virginia line down to Little Washington and on over to Rocky Mount.

"Everything came through here. We had codes and signals. He developed a lot of it. Organized his men well."

"Who were they?" Why was I whispering?

"I don't know. I only met with Quincy. We would meet at night or early in the morning. I could trust him."

I frowned. I'd never thought of Quincy Johnson as trustworthy.

"Trust him? How so?"

"He knew the consequences."

"Consequences?"

"He loved his family."

Did he now?

Abraham stepped away and stared off into the fire. His words came softly. "He didn't take us seriously at one point. Tried to take shortcuts. That is, until—"

The man's shoulders sagged and he ran a hand across his chin.

"Until?"

"Your grandmother's death."

No!

I gasped. Surely he wasn't saying that my grandmother had not died a natural death. I bit my lip. My breathing quickened.

"Did you kill my grandmother?"

He hung his head but didn't answer. His back was still turned to me. My first thought was to do him harm. I glanced at the desk across the room. Was there a letter opener? Or maybe a fire poker.

"What kind of man are you? You . . . ."

He turned to face me with tears on his face. "I went to that prison with John Carter about a year ago to see your father. I knew what God wanted me to do with what I knew about the United Front. I just didn't want to do it."

I sprang from my seat. Abraham was facing me but his eyes were fixed on the rain-slicked French doors behind me.

"God? How could you even talk about God?"

"I hadn't seen Quincy in almost twenty years. John Carter said that your father had found the Lord and he wanted to talk with me. They had been meeting about making the play. I went with John Carter but I didn't know what to expect. I figured it had something to do with the Front.

"Quincy said he'd been praying for me. He'd seen the

news about the Front's leader, Highsmith, being captured. He said God had given him a dream—" Abraham caught his breath. "A dream about me. Said he had to make things right with me before either one of us died."

He stood there quietly, his large hands hanging awkwardly at his sides. I covered my mouth with my hands and let the tears slide down my face. The fire crackled. Thunder rumbled overhead. After several minutes, I wiped my face and spoke.

"You deserve to die."

I was finished with this man. There could be no interview after what he'd told me. There could be nothing positive to come out of this meeting. And this farce of a play. I didn't care about John Carter and his magnificent tribute to my father.

He looked at me with red-rimmed eyes. The creases on his face seemed deeper, longer.

"Celine, I am so sorry."

"Who else died because of you?"

No answer.

"Your father wanted me to tell you these things. And to read you a letter." He wiped his tears away with the back of his hand as he moved toward the desk. There were two sheets of paper there, lying side by side. He picked them up and walked toward me.

"He wrote this to you."

"I don't want to hear anything my father wrote."

"Please sit down."

"Excuse me?"

He took a pair of reading glasses from his shirt pocket and slipping them on, he took his seat.

"My dear Cee Cee. I've tried to write this letter for the

past twenty years. But here I am dying. I want you to know that I love you. I didn't always show you in the right ways but I did love you. Please forgive me for not being the daddy you needed me to be."

"Stop. This is ridiculous." I snatched my bag up and threw the tape recorder and cassette into it.

"I haven't finished."

"I have."

I stalked to the door and snatched it open. "I'm done here. I'll send my cameraman tomorrow morning."

A white-hot light flashed through the French doors and the house rattled. I screamed and dropped my things. The FBI agent's meaty hand steadied me from the other side of the threshold.

"Major thunderstorm, ma'am. I wouldn't be surprised to see some hail. Mr. Hunt says we're under a tornado warning."

"I heard a scream," Isaac said as he descended the stairs. "Are you okay, Celine?"

I nodded. The special agent let go of me.

Catty appeared to my left, smiling and wiping her hands on a dish towel. "That was a big one."

"There's a tornado warning, honey," Isaac told her. "Funnel cloud spotted in Finleigh. Headed in a northeasterly direction. Toward us, in other words."

Isaac opened a closet at the bottom of the landing and pulled out a raincoat.

"Where are you going?" Abraham asked. I moved aside as he neared me. I glanced out the windows on either side of the front door. Pitch-black.

"To the migrant camp." Isaac shrugged the yellow slicker on and stuffed keys in his pocket.

Abraham nodded. "Wish I could go too."

"Isaac, honey. No."

Isaac pulled his fiancée into a hug. "I won't be long." He kissed her cheek and whispered in her ear. She sighed and nodded as they exited arm in arm through the hallway she had come from.

My phone buzzed as another clap of thunder shook the house. I waited for the rumbling to subside. An unseen grandfather clock bonged. I glanced at my watch—4:30 p.m. and pitch-black outside.

"Hello, Bob."

"Celine. Where in the world are you?"

"Benson Ridge Farms. Sorry. Didn't you get my note?"

"The lights are out. Why didn't you wake me?"

I thought of Bob being here during what I'd just experienced. "I just came on a whim. I'm sorry. You'll get better footage tomorrow."

Another sharp flash and boom. The chandelier crystals tinkled and flickered. A chill ran down my back as I peered through a window. A small car pulled along the driveway and onto the road. Its red brake lights burned through the gloom. The tall slender trees bordering the yard bowed to their breaking point.

Another flash of lightning and I could clearly see that there were two people in the front seat of the car: a driver sitting tall in the seat and a shorter passenger with an Afro.

That's not good.

It had been quite a few years since I'd ridden out a tornado warning in the swampy Blacklands but I still knew not to go out. Those two were asking for trouble. I prayed that they'd be safe.

I glanced over my shoulder toward Abraham. He was walking up the stairs. By his reaction I figured he hadn't seen Isaac and Catty driving into danger.

Bob's voice crackled on the line.

"Can you hear me? Listen, Bob, I'll wait for this storm to pass over then I'll head on back. There's a tornado warning. Did you hear about it?"

"Yeah. You be careful." He said some more that I didn't catch through the static.

"I will. Thanks. You too."

I hung up and turned around. Buxton's brown eyes were on me. He smiled.

"Guess you're stuck."

I smiled and looked away. Abraham returned with three flashlights and a transistor radio.

"You'll need this," he said, handing me one of the flashlights. I thanked him with a quiet nod. "Gerome, I'll get some batteries for this one."

He turned to go but stopped midstride at the sound of pounding on the roof. The lights went out.

"Hail," Buxton said.

A familiar wail filled the air. It had been years since I'd heard anything like it but I knew what it was. The siren from the volunteer fire station on Main Street.

Tornado!

Abraham flicked on his light and walked off toward the direction Isaac and Catty had taken. "Catherine?"

"Uh oh," Buxton said. "Sir, we'll need to move away from the windows."

"Catherine."

"Ms. Johnson, can you gather your things, please, and follow me."

I already had my things so I wasted no time following the man. He led me through an arched walkway into a kitchen. A flash of lightning illuminated glossy countertops. Abraham stood near an open back door, a lit flashlight casting a bright circle on the wood floor.

"She left with Isaac, didn't she?"

"Yes, sir." Buxton let out a sigh. "You can't leave, Mr. Benson."

"They're not answering their phones. Probably turned them off." Abraham said something under his breath and placed his right foot forward. The frayed pant cuffs of his jeans caught my eye. "Just this once. Can't you just take it off? Please, Gerome."

I was confused by his pleading tone. Take what off? The jeans? Buxton's shoulders sagged. He shook his head.

"No, sir. They will be fine. Could you please both follow me?"

I followed the men through the dark, feeling helpless and angry. What else could I do? Inside and out, I felt trapped and alone.

Chapter 9

"IS THAT comfortable, Ms. Johnson?" Special Agent Buxton asked. I gave him a tight-lipped smile and a quick nod before shifting my hind parts on the large sack of rice he'd covered with his jacket. With the candlelight reflecting off his holstered gun and chocolate forearms bigger than my thighs, I didn't know where to rest my eyes.

"It'll do for now, huh? Sir, could you hand me that radio?"

Abraham passed Buxton the radio he'd been trying to tune and slumped back against the shelves of food on the far wall.

We were in a pantry the size of my entire kitchen. All manner of boxed, jarred, and bagged food lined the shelves, reminding me that I hadn't eaten since breakfast.

"We're not going to get any reception in here."

My stomach grumbled. I rummaged in my bag. Surely there was a half-eaten something in there. Even a breath mint would do.

Abraham grunted and snatched something from a shelf. A box of cookies. He walked over and held it in front of my face. The candles lining the shelves flickered in his wake.

I rolled my eyes at the bright yellow box. "No, thank you."

"You're hungry."

I glared at him. "I'll live."

Buxton cleared his throat. "I almost got something. Did you hear that?"

All I heard was static.

Abraham shoved the box of cookies back on the shelf and walked away. He eased to the floor and let his legs slide out. Something black around his ankle caught my eye. I squinted. An ankle cuff.

House arrest?

I averted my eyes. Abraham Benson was a prisoner in his own home. Unable even to leave his own yard to make sure his son was safe in a violent storm.

Questions flooded my mind. On what charges was he being held? For how long? Why hadn't this made it to the media? I pressed my lips together as if those questions might just slip out without my permission.

I didn't want to talk to this man, this animal. I wanted to press the reporter-off-duty button. But my mind kept racing.

Our eyes caught. He had the look of a child in pain. I turned away. Was he trying to play me? I wasn't buying his penitent looks. He had killed my grandmother, or ordered her killed. An apology wasn't going to bring her back. He didn't deserve the feelings of sympathy gnawing at my conscience. And house arrest was most certainly not enough.

"So, you're not hungry?" Abraham questioned.

I rummaged through my bag some more and kept my mouth shut.

"I didn't kill your grandmother."

My eyes narrowed. He continued.

"I was out of the country on business in 1988, the year your grandmother died. Isaac's mother and your grandmother were both killed that same year."

My breath left me. New questions crowded my mind. He stared at the ceiling, his hands behind his head.

"I don't think I've paid the price for my sins, Celine. Though the government thinks this is enough for now." He thumped his right ankle against the floor. "I'm not fooling myself. I deserve to die. Gerome is here to make sure I don't until they get what they need from me."

The FBI agent shifted his shiny shoes. I glanced up at his emotionless face. Abraham stretched and pulled some folded paper from his shirt pocket.

The letter from my father.

"I don't want to hear any more."

Abraham leaned forward.

"Celine. Shut up."

"Excuse me?"

"You've been lying about yourself for years. No doubt because of your father's mistakes."

"You know what? I think you should shut up," I shot back at him.

"He told me about Steven, that white boy who tried to rape you."

I caught my breath. *Why, Lord?*

"You have no business talking about any of this." I stretched forward, pointing a finger in the air. "You sent him to prison. He was just doing what you told him. You ruined his life; you ruined my life. This whole town—ruined because of you and your family."

I was standing up now, pointing my finger in his face. He sat there calmly studying the ceiling and talking.

"And then he told me he was sorry for how he had dragged your name through the mud. It wasn't right; the way he treated you. He felt he drove you to tell folks you were from Finleigh. That really bothered him. And all the mess your brother's mixed up in now. It bothered him too. He wants you to help Brother. It's all in the letter."

"I don't care about that stinking letter."

He tapped the folded letter on his outstretched leg.

"Your daddy talked about you all the time. He was proud of you. When he went into prison that second time, he vowed that you would never lack because of him. He had a lot of money. Mostly Benson money, to tell the truth. And in his mind it was all yours."

He looked me in the eye.

"What are you talking about?"

"He made sure I paid your way through Governor's School. And then through Duke. Even your studying abroad during your senior year there."

I covered my mouth with my hands and shook my head. *No!*

It was my mother's hard work. That's what saw me through school. And my trip to Europe—that was me, my hard work. It had to be.

Please, Lord.

"You're lying."

"I have proof, Celine. Receipts and letters addressed to me."

No!

I whirled around and covered my eyes, as if that would stop the tears from coming. My foot hit my things on the floor and I stumbled. Two strong arms held me steady. I buried my face in Buxton's chest and cried.

This couldn't be true. But as much as I wanted it to be a lie, there were times when I didn't know where my mother had gotten such large sums of money on such short notice.

She'd brushed me off when I pressed her about it. And I had, in my childish oblivion, let it slide.

I thought about the shame of growing up in Pettigrew. Carla Celine Johnson, the daughter of that crazy black militant convict. Cee Cee Johnson, that loose black girl. The shame had driven me away—and kept me away. Prompted me to drop my first name and adopt a new hometown. Nothing good came out of Pettigrew.

I thought of my grandmother. She had done nobody harm and yet she had been killed.

Oh, Lord. Oh, dear Lord.

I cried long enough to wet the left side of Buxton's shirt.

"I'm sorry," I said, brushing his hard chest with my palm.

"It's okay, ma'am." He smiled and handed me a folded handkerchief from his back pocket. I thanked him and dabbed at my eyes.

When I faced Abraham, he turned his head. I stared at him for several minutes before I spoke. I let the three words out slowly, calmly.

"I hate you."

"Dad?" It was Isaac's voice. The pantry door opened and a small village of people appeared. Little ones. Big ones. Brown ones. White ones. All drenched from head to toe, straining to see around Isaac. Two little brown-skinned boys pointed at boxes and chattered in Spanish.

Abraham pushed himself to his feet. He frowned at Catty and Isaac. "What the devil were you two thinking?"

Isaac winced.

"Sorry," Catty interjected. "I made him take me. I wanted to check on—"

"Don't you ever do something so foolish again. Do you hear me?"

Isaac was twenty-three. I judged Catty to be a few years younger. Under Abraham's scolding they looked like toddlers.

The others shrank back into the darkened kitchen, except for two men. A white man with a Tigger-like jaw and a paunchy Hispanic man with a wide smile.

"Come on, Abe," Tigger-guy said. "Lighten up. They're safe. We're safe."

The Hispanic man, the oldest in the group, added, "The worst of the storm is over. For us, at least. Twister touched down in Finleigh. Everything is okay, Mr. Abraham."

Abraham started and glared at his son again.

"Okay, Dad, I'm sorry. Never again." He threw up his hands and walked away.

Time to go.

There was nobody to listen to or learn from or love in this place. I stooped to gather my things. "I'm outta here," I announced.

"Celine," Catty said. "You can't leave yet."

"What now?"

Her eyes widened. "Um. Why don't you come into the kitchen and sit down?"

"Why do I need to sit down? I'd like to leave now. I thought you said the storm is over." I pressed my way into the dimly lit kitchen. One of the Hispanic women had placed lit candles on the countertops. Two others had produced a camp stove from somewhere. Catty followed me.

"There are several trees blocking the driveway."

"Oh, Lord, no."

I followed her to a chair and gladly sank into the padded seat.

"I need to help get some dinner together."

I grabbed Catty's thin wrist. "Listen, I'm sorry for snapping at you just now."

"It's okay. You've been through a lot. Probably not what you expected when you dropped in earlier this afternoon. I hope the interview went well, despite the circumstances."

I smirked. *If she only knew.*

"I'll get you something to drink."

The darkened corner of the kitchen gave me perfect cover to watch everyone. The men, with the exception of Abraham and Buxton, hovered near the pantry door. There were five of them, passing the box of cookies between themselves. Tigger-guy, Hispanic elder, and Isaac dominated the conversation. When the women weren't looking, Isaac stopped and slipped a few cookies to the children playing with a ball on the floor.

The women hovered over the stove just outside the kitchen's back door. Smells of roasted corn and beans made me think of rainy days in my grandmother's kitchen. I squeezed my eyes shut.

"Here you go," Catty said. She had appeared out of nowhere.

"What's that?" I nodded to the cup she placed in front of me.

"A little cider. It's not warm, but it's good," Catty said. She placed a hand over mine. "You're going to be okay."

Her manner was so simple. She was a plain country girl, but at that moment I didn't care. I needed plain and simple.

"Thank you, Catty."

She nodded and left.

The cider went down as smooth as honey and just as sweet. The spicy burn that lingered made me want to take off my shoes and lean back. It was indeed good.

The men had moved away from the pantry door and now

stood near the women (and the hot food). Their conversation—a mixture of Spanish, English, and laughter—made me smile.

What were they talking about? Where were they all from? So different, yet all the same—male and hungry.

I figured the Hispanic men were Abraham's employees. Farmworkers of some type, wearing T-shirts, jeans, and boots and carrying curl-brimmed cowboy hats in their hands. Isaac and Tigger-guy stood out like foreigners.

The children's ball rolled my way. It came to a stop under my chair. A little girl in pigtails toddled after it. I set my half-empty cup aside and reached under my seat.

"Here's your ball, cutie." I smiled and she whimpered. "I'm sorry." I looked to the ladies tending the food. Whose child was this? I rolled the ball to the little girl. Her whimper got louder.

Isaac knelt beside her. "Isabel. What's wrong, sweetie?"

The child lowered her chin and pointed at me.

"She's just trying to give you the ball." He picked up the ball. "This is Señorita Celine."

She frowned at me and wrapped an arm around his neck. I had such a good way with children. Usually.

"Sorry," I mouthed as I returned to my chair. He gathered the child in his arms and stood up.

"Don't worry about it. Feeling better?" he asked.

I nodded.

"I think dinner should be ready soon. Man, I'm hungry. Ever had roasted corn?"

I nodded. "My grandmother used to roast corn in a cast iron skillet."

"Some mighty good eatin', as they say. You don't want to eat with strangers. Let me introduce you around."

He invited me with a jerk of his head. I took a deep breath and followed.

76

First he introduced me to the oldest Hispanic man, the man I called the elder. Isaac called him the mayor. His name was Miguel Vasquez.

"It is my pleasure to meet you, Señorita Johnson. We did not mean to interrupt your visit here. Please forgive us."

"No problem, sir," I responded.

"Please call me Miguel. There in the red apron is my wife, Connie. We watch your show often."

The woman in the red apron smiled at me through the steam rising from the mounds of food in various bowls here and there. She offered a little bow. I tipped my head in return.

"My sweet Connie. And these are my five boys."

He named them all quickly and I quickly forgot. "And my two daughters-in-law, helping my wife cook. And this sweet child is Isabel." He reached for the small child in Isaac's arms. She squealed and buried her face in Isaac's shirt.

"You want to stay with your godfather, don't you, Isabel?" Isaac said.

Godfather?

"Naw. She wants to come to Grandpoppy."

Miguel tickled the child and turned back to me.

"She is my youngest grandchild. And eight others over there. . . . I almost forgot. Please forgive me, Trip."

Tigger-guy shrugged and let an easy smile play across his face.

"Celine Johnson," I said, shaking his hand.

"Trip Robertson. Nice to meet you."

"Likewise."

"He is our pastor," Miguel said, gripping the white man's shoulder. "A very good friend. And he's funny sometimes."

The men roared with laughter.

Soon the women settled us all before paper plates of

roasted corn, refried beans, and quesadillas. I smiled and listened to them as I ate. The warmth they shared in the candlelit dining room could not erase the hurt I felt inside. Thankfully, Abraham and Buxton didn't eat with us.

For the first time in quite a while, I thought about calling my mother. How had she survived the storm? How were Tabby and Brother? What were they doing at that moment? Probably not sharing a meal with strangers.

"We will get those trees cleared away in the morning," Miguel said as I rose from the table. "It is too wet and dark now."

"With a couple chain saws and a tractor," Trip added, "we'll have it cleared in no time."

I thanked them for their kindness and food and left, claiming I needed to use the bathroom. Catty caught up with me.

"You look beat," Catty said, resting a hand on my arm. "You can rest in my room. Far end of the house. Not so many little prying eyes."

I nodded, following her along a carpeted hallway off the main entry. "Isabel wouldn't follow me out of a burning building."

She giggled. In the darkness with nothing but the beam of a flashlight guiding us, her laugh made me think of sneaking around in college.

"Those little Vasquez munchkins. They're good kids. There's just so many of them." She placed a hand on her temple and shook her head. I smiled. "Could drive a sister crazy. Thankfully, they don't wander far from their mamas. Here we are." She swung a door open. The flashlight beam revealed mounds of lace and frills. The faint scent of a man's aftershave lingered in the air.

I made a show of sniffing.

She pushed the flashlight into my hands and rushed forward. "I know it's not heaven on earth." She jerked a window open. "But, hopefully, it'll do."

I found my way to a small armchair in the corner and dropped into its soft cushions. She pushed an ottoman under my legs and slipped my shoes off.

"Bathroom's down the hall, second door on the left. I'll get some candles. Just a sec."

I could get used to this kind of service. The B&B lady had nothing on Catty Wright.

Somewhere in the distance I heard the children laughing. The patter of feet made my heart sink.

Children were nowhere on my horizon. Neither was a good man for that matter. I envied Catty, simple though she was. She had a good black man by her side. Happiness rolled off her at every turn.

My life was in shambles. How long could I hold the pieces together? God only knew.

Chapter 10

CATTY RETURNED to the dark room with two large candle-sticks, placed them on a table beside me, and lit them. She hummed as she set out towels and a robe. Her dark skin glowed bronze in the candlelight.

"Now what else can I get you?"

"Catty, you have done too much." I leaned forward and tried to sound genuine. "Do you do this kind of thing for *Mr. Abraham?*"

She laughed. "Are you kidding me? No way. Besides, I think he would fire me. He's a peculiar man. I made him a plate tonight but that's about as far as servitude goes with him."

I hoped she couldn't see my frown in the semidarkness. My insides boiled with memories of my time with the man.

Peculiar. That's an understatement.

"There they go again," Catty said at the sound of the children's distant squeals. "That little Isabel is something else."

I reclined against the cushions again, happy for the change of subject.

"Do you and Isaac want kids?"

Catty repositioned the towels and rested a hip on the corner of the bed.

"Yeah. Maybe three. We want to adopt at least one child."

Adoption? An interesting word from such a young couple. My curiosity ran ahead of me and the question slipped out before my good sense could stop it.

"Why?"

"Well, this is how we see it—"

"Catty, I'm sorry. It's really none of my business. The reporter in me coming out."

"No, it's okay. You see, Isaac is adopted. Children need homes badly. Especially biracial children. That's the way we see it. Doesn't work for all African-American couples . . . but for us, that's the thing."

"I see. Thanks. That satisfied my curiosity," I lied. Ten million questions flooded my mind. Who was Isaac's mother? When was he adopted? There was a tale here. A nice, warm, human interest story. Too bad it involved Abraham Benson.

I closed my eyes and sank deeper into the pillows. Scents of aftershave floated around me.

Catty cleared her throat. "I . . . um . . . I can remove the pillows if you like."

"The pillows?"

"The smell. If it bothers you. It's in the pillows, see. If it bothers you, I can just put them in the closet."

"No, they're fine. Old Spice?"

"Um . . . yeah. My father's. Unfinished grief, or some such nonsense. That's what Pastor Trip calls it. My father died in a farm accident about three years ago. Trip says I didn't properly grieve his sudden loss. So I cling on to his memory.

"He tells Mr. Abraham the same things. So it's like one

size fits all with him. He's a crazy preacher man." She stopped short and clapped her hand over her cheek. "But I'm babbling. I should go and let you rest."

"No problem. Nothing wrong with hanging on to smells. Tell me something." Here my mouth was running ahead again. But who could blame me. Catty was a primed pump, ready to fill me with information galore. My cup was about to run over.

"How was Isaac adopted?"

"It's kind of complicated." She stood up.

Uh oh. You've pushed her too far, Celine.

"I'm sorry for prying."

"No, no, no. You're not prying. It's just that I don't like talking about folks' stuff, if you will, without them knowing about it. Isaac and I, we talk about his being adopted a lot. But I'm not sure how he'd feel about me telling his story. Or in his words, 'his making.'"

His making?

"Well, if you don't feel comfortable with it, we can just drop it."

A knock on the door made me jump.

"Excuse me, ladies." Isaac's bright face and shirt hovered in the darkness. Catty sprang to her feet and wrapped her arms around him.

"You scared me, sweet."

"I'm sorry, honey. Just checking on you. Then I heard someone talking about me." His teeth flashed in the dark.

"Were your ears burning?" Catty asked.

"On fire." He bent his head and kissed her earlobe. She gushed and kissed him back on the lips.

"Should I leave?" I asked.

They laughed.

"Celine wants to know about your 'making.'"

"My making, huh?"

"Well, that could take a while," Isaac said.

"The short version will be fine," I said.

"I think I need to warn you, Celine," Catty interrupted, "this man tends toward the theatric."

Isaac pushed his fiancée gently toward the bed and stood on the rug in the middle of the room. He adjusted his collar and cleared his throat.

"Let's see. First off, what I'm able to tell you about the making of Isaac Hunt is so way out there, you won't believe me. Are you a believer, Celine? A Christian?"

"Yes."

"Well, this is a story that'll increase your faith. It's not only a tale about how I was adopted but how God pursued me and showed Himself big in my life."

Clearing his throat again, he began. Over the course of several minutes, he told me about finding out "by accident" just two years ago that he was adopted. For many months, he turned his back on the Hunts, the prosperous but distant couple who adopted him at age four. He described the sad journey to Pettigrew in search of the mother he never knew.

He spoke in vivid detail about being pursued by Benson men, white males in Pettigrew loyal to the old ways of the South. The journey ended with his birth father, Abraham Benson, killing his cousin, Ben Jacob Benson, to save the son he hadn't seen in almost twenty years.

"I survived it all by God's grace, His power, and His love. The biggest change was in me. I know a bigger God now than I ever believed existed. He's bigger than any of my struggles. Bigger than the darkness and emptiness that I'd lived with for so many years. And certainly bigger than hate."

Bigger than hate.

The words I yelled at Abraham in the pantry came back to mind.

"Do you hate your birth father?" I heard myself say.

Isaac took a deep breath and let it out slowly.

"No. I love him. Most assuredly. He knows how to rub you the wrong way sometimes. But that's his way. He's a Benson."

Isaac chuckled and sat on the bed beside Catty.

I continued. "He's admitted to killing people and for so many years he stood at the head of this horrible family. The Benson family—known for supporting hate groups like the United Front. How can you say you don't hate him?"

"It's hard to explain. I know what he's done. He's told me things that have been hard to accept. Your grandmother, for instance."

Catty started. He glanced at her and then back to me. I was grateful for the cover of darkness. Tears stung my eyes.

"I'm sorry for your loss. I'm sure he is too. The Word says for those of us who know the right thing to do and don't do it, we are in sin. To me, that says we are to do that right thing without hesitation. That's a hard thing sometimes. But that's the price of justice. I trust that Abraham is genuinely striving for justice. And that it's not just a show.

"He didn't have to shoot his cousin to save me. He didn't have to work with state lawmen to bring the Front down or testify before Congress. Or even wear that ankle cuff. He could have let me get killed. He could have kept his mouth shut and let the Front continue to wreak havoc."

Catty sighed and dabbed at the corners of her eyes.

"He wants to make things right. I respect him for that. He's made a hard decision and he's sticking to it. Chances are he'll never see Patrick, my little brother, again."

What little brother? Where is he? Why haven't I seen him yet? Don't get sidetracked, Celine.

"So to answer your question, Celine—I don't hate Abraham. I love him. Sure, it's not the same love I have for my adoptive father but it's a real love. A big love. Given through me by a big God."

He sat there with his head down and his fingers entwined with Catty's for several minutes.

For the first time since I cornered Catty in the room, I didn't feel pressed to ask another question. Sure, I was curious about this little brother, Patrick. And yes, I did wonder about his biological mother. But the need to know was gone.

And in its place came the need to be alone, to feel the breeze from the window slip through my toes. I just wanted to hear the night sounds and nothing else.

Nothing else, Lord.

No more pain. No more discoveries. Just a quiet place where I could pretend I was still a little country girl with nothing to do on a summer night but listen to frogs calling for rain.

Finally, Isaac and Catty blew out the candles and said good night. Amazingly I drifted off to sleep without a struggle and woke the next morning to crowing.

Chapter 11

AT FIRST I thought the crowing was part of my dream—a vision of me on the dirt lane headed to my grandmother's ramshackle farmhouse. But as I stretched my stiffened leg muscles across the ottoman, the animal crowed again.

"Good morning, Celine," Catty called through the door. "Are you up?"

"Yes."

"What did she say?" asked a man. Tigger-guy Trip, I figured.

"She's up." There was impatience in Catty's voice. I heard someone walking away from the door.

I sat up and looked around the room. Almost seven o'clock and overcast judging by the dim light that filled the room. The smell of aftershave still lingered even in the light breeze that fanned the lacy pink curtains. Little Miss Catty loved herself some lace.

"They're gonna start cutting the trees up to clear the driveway," Catty said through the door. "It'll be a little noisy. Might I come in?"

"Please do."

I wiped the sleep from my eyes and brushed my hair

back. Catty entered wearing a black silk robe and carrying a dragon-print kimono on a hanger.

"You slept in that chair? You must have been tired. I thought about this kimono after I left last night. It's too big for me. Might be nicer to walk around in than that cotton robe."

She laid the kimono on the bed and took a few steps toward the window before spinning around.

"Oh, I almost forgot. John Carter called."

John Carter. I'd forgotten about the man with all the other shocking things that had happened yesterday. He had slipped out of my focus for sure.

"He's on his way to meet with Mr. Abraham but when he heard you were going to be here, he got really excited."

Oh, did he?

She lowered the window and pulled down a pink shade.

"We have power back. I can wash your dress and . . . um . . . undergarments. If you'd like."

My eyes twinkled. "That would be nice."

She talked as she moved through her small walk-in closet across the room. "There's a spa tub in the bathroom. Check the cabinet in there for a new toothbrush. I try to keep some on hand. Never know who's gonna drop in for the night."

She emerged, wearing white jeans and a pink top, with a wicker basket under one arm. Silver hoops dangled from her earlobes. And I thought I was the quick-change queen.

"You can put your clothes in this basket. I'll start a load in a few. What would you like for breakfast?"

I stared at her and laughed.

"What's so funny? Something caught in my hair?" She patted her Afro. A pink polka-dotted scarf held it in check.

"No. I'm laughing because I'm paying seventy-five dollars

a night for a B&B in town and I wouldn't get this kind of—"
I stopped short. The word service had caught in my throat. I
didn't want her to think she was my slave. I winced. Her dark
face widened into a grin.

"Service? No problemo. I don't mind serving. It's my gift.
The gift of helps. You know, from the Bible. Besides, all my
friends will have a fit when I tell them I got to cook you
breakfast.

"I get paid well. I get to see my sweet when he's in town.
I can keep an eye on Mr. A. I get to be in Pettigrew just a little bit longer. And I get to paint in the afternoons." She fanned
a hand Vanna-style toward two paintings on the wall. They
each showed magnolia blossoms the size of watermelons.
Even in the limited light I could see the quality of the strokes.

I stood to inspect them. The initials C.W. graced the corners.

"Very nice."

"Thanks."

She set the basket at the foot of the bed.

"Well, what'll it be? Coffee? Tea?"

I gave my order and she left, smiling and humming. For
all her childishness, Catty was an okay kid. If I could have
chosen a younger sister, she would be on the top of the list.

I called Bob while I slipped into the kimono. He was
okay, so he said. But by the sound of his voice, he was on
edge and plenty hot at me.

We planned to meet at ten to drive over to survey the site
of the Pettigrew Homecoming, Finleigh State Park.

As I ran water for my bath, I jotted down questions for
Bob to ask Abraham. It would be a monologue. That would
work. I'd explain the change to my boss later. I didn't need
to be involved in this at all. She'd understand. Maybe.

I tried to stay objective but the rage kept getting in the

way. After several minutes of sitting on the edge of the tub, all I had was a sore behind and one tepid question: What do you love most about this land?

This is crazy.

Bob would have to become a photojournalist for one day. He'd hate it, but that's tough.

I slipped into the water and closed my eyes. The scents around me—the herbal bath salts, the spicy potpourri, the musky scent of the water itself—they all took me back to the swamp. The many days Tabby, Brother, and I would spend tramping through the soggy backwoods. Looking for baby turtles and running from copperheads.

The memories just slipped by like clouds on a wind until one memory stopped me cold. Where had I left my journal?

It was a fuzzy memory of meeting Abraham Benson in the swamp one day a few months after Daddy went to prison for manslaughter. Many of the mobile homes in our trailer park had been replaced after the fire he set.

But we had moved across the lake to a different trailer. Three bedrooms with a carport. The rental that my mother eventually bought. We could still go on our swamp outings. And we could still see Benson Ridge Farms' red barn in the distance.

Was it morning? Afternoon? Late summer? Early fall? Many of the details escaped me but as the smells of water and herbs surrounded me, my mind went back.

❋ ❋ ❋

"You need to get yourself a stick," I told my sister as I looked down at her sprawled on the damp ground. "Wait here a minute."

My sister, Tabby, had twisted her ankle running from a water snake. Brother, like the quick brown creature he was, had run on ahead. He was probably enjoying a soft drink sitting on the sofa in our new home while Tabby sat on the moist ground squeezing her ankle.

"Why do I need a stick? Just let me lean on you."

"Tabby, you too big to lean on me." I yanked at some underbrush. "Gonna break my durn back." Then I yanked a stick about my height from the thicket and gave it to her. "Here."

She wrapped her fingers around the gnarled vine. "How I'm gonna use that thang?"

"Just lean on it. See?" I demonstrated.

A rustling in the brush nearby made us scream and clutch for each other. Abraham Benson emerged from the thicket, carrying a gun. It was similar to the gun my father kept behind the front door. The barrel didn't shine in the sun and the wooden stock looked as beaten up as the stick Tabby held. He set the gun down on the ground and approached us.

"You hurt, girl?"

"Yes, sir," Tabby said. She gulped.

He crouched down on his heels and steadied himself with a hand on the ground. A chilly wind picked up his hair and whipped it about his head. His cold blue eyes caught mine— I held my breath. He looked like a wild man.

"Where?" he asked.

Tabby pointed at her right ankle. He rested his fingertips against the spot. She yelped and he drew his hand back.

"Ain't that bad, is it? I just wanna see if it's swole. Can I look at it?"

She pulled up her pant leg. He leaned in closer and looked at her ashy ankle.

"You ain't no doctor," I said.

"Never said I was, Carla Celine."

Tabby and I exchanged wide-eyed glances.

"How you know my name, Mr. Abraham?"

"You know mine, seems like." He squeezed her ankle gently with his big fingers. Tabby winced.

"Everybody knows you, Mr. Abraham," Tabby said. "Most folks get us two mixed up."

It was true. Most folks in town called me Tabby for years even though she was so much taller than me.

"Well, Tabitha, I know y'all apart easy. I know all your people. Don't think your ankle's broke. Try and stand up now."

He held her hand and let her lean on him as she stood up. She bit her bottom lip and winced again.

"Try and take a step," he said.

She hobbled a few feet. "I'm fine."

"No you ain't, Tabby."

"I is." Her eyes watered. She took a few more steps, hiding her wince with a thin smile. "See."

I grunted and tried to shove the stick into her hand. She jerked her hand away and shook a finger at me.

"Sit down," Abraham said. He had unbuttoned his blue cotton shirt and flung it to the ground. I stood leaning on the stick, staring with round eyes at my big sister.

"Oh, my God. Mr. Abraham, what you about to do to us?"

He had a pocketknife and made a downward slice in the bottom of his T-shirt about the width of his hand.

"Ain't gonna do nothing to y'all. I'm trying to help your big sister walk home. I could carry you home but you can bet your Barbie doll that if your mama sees you on my back, Tabitha, I won't walk home alive." He chuckled and ripped a long strip from his white undershirt. "Now, sit down."

Tabby sat down and he wrapped her ankle, using the strips like when Grandmamma used to bandage her knee.

Little beads of sweat formed on his temples as he wound the makeshift bandage around her heel and up her ankle. He smoothed it with each turn and tied the end off.

"There. Now stand up. Good. This is our little secret, okay? Don't ever tell nobody."

We nodded and watched him pick up his gun and leave.

❈ ❈ ❈

We left Abraham in the woods that day. Tabby limped home without the aid of the stick. She and I promised to never talk about the strange incident.

What had prompted the man's kindness in the woods that day? Remorse? Pity? He had turned us away the day of the fire. Did he feel responsible for withholding help in the time of great need?

In spite of all my hatred for him, I couldn't help but be curious about his motives, his endgame. He was up to something bad. There wasn't all that much self-sacrifice in the whole world. This "Jesus act" wasn't working for me. Something was up and I aimed to find out just what it was.

Maybe Tabby could help me get to the bottom of it all. Something was nagging me about that day in the woods and the day of the fire. But I just couldn't put my finger on it. I made a mental note to call my sister as well. Hopefully Mama would give me her number again.

By the time I emerged from my divine bath, the whine of a chain saw had mingled with the chatter of little children from the front yard. I made myself presentable and ambled to the kitchen.

"Mamacita Vasquez used up all the eggs," Catty whispered while shaking what appeared to be an empty egg carton. She tapped a carton of egg substitute. "Hope you don't mind fake eggs. Gotta thaw it out, though. Sorry."

I shrugged and reached for the *Virginian Pilot* on the counter. Abraham's face stared back above the fold. I turned the newspaper over and pushed it aside. Catty hummed as she went about buttering a loaf pan. She filled a cup with hot water, set it down, and dropped in a tea bag. Then she swiveled on her heels to tend to the hash browns sizzling in a pan.

"Please feel free to enjoy some green tea on the back patio while you wait. A little ray of sun is trying to peek through. But they're calling for more bad weather later." She tied an apron around her narrow waist.

Maybe I should leave soon. I thought of how anxious Bob had sounded on the phone as I stirred sugar into my tea and brought the thick mug to my nose.

Mmm. Bob can wait.

A luxurious, nutty scent filled my head. I closed my eyes and let a moan rumble up from the bottom of my tired soul.

Do I have to leave?

"Catty, this smells so good. Was there much damage last night from the storm?"

No response. Catty was nowhere in sight. Half a dozen hash browns still sizzled in the pan. The carton of frozen egg substitute swam in a bowl of water in the sink.

Where was everyone? I heard voices through the screen door. Catty was talking with someone.

After making sure that the other voice didn't belong to Abraham, I stepped out. The sun felt good on my skin as I set foot on the patio's wooden decking. The wind whipped the tops of the distant pecan trees. Smooth dark clouds hung overhead. A cool breeze cut through the kimono's thick silk. I wrapped an arm around myself and sipped from my mug.

Catty stood on the grass a few feet away, talking to a thin white man in wrinkled clothes. She glanced at me, her forehead creased.

The man wheeled his ten-speed bike closer to me, his blue eyes stretched wide. I'd experienced that before. The look of awe from a fan.

"You some kin to Harvey?" he asked me.

What?

I turned my questioning look on Catty. She rolled her eyes and grabbed the man's arm.

"Just go get half a dozen eggs, Eddie. Okay? Tell Miss Nichols I'll pay her later."

"Pay her later? Right. Right. Later," he said.

"Could you go now?"

"Go. Yes. Go. Now." The man was staring at me like I had green hair. Had I put the wig back on right?

"Eggs, Eddie," Catty urged.

He moved beyond the reach of her arms, spit on his palm, and extended the moistened hand to me as he bowed.

"Charmed, I'm sure, madam."

"Eddie, this is Celine Johnson."

"Oh, my. I must accoladify you on your fine perfume. I bought some at Belk Tyler for my mama, God rest her blessed soul, the other day."

Catty slapped her forehead. "She's not Céline Dion, Eddie. Go get those eggs."

Eddie stood there smiling, his hand outstretched. The wind billowed through his baggy T-shirt and brought the faint scent of corn chips to my nose. I smiled back at him and kept my hands wrapped around the mug.

"It's a pleasure to meet you too, Eddie."

The smell of corn chips got stronger as he leaned in closer. "That's Crazy Eddie to my good friends."

My good friend Crazy Eddie pedaled away, calling over his shoulder as he went. "Miss Nichols don't sell her good eggs after a tornado. Everybody knows that."

"I'm gonna tornado him," Catty grumbled as she stomped into the house. The bang of the screen door made me jump.

"So much for Plan C," she yelled through the screen door. "Sorry, Celine."

"That's okay."

I gathered the folds of the kimono around me and settled into an Adirondack chair a few steps away. The smells and sounds of the morning were soothing. I looked out over the expanse of the level green lawn to the cornfields and farm outbuildings.

The young plants seemed to shiver in the breeze. I took one last gulp of warm tea and placed the empty cup on the table next to me. A folded newspaper underneath caught my eye. I picked it up.

The Wall Street Journal?

Someone had opened it to the crossword puzzle. Several blocks had been filled in. Like an invitation I couldn't decline, an ink pen tumbled onto my lap.

Don't mind if I do.

I heard someone in hard-heeled shoes walking across the kitchen floor. Catty's voice rang out, "Morning, gentlemen."

"Morning, Catherine," Abraham replied. I dropped the pen. My heart stopped.

"Morning, Cat Woman," said another man. It didn't sound like Buxton, Trip, or Isaac.

Cat Woman?

"I told you about calling me that. Coffee?" she replied.

There were sounds of something being poured into a cup, then the clink of china.

"Thank you, Catherine. Fake eggs with fake cheese for my pitiful, congested heart, please."

"Yes, sir."

"Cat Woman, give me some of that green tea I had last time."

"Sorry. Gave the last one out just this morning."

"Well, that wasn't nice. Coffee then. No sugar. No cream. Big Abe, with all this rain we're getting, you should have a great harvest this year."

Abraham grunted. "Why's my harvest a concern of yours?"

"Thanks for reminding me that I am no longer in your employ."

"Or my debt."

"For which I am heartily sorry, sir."

"Behave, gentlemen," Catty interjected.

Abraham chuckled. A phone rang.

"It's Washington," Abraham said after a pause. "I'll take it in my office." With the sound of a chair being moved across the floor, I hoped it meant Abraham was gone. I let out a breath and picked up the puzzle again.

Catty's voice rang out, "I'll keep your eggs warm, Mr. Abraham."

"Yeah, in my belly," the other man said.

"Let go of that plate and get on outta my kitchen." Catty laughed.

"Why you gotta treat me so badly, Cat Woman? You mad at me, too, for quitting?"

"Just go outside and wait."

"You don't own the kitchen, you know."

"Git out of here, man! Celine, I'll have your breakfast ready in a few. More tea?"

"No, I'm fine," I yelled over my shoulder before turning back to the puzzle. "A shepherd's lunch?" I mumbled.

The screen door swung open. I saw a white hand gripping the knob and the back of a red-checkered shirt pressed against the mesh of the screen door. "Hey, I thought you said you were out of tea," the man said.

"Outta my kitchen."

The man laughed and sprang out onto the patio. A dishcloth came whirling after him. He jumped aside and flinched at the slap of the screen door.

"Somebody should fix that door." The man's boots clicked across the decking. "Oh, I see you found my puzzle. One of the kids hid it out here, I guess."

With expensive sunglasses hiding his eyes, he reminded me of an Italian model I once shared a wild Lower Manhattan cab with. From the neck down, though, it looked like he and Crazy Eddie frequented the same thrift shop.

We exchanged a morning nod. The wind tousled his wavy brown hair. He had what looked like a few days' growth of beard but, unlike my good friend Crazy Eddie, he wore it well.

"Well, you had 1 across wrong. And 4 down wrong," I said.

"Huh?" He placed one brown scuffed boot in front of the other, whipped off his shades, and rested an elbow along the back of my chair. His body heat folded around me and I looked up into the oddest eyes I'd ever seen on a man. Deepset, caramel brown; rimmed in long dark lashes.

Oh my goodness. How beautiful.

"Yep, I see it now. A shepherd's lunch." He tapped 2 down. "That's Alpo. You know, as in German shepherd."

Tearing away from those eyes, I realized I could have figured it out.

Okay, let's stump this guy.

"How about 8 across?"

"Poignant quality? Six letters? Oh, that's easy. Pathos."

My eyebrows shot up. "Pathos?"

"It fits."

This tall and tan farmhand had some nerve.

"Just because it fits doesn't mean it's right."

"Look here, 8 down. 'Palm product.' That's a PDA. You know a personal digital—"

"I know what PDA stands for."

He laughed. "You're pretty good. You certainly know your way around a puzzle, Celine."

I glanced at him, not trusting myself to look at those eyes again but not quite liking his ease with my name. A man, even a good-looking one, should not expect to meet women over crossword puzzles and instantly be on a first-name basis.

"Thanks. You're not half bad yourself. Celine Johnson." I stretched out my hand.

He wrapped large warm fingers around mine and squeezed, a small smile playing across his full mouth.

"John Carter Manning," he said.

I sputtered. "What? Why, I thought you were a hired hand."

"Sorry. I should have worn my tuxedo." Shoving his shades on, he stood up straighter and pulled at his shirttails.

"Don't make light. You knew who I was all along." I stood up too, pointing my finger in his face.

"Catty called you by name."

"You knew who I was before she said my name. You've seen me on TV. Why didn't you identify yourself—"

"Seen you on TV, huh? I'll have to remember that one. You started in with 'you did 1 down wrong and you did 4 down wrong.' I didn't have a chance to identify myself." His tone was snide and mocking.

"Don't you dare talk to me like that."

"Don't what?" He bared a set of perfect white teeth at me. "You sit out here in your kimono drinking the last cup of good tea in the house. A little black woman waiting on you like a Hebrew slave. Brown-skinned men breaking their backs cutting trees out of the driveway so you can drive all over town cutting everybody down. You are such a diva."

My hands were on my hips. "Diva? Diva! Well, you are nothing but a fool."

"A what?"

The screen door's bang cut us both short. Abraham stood behind us.

"That's enough. John Carter, take your paper and leave."

"My pleasure."

He reached for the paper. I threw it at his chest. He glared at me, then with a huff, bent down and snatched it up.

"Your daddy would be embarrassed at your behavior," he said and marched back inside. I followed.

"News flash, John Carter Manning—Quincy Johnson is dead."

On a dime, he whirled around. "No, Carla Celine Johnson, Pettigrew native, I've got news for you. Part of the old Quincy is still alive. In fact, it's thriving inside your cold, lying heart."

100

Chapter 12

MY LYING HEART?

I had been lying for a long time. I knew that. So many times I had planned to set the record straight, claim Pettigrew as my home. But the words and the circumstances had never been right.

But cold heart? Diva?

The man just didn't know me.

"Who does he think he is?" I grumbled as I tossed lipstick and mascara back into my bag. "Diva, I ain't. He comes up in here looking like a raggedy-tail bum and expects to be taken seriously. He's got another think coming. Calling me a—"

"Celine?"

I started and turned around. Catty stood in the bedroom doorway, holding my clothes, which were folded and neatly stacked. She placed them on the bed and shot a glance my way; then she stared at the floor.

"Oh, thank you so much."

Would a diva show gratitude? I ask you that.

"There's another tornado warning."

I looked toward the window. A downpour had started. Bob would be furious.

"You gonna stay?"

"I can't stay, Catty. I'll just go back into town and ride out the bad weather there. My cameraman is itching to work. This will probably blow over by noon."

I glanced at the clock—9:38 a.m.

"I've got to get going. Thanks for all you've done for me."

"You're welcome, ma'am."

"Ma'am?"

"Sorry." She turned sad eyes on me and shrugged. My behavior had driven a wedge between us, it seemed.

Bye, little sister.

I hugged her and let her leave without a word.

❅ ❅ ❅

"Now, Bob, I know you're ready to wring my neck."

I cradled my cell phone under my chin and steered the van slowly around the logs and tree limbs that littered the Benson Ridge Farms driveway. The tree-cutting crew had not done a very good job.

"No . . . well, yeah I am kind of upset and stuff. But I was able to get out earlier. Got some nice footage of Main Street. Even interviewed some folks."

"Well, go on with your bad self. All my expertise has rubbed off on you."

"You're the best, Celine."

My stomach did a funny dip.

Diva.

"I was joking, you know," I responded.

Rain pounded the windshield. The wipers, on high, did nothing to clear my field of vision. I lifted my foot off the gas.

Slow down, Celine.

"What did you say . . . couldn't . . . "

He was breaking up. I hung up and tossed my phone in my bag. A ceiling of dark clouds hung low. Goose bumps rose on my bare arms as lightning split the sky over the cornfields on either side. Why had I left that sweater on my bed at the B&B? The mugginess had left the air. It was downright cold.

Leaves and twigs plastered the windshield. A few up-rooted corn plants tumbled across the road. I slowed down even more and squinted through the rain-slick windshield at two signs several yards ahead.

"Pettigrew, 2 miles," the first read.

"Finleigh State Park, 10 miles," read the second.

Thoughts of turning back crossed my mind. I had no way of telling how far I'd gone but the weather had turned nasty quicker than I thought possible. I didn't need confirmation that the situation was bad but I turned the radio on anyway.

A recorded message was playing:

". . . issued a tornado warning affecting Pettigrew, North Carolina. This information is valid through 11:59 a.m. The National Weather Service has issued . . . "

Pettigrew, 2 miles.

I stopped the van. It shook with the gusts of wind blowing across the road.

"Lord, what should I do?"

Behind me, I could see the Benson Ridge farmhouse like a toy in the distance, stark white under the gloomy clouds. The farm wasn't close but certainly not two miles away.

A small brown bird flew up to the back window. It beat its wings but went nowhere. A gust blew it sideways into the cornfield beyond. The van shuddered and rocked as corn plants, small branches, and leaves pelted and plastered every side.

"Should I turn around?" I said out loud.

A large limb fell across the front windshield. I screamed and turned the wipers off. Other parts of the tree that had once held the limb now blocked the road. To go around it I would have to drive onto the rain-drenched shoulder. One slip down the soggy embankment and I would be hip deep in the drainage canal that paralleled the road.

"Well, that's my answer." I put the van in reverse and looked in my rearview mirror. The landscape of clouds behind me had grown a large wedgelike foot. The sky beyond the farm glowed a sickly yellow-green.

All debris had stopped flying. My ears felt stuffy. I held my breath and gripped the wheel to steady my shaking limbs.

There was that thing that looked too much like a tornado behind me and the tree blocking the road in front.

"Oh, help me, God."

I bit my lip and cried.

"Okay, Celine. You can't just fall apart. Think. Okay, it's not a tornado. I don't hear freight trains bearing down on me."

In an instant, loud winds hammered the van again. Once again leaves and dust mingled with the lashing rain. Small icy pellets sliced through the air. My wipers were still pinned under the limb across the front. Useless.

I glanced around. From my childhood days, I recalled another house close to Benson Ridge. It was a smaller house set back from the woods in a grove of trees. I remembered a dirt road leading from the main road to that house. What had it been called? The Ross house. Yes!

"There it is."

Just beyond the road signs, obscured by bushes, I saw a break in the trees and what looked like the rear end of a small truck.

I needed shelter fast. Gunning the engine, I drove toward the tree debris in the road. The front wheels crunched and skidded over the wreckage. I gunned it again to overcome the spin. The back wheels hit the wet earth of the shoulder. The van started to slip out of control. Down. Down. Down. I braked hard. The sliding stopped.

"Oh, Lord. Please."

I gripped the wheel and floored it. Chunks of earth flew from the rear wheels. I was slipping again.

I had only one choice. I opened the door and jumped out. I scrambled up the slippery shoulder and onto the road. But then I looked back. My feet froze.

The wedge in the cloud had turned into a gigantic V the size of the entire county. A cloud of dust hovered on the ground below it, rising like magnetic debris to touch the bottom of the funnel. Would I see the farmhouse swirling through the air. The barn? A tractor?

"Oh, my. Oh . . ."

I was crying and drenched—blind in the storm. I felt like Dorothy in that movie, except I didn't have a bike or a cute little dog or a script.

"Celine!"

Lord?

"Celine! Over here!"

Where?

I turned around. A man was standing in the road a few feet from the van. The wind whipped his brown hair around his head. He reminded me of pictures I'd seen as a child of Blackbeard. Mud clung to his red-checkered shirt. He reached for me. I came to my senses and pulled away.

"John Carter?"

"Yes. Come . . . please."

"Where?"

He grabbed my arm and pulled me toward him. "Does it matter, woman?"

John Carter held my wrist and ran past the van. He slid feetfirst down the muddy bank. Still in his grasp, I slipped and stumbled forward. My foot hit something solid. His head? His back? My shoes slipped off my feet. I groped for them but they were gone, flung hither and yon by the harsh wind.

My wig caught on something and came off. I reached for it but it had taken flight. Mud caked my bare legs and backside. Suddenly I landed knee-deep in the water beside him. Cold, thick mud surrounded my feet.

"Are you okay?" he shouted.

The noise around us had increased. I could barely hear him yelling in my ear. "I'm okay. You're bleeding."

A little blood trickled from a cut on his jaw. He touched it.

"It's nothing." He looked over my shoulder with round eyes. "Oh no."

I followed his gaze and screamed. The funnel was closer to us now, ripping corn plants from the earth like a giant mixing hand. Dust stung my eyes and caked my teeth. My hair was slapping my face; it felt like tiny knives. Stalks and unshucked ears of corn pummeled us. I closed my eyes and turned away. John Carter pulled me into him and fell back against the side of the ditch. He held me tight and buried his face in my hair.

"Lord, help us," I sobbed. His chest was hot against my cheek. I clung to his upper arm with my right hand and the ground with my left.

John Carter rolled and pulled me into the shelter of his body. He stretched his arms wide across the ditch bank and grabbed half-exposed roots. Shaking his hair back, he looked into my eyes and spoke. The wind carried his words away. He winced then once again buried his face in my hair.

The wind rocked our bodies. John Carter groped for a better handhold.

"Yea, though I walk through the valley of the shadow of . . ."

Debris tore at my skin. I struggled for breath.

"Shadow of death, I will fear no evil." Oh, Lord, please help us.

Sounds of limbs being ripped from nearby trees made me flinch. I wrapped my arms around John Carter and pressed closer.

"Yea, though I walk through the valley of the shadow of death."

I squeezed my eyes shut and prayed. His mouth moved against my hair. It seemed he was praying too.

"I will fear no evil."

Like the settling of heavy velvet, the roaring lessened and the winds subsided. I moved my head to one side. John Carter's heartbeat thundered in my ear. My chest rose and fell with his breathing.

He drew in a deep breath and released it slowly. Was he smelling me? Or simply expressing relief? I let go of him and glanced up. He turned his head and rolled away.

For several minutes we sat on the muddy slope, side by side, watching the ragged clouds floating by. As my breathing steadied I began to look around. Cornstalks and tree limbs were strewn all about. Some eight or ten feet over us, a tree trunk dangled from the electric lines like an incomplete bridge. What did the landscape above look like?

"You okay?" he asked, his voice raspy.

"Yes."

"Your dress. You've lost a button . . . " He lowered his eyes and turned his back to me.

Indeed I had. I pulled the opening closed and held it flat with my palm. Unsure of whether to thank him or slap him, I walked away.

My foot hit something hard under the murky water and I fell to my knees. John Carter rushed forward and helped me up.

I pulled away and struggled to my feet alone. My once-blue dress was now blue with large brown spots. Mud coated my hands and arms. Grass and leaves clung to my skin. I wiped mud and trash from my face with my muddy hands.

"Leave me alone."

"Fine. I just saved your life. I'll leave you alone."

I left him talking and walked toward the rocks piled against the culvert under the dirt road that led to the Ross house. I would use the rocks to climb out of the muck and mire. Then something occurred to me. I whirled back around.

"And why in heaven's name did we not ride out the storm in there?" I pointed toward the culvert. Maybe four feet high, the sturdy metal tube would have been better protection.

"Well, Ms. Diva, if I had wanted to drown, I would have gone in there. But then again, I am foolish."

"The water didn't get that high. Look." I pointed to the waterline, lapping just above my knees now. "I might be shorter than you but . . . "

"Oh yeah, and I would have known just how much water that monster was planning to drop on us." He pointed toward the parting clouds overhead. "I'd love to debate this ad infinitum but I have need of a bath."

He splashed past me, his mouth working. He glared at me over his shoulder then he spun around.

"And, FYI, I wasn't looking at you *there*." With a quick glance, he indicated my chest. "Yes, I saw . . . *there* . . . but I wasn't looking *there*."

"And that's supposed to make a difference?"

"So you'd rather I keep my mouth shut while you go around exposing yourself. Now, that would be downright *foolish*."

He stomped away.

"Coming or not, Ms. Diva?"

Chapter 13

JOHN CARTER, the humanitarian, left me to clamber up the rocks alone. I stood in the middle of the dirt road, adjusted my nasty clinging dress, and looked around.

"Oh, look at this mess."

Much of the corn in the fields on either side of the road was flattened. Great patches of earth had been gouged out. The electric poles leaned this way and that; the lines sagged close to the ground like forgotten clotheslines. The roads were littered with destruction as far as I could see.

By some miracle, my van hadn't slipped any farther. But the amount of tree and corn debris littering the road had made moving it nearly impossible.

In the distance, the Benson Ridge farmhouse seemed to be intact. The red barn was not. I could only stand and shake my head.

"Thank You, Father, for Your mighty hand of protection," I prayed.

The rumble of an engine made me turn around. John Carter had started the little truck tucked in the brush. I walked closer.

"Where do you think you're going?"

He glared through the open window at me.

"I'm trying to get an update on the weather. Any *fool* can see we're not driving anywhere anytime soon."

"Can we drop the fool nonsense?"

"Shhh!?"

He held up a hand to silence me as he adjusted his radio.

". . . reports of serious localized damage in several areas," a man announced. "The National Weather Service says that there were at least three sightings in Washington County alone. They're calling the past two days of severe activity a major tornado outbreak. A tornado watch will stay in effect until 5 p.m. The squalls that triggered the tornadoes are starting to move out over the Atlantic so we can only hope and pray that the worst is over. Until our uplink to the TV station is restored, we'll be suspending our regular programming. It's been a crazy couple of days . . ."

John Carter switched off the radio and sat back, his shoulders sagging. He wiped mud from his lower lip and looked at me.

"Come here," he said and opened the door. He uncapped a plastic jug of water.

I raised my eyebrows.

"I'm not gonna kiss you." He stood and spit to one side. "Cup your hands. Don't worry. I'll close my eyes. Wouldn't want to see anything."

I huffed, my eyes narrowed. "You are something else, John Carter."

He closed his eyes and smiled. "That's what all the divas tell me. Are your hands cupped?"

"Yes." I cupped my hands under the water pouring from the jug. My dress fell open down to my waist. Another button had fallen off. I stifled a gasp then glanced up at John

Carter. Eyes still closed. Water spiked his long thick lashes.

I turned my attention to the cool water splashing over my hands and scraped mud from my arms. Then I splashed my face and neck, and let it run down inside my bra.

From what I could tell by patting my hair, a good washing was in order. Maybe five good washings.

"Done?"

I cinched my dress closed with both hands. "Mmm hmm."

"Okay. Now you pour for me." He shoved the jug toward me.

"I . . . um . . . I lost another button."

"Another button?"

"Yep." I stared at the ground.

"Well, that might complicate matters. If you pour, then you'd have to release that death grip you have on your dress and I'd surely see *something* then."

"Just close your eyes."

He cocked an eyebrow and chuckled.

"You're a sad, demented man."

He reached in his pocket and pulled out a little zippered sandwich baggie, full of sewing supplies. A poor man's sewing kit, no doubt. Then he fished out several safety pins.

"You had that all along."

"No, I found it in my glove compartment while you were taking your sweet time climbing those rocks. Do you want them or not?"

He dropped them into my waiting hand. I thanked him with a nod and turned around.

"You're welcome, Ms. Diva," he responded as he climbed out of the truck.

"Please stop calling me that."

I heard the sound of water hitting the ground and looked

over my shoulder. He was squatting with the jug between his knees, rocking on his toes to get water to flow over his hands and arms.

"That's your name, isn't it?" he asked. "Why should I stop calling you by your name?"

I'd finished with two pins and was struggling with the third. "Because I asked you."

"Hmm. I'll take it under advisement."

Having added extra pins to reinforce the existing buttons, I turned to face him. He stood with his eyes closed and head back, pouring the last bit of water over his head.

He opened his eyes and looked at me. The sun broke through the clouds, making me squint. He frowned at my hair.

"I've got another jug of water," he said. Water dripped from his shirttail and the tip of his nose.

I frowned at him.

"For your hair."

"Is it that bad?"

"Yeah." He jerked a thumb at the truck's rearview mirror.

Caked on one side and the back with thick black mud, spiked with twigs and leaves—my poor hair looked as bad as I felt.

"You ready?"

John Carter unscrewed the cap and stepped forward. I grabbed the jug with my right hand. He held fast.

"Wait a minute." He poured about half the water into the first jug and placed it on the hood of the truck. "We might get thirsty. Now bend over."

I shook my head and reached for the jug again.

"I can rinse my own hair."

"You won't be able to see what you're doing. Bend over, please."

I needed a relaxer and a trim. There was no way I was going to let this white man care for my nappy hair. I stood there, crossed my arms, and looked him in the eye. He shook his head.

"Will you just let me help you, Celine? Please?"

His use of my actual name melted my resolve. I bit my lip and shrugged. "You pour. I'll comb." I bent over and finger combed my hair, pulling out the bigger clumps and sticks as I went.

John Carter poured slowly across the nape of my neck and worked his way toward the crown. I rolled my head from side to side and let the cool stream caress my forehead and temples.

When I could no longer feel the grit, I stopped combing and just let the water fall across my neck. The water stopped but I didn't straighten. I closed my eyes and inhaled the scent of the mud at my feet. Memories of mud pies came rushing back.

The pressure of another hand in my hair startled me. I whipped my head back.

"What are you doing?"

He held an empty jug in one hand and a bright green leaf in the other. "You missed this." His face was red.

"Thank you." I leaned to one side and squeezed water from my hair.

"You're welcome." He tossed the empty jug into his truck and slammed the door. "We'd better get going."

"Going?"

"Back to Benson Ridge."

He grabbed the half-full jug of water from the truck's hood and headed for the blacktop. I'd long since lost my shoes so following his long strides took some doing. I picked

115

my way around the sharp, ragged objects that dotted the pavement.

"Slow down, John Carter."

He said something but I didn't catch it. He stopped in front of my van and put his foot on the bumper. The van bounced and creaked. I ran ahead, wincing all the way. The fool was going to push the van in. Did he hate me that much?

"Don't do that. You're going to push it in."

"You want me to get your van out."

"Out of the ditch once you push it in, you mean?"

He walked around and opened the door. "Good. The keys are still in there. Not much else though. Where's your equipment?" He gripped the steering wheel and lifted himself into the driver's seat. The van creaked again.

"You're crazy, John Carter. It's going to slide in." My heart stopped as the van slid a few inches along the wet shoulder. "Get out!"

He rolled down the window and tossed me my bag.

"So you left your cameraman in town? Give him a call." He started the engine. "Call your mama and them. Call Benson Ridge. Make sure they're all alive. And, oh yeah, call for help if I don't make it."

He flashed a grin and gunned the engine. Mud flew everywhere. I leapt backward.

"You've got to be the craziest man I've ever met."

"Then I guess you haven't met Crazy Eddie yet," he yelled.

The van slid back another inch or so. John Carter glanced in the mirror like he was only parallel parking. He gunned the engine and leaned forward.

"You're gonna kill yourself."

The van slipped to the right, then the left. It inched forward until finally all four wheels were on the road.

116

I exhaled and relaxed my shoulders.

John Carter flashed a smile as he pocketed the keys and jumped out with the water jug in hand. "I think it'll be safe here."

"That was the most foolish thing I've ever seen."

"You're welcome." He walked away, glancing at the tires and rocking the vehicle.

"Are you just going to leave it there?"

"Well we can't drive it. Unless you want to blow all four tires." He looked at my bare feet. "You can ride my back."

"You can eat my cell phone." I fished through my bag for a silk scarf I'd seen earlier. "Why do men have to be so durn crazy."

"Carla Celine, what language!"

I tried to flash him my "back off, fool" look but a giggle bubbled up instead. "I haven't said that word in years. Durn, that felt good!"

"Durn!" He smiled. "That's a mighty powerful word."

I laughed as I tied the scarf over my damp wild hair. "You are a crazy man."

"All that crazy makes a man thirsty." He uncapped the jug and offered it to me. "Divas first."

"Watch yourself." I wagged a finger at him as I took the jug. He watched me hold the jug just above my lips and let the water fall freely into my mouth. With a nod of thanks, I handed it back.

He turned the jug to his head and let water fall into his mouth just as I had. Water ran down his chin. He wiped his mouth with the back of his hand and screwed the cap on.

Not the polished playwright I thought I'd find.

Had his return to Pettigrew the previous year changed him? What had prompted the return? I fingered my tape recorder. How could I start questioning a man with such a lax attitude? Interviewing Crazy Eddie would be more productive.

"Sure you don't want a piggyback ride, Celine?"

I gave him the real "stop the foolishness" look. He mocked me by jumping back with a high-pitched shriek. Laughing, he walked away, kicking piles of rubbish as he went.

"Very funny," I said, following on tender feet.

"You wouldn't happen to have a cheeseburger in that purse would you?"

"Do you ever turn it off?"

"What?"

"This wise-cracking Rambo thing. You don't look like the 'break necks with your bare hands while you're cracking jokes' type."

He pushed back a sleeve and flexed a brawny arm. My heart did a funny flip and I found myself staring.

"I don't?" he said. "You're right, it's all an act. I did quite well in acting class, you know."

"I know."

"Don't believe everything you read on the Internet."

"So all those awards . . . "

"All fake." He bent down to move a large section of tree out of the way. I stooped to help. He elbowed me away. "Stop that."

I gave him the eye and continued to push. Two of my nails broke.

"Durn," he muttered.

Chewing on a ragged nail, I glared at him and walked by.

"Pretty is as pretty does," he said.

"What's that supposed to mean?"

"Divas do diva stuff."

"What!"

"I just called you pretty."

Not really.

"And?"

"Say thank you like a good diva."

"What kind of foolishness is this? No more diva anything. I'm supposed to interview you. And I'm asking myself how am I going to do it? You are as unprofessional as they come.

"Do you have an evil twin or something? One that's more serious and believable? We've just lived through a harrowing experience and all you can do is joke. You were praying over me, back there. I know you were. What happened to that man?"

"Okay, if you are not a diva, then I'm not a fool."

"Stellar logic, Einstein."

"Spoken like a true diva."

"Foolish is as foolish does."

He slapped his forehead and let out a howling laugh.

❊ ❊ ❊

A pile of red lumber. That's what the Benson Ridge barn was. Across a leaf-littered yard, the main house stood solid. Curtains wafted through broken windows in the front of the house.

The few tall spiky trees bordering the front yard that had survived last night's storm now lay like toppled dominoes across the grass.

As John Carter and I picked our way across the front lawn, he called out. No one answered.

"Maybe they're in the pantry," I said.

119

He nodded and started unlacing his boots. "Do you want my boots or my socks?"

"What are you doing?"

"The windows are broken. There's bound to be broken glass everywhere."

"Socks, please."

I slipped the muddy socks on and followed him across the yard and into the house. A radio was playing somewhere. *The kitchen?* John Carter broke into a run for the kitchen, calling out as he went. I stayed in the front entry. A sense of not belonging had gripped me.

Sounds of a happy reunion reached me from the kitchen. Their shouting and laughing was proof that I didn't fit in. No one was looking for me.

I was the outsider who had alienated myself. No one really wanted me here, I figured. Not even Catty. Her pleasant reception had only been part of her job, no doubt. She'd called me ma'am just before I left. I was being treated like any visitor, not like a friend.

I sat at the bottom of the stairs and flipped my phone open. No signal. I remembered seeing a phone in Abraham's office.

Glass littered the office floor. Puddles of water stood here and there. I closed the office door behind me and tiptoed around the shards and water to the large desk. The phone sat under a pile of damp windblown papers. There was a dial tone. Good.

"Hello, Bob," I said.

"Oh, my God, Celine. You're okay. Oh, my God. I've been trying to call you . . . the news reports and then we walked through town and . . ."

"Calm down, Bob. I'm fine. Nothing broken. The van is

fine. A little muddy. Okay, a lot muddy. I'll tell you about that later. Where are you now? Are you okay?"

The man was gulping for air. Did I hear sniffling?

"Yeah, I'm fine. We didn't have any real damage in town. A few signs down and an old tree fell into the street. Summer and I walked down to Benson Ridge Road. She said it leads to the farm. You're still there, right?"

"Yeah. But something happened . . ." I trailed off, searching for words to describe my experience in the storm. The sights and sounds of the tornado hovering so close. The sounds and smells of John Carter stretched across me. My breath caught and tears stung my eyes.

Bob continued. "She drove me down the road but couldn't get far. There were trees and stuff just covering the road. Power lines down. It's incredible. But I guess you know that."

"Did you get footage?"

"Yeah, you know it."

I smiled at the excitement in his voice.

"It's good to hear your voice," he said.

"Yours too, Hollywood. They say the worst of the storm is over. Try to get to the park and get footage."

"Way ahead of you. Summer's letting me borrow her car so I'm going after lunch. There's a little flooding in town so I'm hoping it'll be down and stuff by then."

"Good." I bit back the tears.

"You okay?"

"Yeah. It's been a rough morning."

A colossal understatement.

"Some townspeople are starting cleanup already. And I just saw an electrical crew from the power company drive by. Hopefully you can join me soon."

"Maybe. Take care, Bob." My voice cracked.

"You too."

Trembling, I hung up and sat in the wooden chair behind the desk. The tears turned to sobs. I buried my head in the crook of my arm and wept.

The door opened. I started and looked up. It was Catty.

"Celine?" She rushed over and wrapped her arms around me. "We've been looking for you."

She wiped the tears from my face and kissed my neck. I sank into her arms.

❋ ❋ ❋

"Close your eyes and turn around," Catty said. I looked up at her smiling face. "You might want to hold your nose this time."

Pinching my nose, I closed my eyes and tilted my head back. The water from the plastic bucket suspended overhead splashed down over me.

The makeshift shower didn't quite compare to my divine bath earlier but I wasn't complaining. Clean is clean. With Catty's herbal body wash, even the cold water from the well was tolerable. The shower stall, two blue tarps hung in a circle from the branches of the pecan tree, popped in the breeze. One of the curtain weights, a metal clamp, fell from the bottom edge, revealing the toe of a scuffed muddy boot inches from my toes.

John Carter.

I stifled a squeal.

"Is our diva clean yet?" John Carter asked. "Don't worry, Celine. I've got my eyes closed. I wouldn't want to see anything, you understand."

A soft thud shook the rough wooden pallett that comprised the shower floor as a plastic bucket was set down.

Catty giggled. She steadied herself on her platform, which happened to be thick boards stretched between two metal ladders. Catty then unhooked the empty bucket from the pulley and rope system Isaac had rigged. "What do you think, Celine? Another rinse?"

I crisscrossed my chest with my arms and shivered. "Good-bye, John Carter."

The toe of the boot tapped on the pallett.

"Pretty please with sugar on top. Go on, say it," he teased.

"What kind of foolishness . . ." The toe continued to tap. I continued to shiver. "Pretty please with sugar on top."

"Thank you, ma'am."

He walked away whistling.

"Is he always so goofy?"

"Nope." Catty handed me a large thick towel. "Can't say that I've seen him quite that goofy. Makes me a little worried. I wish Pastor Trip was back. Maybe he could help John Carter."

Trip had weathered the storm in the pantry with Abraham, Isaac, Catty, and Agent Buxton. After the all clear, the minister had left in search of his new bride, Frieda, who had been visiting family in Finleigh.

"What do you mean, help him?" I asked, slipping my feet into a pair of Catty's flip-flops. My heels hung over the back edge more than an inch.

"You said that you were close to the twister. How close?" Catty handed down the kimono I'd worn after my bath this morning. She untied a cord at the top and let the tarp down like a magician in a magic show.

I stepped over the ring of blue plastic and cinched the brocade sash around my waist. The sky was blue and clear.

The wind played among the leaves of the pecan and syca-mores overhead. But in my mind, the storm still raged.

I felt the pressure in my ears. The grit in my mouth. The warmth of John Carter's body against mine. Part of me was still in the storm.

"Mmm hmm. Pretty close." I pointed beyond the jumble of tree limbs and shredded corn plants stacked around the yard to where John Carter and Isaac struggled to clear the driveway. It looked like four or five city blocks away. "Maybe the distance from here to the men."

Catty let out a low whistle as she climbed down.

"Wow. That close? The sound of the wind inside the pantry was scary. Then when the windows all shattered, it was like an explosion. I can't imagine being out in it.

"Coming through something like that is bound to make you act a little different, I imagine. I'm glad you're alive. If you wanna talk about anything, I'm here. But Pastor Trip might be better, being a minister and all." She gave my shoul-der a quick squeeze.

I knew she meant well but I wasn't that bad off. I didn't need professional help. That shower had done wonders to re-turn me to my old self. Some food in my stomach and I'd be ready to catch up on work.

"Thank you, Catty."

"I'd better get lunch started."

I shook the water from my hair and wrapped it in a dry towel as I walked to the house. The kitchen smelled of freshly shucked corn. And except for the buzz of a fly against the screen, the house was quiet.

Catty stood at the sink, her hands in a sink full of sub-merged cobs of corn. A breeze through the open window blew strands of corn silk across the countertop and into the water.

"Hopefully, the power will be back on tomorrow. Mr. Abraham wants to stick it out here. He wants you to go." She told me all this with a flat tone, her eyes fixed on the corn. "If you want to, that is."

I hadn't seen Abraham since I'd left earlier in the day. So much had happened since that time. The storm had opened me up and stripped so much away. I felt exposed and raw, tired clear to the core.

And the rage from this morning still loomed close, keeping the tears in check, helping me focus. I did have a job to do and I aimed to do it, despite the circumstances.

"Catty, can I ask you something?"

She made circles in the water and nodded.

"This is kind of personal. Is that okay?"

"About Mr. Abraham?" she asked.

Either she was more clever than I thought, or I was more shallow.

"Yeah. It is." I took a breath and moved closer. "Has Abraham ever harmed you?"

With wide eyes she looked at me and shook her head. "Never."

"How long have you lived here? Just the two of you?"

"About a year and a half. And every day has been aboveboard. He's like a father. Never touched me in any way that made me uncomfortable. You could call him old school to a fault. He doesn't even allow Isaac to stay here when he's in town. In this big house. Imagine that. Every night he makes me lock my door."

That wasn't the answer I'd expected.

"Celine, can I tell you something?"

"Sure."

"Not too long ago, a young white guy used to work here. He was a farmhand like John Carter used to be. Isaac talked about him last night but didn't call his name. His name was Jack Kepler. Jack was a hateful fella. Hurting folks, especially black folks, just to be hurting folks. He was in pretty deep with the Front.

"He almost killed Isaac one day. He killed my grandmother. He's in prison now."

My mouth dropped. Catty's voice was flat but she was telling me some far-fetched things. When had Pettigrew become such a gruesome place? She dried her hands on a dish towel and continued.

"It was the hate in Jack. In the end, he had less than what he started with. A while back, Mr. Abraham had a lot of hate bottled up too. And hate only thinks about killing. One day I walked in on Mr. Abraham. He had a gun to his head.

"That was a few days before Isaac came. God sent him back to show Mr. Abraham another way of dealing with the hate. Isaac was full of a lot of hate too. But God—"

"Catty, you can't be serious. Abraham is a confessed killer. He's lied for many, many years. God knows what he did to Isaac's mother."

"Listen, Celine. I may not have a college degree and I've never been to seminary. But it's plain to see that hate kills. Hate leads you quickly down an ugly path. The hate inside of you, it'll justify its existence. It's trying to survive at all cost. Hate will always be in the world, Celine. We live in a fallen place. So let it be in the world and not in you—not in your heart. How can it be there when Christ is there too? You don't want to pay the ultimate cost. Your health or even your life, your connection to God."

I shook my hands in the air like I could erase her words off an imaginary blackboard floating in the air between us.

"Catty, Abraham Benson killed people. He lived with that knowledge for years. Lied through his teeth."

"He's not the only one. Murder is sin. So is lying."

I bit my tongue and glared at her. She was definitely not a harmless country bumpkin. Or a cute little domestic who kept her mouth shut.

"Excuse me, ladies." We turned to face Isaac, concern spreading across his face. "Celine, your mother's on the phone."

Heat rushed to my face. I glanced at the cordless on the opposite wall. I hadn't even thought to call my mother.

"You can take it in Dad's office. The phone's not cordless."

I excused myself and went to Abraham's office. With the door locked behind me, I picked up the phone. How would I explain why I hadn't called?

The truth, Celine. Speak the truth.

"Hello, Mama."

Chapter 14

"I'M YOUR MOTHER, remember?"

"I'm sorry I haven't called. My cell phone isn't working right now. I guess the tower is down. How are you doing?"

And how did you know to call me here? I wondered.

"Don't switch the subject, Cee Cee. I'm coming over there as soon as they get Benson Ridge Road clear. I don't know what you think you're putting down."

"I'm doing my job, Mama. I do work for a living."

"Don't get smart with me, child."

The office was stuffy and my head hurt. I pushed broken glass and papers aside and sat on the desk.

"How are you doing, Mama? And Tabby? How are she and the twins?"

"They're fine. A little wind damage to their house. When is your family going to come first, Cee Cee? When we're all dead?"

I rubbed my neck and rested the phone on my thigh. Her irritated tone echoed off the paneling.

Lord, help me.

I lifted the phone to my ear again and steeled my nerve. She was still ranting.

"You don't ever listen, child. You're going to put me in an early grave. Or worse—"

"Mama, how much money have you received from Abraham Benson?"

Her answer came quick and sharp.

"That's none of your business, Cee Cee."

"So, you're not denying it?"

"I'm not talking about Abraham Benson right now."

"He says he was there when Daddy died. He says he gave Daddy's eulogy. He claims he paid for my education. Is that true?"

"It's too late to be asking me about Abraham Benson."

"What's that supposed to mean, Mama?"

"You need to focus on what's important, Cee Cee. Figure that out. I'll see you tonight."

She hung up. Why was she being so stubborn?

My head was killing me. The conversation had been long and painful. The grandfather clock was striking noon as I left the office.

After I dressed in a borrowed pair of oversized sweats, I combed some of Catty's moisturizer through my hair and pulled it back into a ponytail. Little flashes of light danced before my eyes as I returned to the kitchen.

I sat on a bar stool and pushed cans of beans aside to rest my elbows on the bar countertop. "Catty, I'm sorry for how I behaved. The way I spoke to you was inexcusable."

Catty turned to face me, a can opener in her hand. "Oh, Celine. I'm the one who should apologize. I had no right speaking to you the way I did. I'm sorry."

She put the can opener down and came to sit with me. "I wasn't very empathetic. In your shoes, I'd probably be thinking and saying the same things. Or worse. My mother is still

130

alive. She divorced Daddy when I was in second grade. The last thing she said to me was that I'd never amount to anything. She never hit me but she never had to. Her words were worse than any beating. I was glad when she left. It was hard with just Daddy and me but it was better. We moved in with Grandma Lucretia and I never saw my mother again.

"I never heard another word from her. But the hurt was still there. And the hate only grew bigger. As a child, I was always thinking about how I'd pay her back when I grew up. Until one day I realized that I'd never be free if I didn't let go of that hate. I would never amount to anything with all that meanness inside me.

"I don't know all of what your daddy did to you. I've heard things."

I opened my mouth to interrupt. She held up a hand.

"Truth is truth, Celine. I'm not trying to get in your business. Maybe you had good reason to tell folks you were from Finleigh. I don't know. That's none of my business.

"I'm just saying follow the truth and let go of the hate. Neither one of those things will be easy but God is able. Like my sweet says, God is big enough. . . . Enough sermonizing."

Confusion and embarrassment churned inside me. No doubt it showed on my face.

"You don't look so good," Catty said.

I rubbed my temples. "Do you have anything for a headache?"

"I don't keep a whole lot in the house 'cause Mr. Abraham might . . ." Catty glanced toward the open back door. Men's voices, low and serious, came from the patio. I heard the sound of boots on the wooden decking. "Look in my top drawer," she whispered.

I found the medicine tucked amongst her underwear and

love letters. A snapshot, rubber-banded to a grade school composition book marked "Betty's Wedding," caught my eye. The photo was of an old woman standing on the porch of a wood frame house. She smiled down on two large cabbages in her hand. Her dark skin glistened with sweat.

This had to be Catty's grandmother. But why was it in the drawer? She'd been killed by a United Front member. What had Abraham to do with that? All this was beginning to be so complicated and tiring. When did life get so crazy? The more I knew, the more I didn't want to know.

And then guilt settled over me. My mother had worried me to the point of pain, but I didn't want her dead. I still wanted her in my life. I'd see her tonight if I wanted to or not. From the fire in her words I could tell she was coming whether the roads were clear or not. I needed to finish this assignment as best I could. Then we'd set things right again. Start anew.

Lord, help me to get along with my mother.

I downed three pills and returned to the kitchen. Catty's voice drifted in from outside. She was talking to Buxton and Isaac. I hadn't seen the FBI agent since I returned to Benson Ridge but I figured Abraham wasn't too far away.

I was in no rush to join them on the patio. I just stood and listened to their laughter, trying hard to ignore that empty ache in my heart.

Left out again.

"You clean up right nice, Celine."

It was John Carter. I turned to face him. He seemed taller. His shoulders seemed wider. He smelled better.

"Thank you."

Except for a small patch of hair under his bottom lip, his face was clean shaven. A small adhesive bandage on his chin caught the light. He rubbed it with a thumb and smiled with softness in those bewildering eyes.

"I'm glad you lost those high heels."

I frowned. "I didn't do that."

"When you slid down the ditch bank on top of me. Feet-first." He tapped the spot with a finger. "That's a diva size-8 divot right there."

I smiled.

"I'll miss those shoes. Hard to find a sexy three-quarter inch heel."

His eyes flashed with humor but there was something else there behind the jesting. A hint of sobriety.

Finally. Here's my chance.

"Why did you write the play, John Carter?"

"Boy, you know how to spoil a mood."

"What was it about my father that made you think—"

"Now is not the time. And you know it. I'm not going for your shock-jock technique."

"Shock jock!"

"I didn't agree to an interview to begin with. Abraham did. You got questions, ask him."

My mind went back to my interview with Abraham. No memories there that I wanted to revisit.

"What made you think that this town was ready for a play about a former black militant activist? No one would have described Quincy Johnson Sr. as a town darling."

"Especially not you."

He started to leave. I planted a foot in his path. He stepped away. Ignoring the glare, I wrapped my hand around his forearm. Feeling the heat from the solid arm stirred something deep inside me.

Focus, Celine.

133

"You're not getting off so easy."

He pulled his arm free and took my wrist. Narrowing my eyes, I fought to steady my breathing.

"What do you really want, Celine?"

That was a question I didn't want to answer. His eyes softened. All manner of wants stirred within me. I gulped and averted my eyes.

"Your father found something that few people find in life. Peace with God and peace with themselves. He wasn't happy with his life but he was ready to die."

Ready to die?

I stiffened. The lump in my breast. A brush with a twister. My mortality had to be put on the back burner. Looking him in the eye, I asked, "Why did you write the play? Why that title?"

"I said no interviews."

"Please." I relaxed in his grip. "I'm not interviewing now. I just want to know. Why him? Of all the prisoners in that jail. Why my father?"

"Truth finds truth. God led me to Haiti a few years ago. For a film project, I thought. He led me to find His truth there. God led me to Quincy. Just another project? Hardly. More truth. I'm a better man because of your father. That's all I have to say."

It wasn't enough for me. Why did he choose my father? What of the title: *Black Jesus: The Quincy Johnson Sr. Story*? Did he know about my fire-blackened Jesus?

I opened my mouth to ask another question but he let me go, turned his back, and left.

* * *

What do you really want?

John Carter's question had echoed in my mind throughout lunch. With Abraham ogling me from across the table, I couldn't concentrate.

What had he meant about truth finding truth? That was too cryptic to make good sense. I yearned to talk with him more. So we wouldn't do a formal interview. Okay. That was fine. We wouldn't have to put him on camera, front and center, but maybe working alongside others. Yes, that would fly. The humanitarian angle. We would work that.

"I need to call Bob back," I thought aloud as I stood on the porch after lunch.

I rummaged in my bag for my digital camera.

"Celine, did you say something?" Catty asked. "Are you feeling better now?"

She was sitting on the front porch swing with little Isabel at her side. An infant in her arms sucked noisily on a bottle. The children's parents, along with a village of other brown-skinned folks, worked the yard. Picking up corn, leaves, and branches were all ages of women and children. They piled the debris in the bare fields.

Men—brown, black, and white—were dismantling what was left of the barn, carrying the longer pieces inside where Abraham and Buxton used them to board up the windows.

A definite photo op.

"Thanks for asking, Catty. I'm feeling much better. I was just thinking that I should get my cameraman here. This digital will have to do for now."

I snapped a few pictures. Leaving my bag on the step, I walked among the women and men, chatting and taking candids. The sound of a tractor behind me made me jump.

"Move out the way, Ms. Diva."

135

John Carter smiled down from a window in the glassed-in cab. He winked at me and, despite myself, I smiled back. Another smaller tractor followed with Isaac behind the wheel. Instead of the big farm implements attached to the back of the tractors, each one had large bulldozer-like blades on their fronts.

Isaac tipped his wide-brimmed hat as they passed by. "Want a ride into town?"

"Sure."

I stepped up and slid across the seat.

"We're going to clear the road," Isaac shouted.

I nodded. The rumble of the tractor was threatening to resurrect my headache. I braced myself against the front roll bar and the seat back and held on tighter.

"Celine, I bet you've never been on a tractor before. Being from Finleigh."

"Isaac, I've got a confession to make." Children chased the tractor, tossing unshucked ears of corn to me. I caught them and threw them back. The wind lifted my scarf and I felt free and happy.

"What's that?"

"This is not my first time on a tractor. I'm not from Finleigh."

Taking off his hat, he looked me in the eye. A breeze ruffled his hair and he flashed a wide smile. Despite his likeness to Abraham, I liked the young man.

"I've lied all these years. I'm really from Pettigrew."

"Well, that confirms some things."

He looked away and waved at some children running alongside the tractor. A scruffy dog came from nowhere and started yapping happily among the group. Isaac whistled to the animal. It barked once in reply and sat on its haunches.

Curious about his comment, I touched his arm and asked, "What do you mean? Confirms what?"

He turned around and waved across the yard at Catty. She shifted the baby in her arms and blew her fiancé a big kiss.

"Pettigrew girls are mighty fine."

I smiled and thanked him. He didn't know my history in this town, did he? It didn't matter. His words had flipped a switch. A weight had lifted. A door had opened.

I didn't need to run away anymore.

Stay and help.

"Isaac. Stop."

He glanced over at me and cupped a hand behind his ear. The larger tractor in front of us was moving at full speed and making such a racket I only saw his lips move. "What?"

Smiling, I tapped my finger on my chest then jerked a thumb back toward the farmhouse.

He nodded and slowed the machine. I kicked off Catty's flip-flops and hopped down into the dirt. Barefoot, I trotted across the yard and up the front steps.

"Changed your mind?" Catty asked, her head to one side. "Better put those shoes back on. There are still little bits of glass on the floors."

"A change of mind and a change of heart." I slipped my feet back in the short sandals and giggled.

I raced into the house and burst into Abraham's office. His voice stopped me short. I stood with my hand on the doorknob, my happy mood evaporating.

Abraham was at the top of a step ladder, bracing a barn plank with one hand. He held a hammer and wore cutoff jeans. Special Agent Buxton, wearing jeans and a T-shirt, squatted over a wooden toolbox. He looked more like a line-backer than an FBI agent.

"Thought you were leaving us, Ms. Johnson," Buxton said, standing and brushing dust from his thighs.

The room was near dark. They had covered the French doors and all but one window with wood from the barn. In the dimness I could sense Abraham's eyes on me. I held my head high and addressed Buxton.

"I changed my mind." I glanced toward the phone sitting alone on the cleared desk. "Could you give me a few minutes of silence while I use the phone?"

Buxton nodded.

Summer Courtland answered on the first ring.

"We were expecting your call. Bob's right here."

Expecting my call?

"Hi, Celine." He sounded down. "Word is there's been quite a bit of damage at the park. The homecoming's called off. Sharon has called me back in."

"She can't do that. There was a storm. People are crossing barriers to help each other. We've still got a story here."

There was a pause. I sat on the edge of the desk. Bob groaned and continued.

"You know how she gets and stuff. Coulton should be back in the country in a couple days. He'll probably just go along with her."

My turn to groan. I knew he was right but I didn't want to go back to Raleigh just yet. This was borderline for Public TV. Sure, it was the kind of story that local news covered. But the local yokels weren't here yet. I was.

Carla Celine Johnson.

"I'm staying on."

The questions about John Carter still nagged me. And there was still my suspicion that Abraham was up to something right under the FBI's nose. Maybe my mother knew.

Maybe Isaac or even Catty. I still had answers to search out.

"Celine . . ."

"Sick leave. Vacation leave. Me leave. Whatever."

He chuckled. "I'll take some 'me leave' any day. All right, Celine. Summer's gonna bring me over as soon as the road is cleared and stuff. The van okay?"

I assured Bob the van was ready to go and hung up. How could Sharon pull the crew? Okay, so what that the crew was just me and Hollywood, but there was still a story here. Bob could go. He was young and I didn't want him to lose his job. But as for myself . . .

I jumped at movement behind me. It was Abraham. I turned away.

"Just need a few more nails." He pointed to two small cardboard boxes on the floor at my feet. I moved out of the way and glanced around the room.

"Where's Buxton?"

He hefted the boxes in his hand. "Bathroom break."

Alone in the room again with Abraham Benson. My skin crawled.

"I'm glad you're okay," he said as he walked away.

I swallowed the fear and disgust rising up like a hot baseball from the pit of my stomach and followed him. "Why didn't you turn state's evidence back in '88? Black folks were dying left and right. Their houses and churches were being burned.

"Unexplained deaths and fires. That's what the media called them. It was the Front, wasn't it? You knew it. Why didn't you step forward then?"

He faced me, a smirk playing across his face.

"'I'm not trying to ascertain your culpability here, sir. You had these damning documents for decades,'" Abraham said, mimicking Senator Fenton Barstow's words. "You sound like a meddlesome politician, Celine."

With his back to me, he took a handful of nails from a box and shoved them in a hip pocket.

"How does your son Patrick play into this plan?"

"Patrick? Is that what this is about? You figure he's my ace in the hole? He's a young, innocent boy."

"Your son?"

Buxton walked in and pulled up short in the doorway.

"You can stay, Gerome. Patrick was the only child that Olivia and I had who lived."

My heart sank. The FBI agent had assumed his position over the threshold. I cleared my throat and pressed on.

"So where is he now?"

"Holed up in Amsterdam, plotting the return of the Benson regime." Abraham's voice was flat as he climbed the ladder with hammer in hand. "He's a menace to society. Faith and purity forever stamped on his hateful soul."

Abraham raised a fist in a salute that made me clench my jaw.

"So why's he in hiding?"

He lowered his fist, placed one foot ahead of the other, and stared down at me. "For his protection. As you can imagine, there are folks who don't want me to testify. Folks who would kill my two sons to get at me."

That's what I suspected. No surprise there.

"And why not Isaac?"

"He's hardheaded and he's a grown man." Abraham chuckled.

Here he was laughing and brushing me off with snide remarks. He knew the power he had. Over this town and over me. I narrowed my eyes and stepped forward.

140

"So you love your sons. If this change were for them, why didn't you turn evidence years ago?"

"I had a different heart years ago."

It was all I could do to keep my tone professional and objective. My hands were on my hips and my head had tipped to one side.

Do you have one now?

"A different heart?"

"Olivia's faith drew me to Christ even before we got married. During those early years I did consider going to the government with what I knew. My concern for Olivia and Patrick held me back. But when she died over two years ago, my world crumbled. I sent Patrick to stay with Catty's grandmother. I was going to end it all."

My hands were still on my hips. I couldn't believe a word I was hearing. Change of heart? Sending a Benson child to live with a little old black woman?

Intent on remembering every inflection in his voice, I leaned forward and let him continue.

"The Lord spared me many times. Then He sent Isaac back. That's when I knew I had to turn state's evidence. I couldn't kill myself. I'd do the right thing even if it meant never seeing Patrick again.

"When John Carter came here talking about going to see your daddy, I thought, 'What more can I give, Lord?' You see, I figured I'd given the Lord all I could. My money, my land, my house. All of it was no longer mine. The government had seized everything.

"But when Quincy called me brother that day, I cried like a baby. He'd told me about how he'd found the Lord. Stronger than hate. Stronger than the blackest coffee. That's what he said. Right, Gerome?"

"Yes, sir."

Abraham shook his head and sat on the top rung of the ladder, his head hung low. His lips moved and I strained to hear his words above the commotion outside. The tractors had returned. Children were on the porch running and laughing.

"What was that?" I asked Abraham.

He lifted his head—his face was wet with tears. Okay, not the tears again. I bit back a groan and waited for him to compose himself.

"I said, praise God for Quincy."

Chapter 15

❦

"DIDN'T KNOW how big this place really was. Look at all this land and stuff." Bob had his camera off but it was still sitting on his shoulder. I'd convinced him to stay and get a little footage of the damage and the cleanup.

He sighed and pushed his imaginary glasses up his nose.

"Wow, greenhouses? This place is big."

"Mmm hmm. It's big," I said.

Isaac had told me that the farmstead was five square miles, most of it being behind the house, and included ornamental, fruit, and nut trees. Cornfields normally bordered on the east and west and a line of trees along the front border. But the twister had taken out many of the trees and most of the bordering crops, making the house stand out like a beacon.

"Man, it's nice around here. I mean even with the storm damage. Just look at that black earth. And these people are so friendly."

I followed his gaze to the little Hispanic children playing hide-and-seek among the pecan trees. A few adults—parents and grandparents I figured—lounged under nearby trees.

My mind went to my own family and the townspeople.

Would they be as friendly as these migrant workers? The few folks from town who had come today to help out were youngsters who really didn't know my story. Or should I say, my lie? They hadn't seen me as anything other than another black face. The obscurity felt good.

I'd faded into the scenery in my baggy clothes and flip-flops. The scarf covering my knotty hair had been my crowning glory. For one day in my entire life, I'd been happy to be nappy. And boy did it feel good to help out. To be needed in a real way.

What do you really want, Celine?

"I'm not planning to report back until tomorrow morning," Bob said.

"Don't lose your job on my account."

He shrugged and pulled a pear from a nearby tree. "No big." After rubbing it on his jeans he took a big bite.

"Taste good?"

"Yep," he mumbled.

"Don't come to me begging for a job. I warned you." I plucked a pear and held it to my nose. Its perfume took me back to days of longing over Benson's bounty. "I'd better get back inside. I'm supposed to be helping clean floors."

Bob caught his breath and nodded toward the open bay door of the tractor shed that was near the most distant greenhouse. "Who's that?"

John Carter had stepped out from behind the big tractor he'd driven earlier. He took the baseball cap from his head and wiped his face with a bandana. He then rolled his shoulders and leaned back against a tire.

"That's John Carter Manning. The infamous playwright. Won't give me an interview . . ." I looked up at Bob, astonished at the goofy look in his eyes.

144

"If that's who I think it is, I met him once. He was going by John Carter back then. I could kick myself. John Carter and John Carter Manning are one and the same. Explains why we couldn't find anything on John Carter Manning."

"So what *do* you know about John Carter?" I asked.

Eyes stretched wide, he faced me and explained. "He was part of a lecture series at UCLA. It was shortly after the premiere of his film, *Black Boy in Shorts*."

"*Black Boy in Shorts?*" I repeated.

Bob fussed with his hair, brushed wrinkles from his T-shirt, and pushed up his imaginary glasses.

"Man, I should have worn a different shirt. Celine, how do I look?"

"Why? You look *maaaahvelous*, baby."

"Celine."

He hadn't seen the man like I'd seen the man. Or dealt with his silly, petty attitude—and that *durn* temper.

Lord, help me.

"What's all the fuss about? I mean, look at the man," I prompted.

John Carter had taken off his boots and rolled his jeans up to his knees. Two little brown girls were running water from a hose over his bare feet. His noises of satisfaction could be heard across the yard. In fact, the next county could probably hear his hoots of joy. Talk about overacting.

And he calls me a diva!

I swallowed a snort.

"That can't be the same guy. He graduated from Pettigrew High a couple years before me. Then he met my dad in prison and then he just happened to write a crazy play. No big deal," I said with obvious sarcasm.

"No, it's gotta be the same guy. Either that or he's a dead

145

ringer for John Carter." Bob stopped short and looked at me. "Hey, you never said you went to Pettigrew High."

My heart skipped a beat. I licked my lips and told him the truth. That I'd lied all these years and how sorry I was because of it. No lightning bolt struck me down. Actually, it felt good to tell him about it.

"Oh. Okay," was all he said and went back to fussing over his hair.

"Man. I wish I'd dressed better."

"The man's in a dirty T-shirt and jeans. He probably smells like a goat. Just walk over there, Bob."

"Celine, can't you just introduce me?"

I huffed and rolled my eyes.

"Come on."

"Thanks."

He fell in behind me, mumbling all the way.

"You would love *Black Boy in Shorts*, Celine."

"What kind of movie title is that? Get real."

"It's so realistic and stuff. And funny. And sad."

"Why don't you tell me what it's about, Bob?"

"It's about this little Haitian orphan who mysteriously appears in America wearing nothing but a pair of yellow shorts. John Carter bases the film on a folktale told by one of his Haitian-born Manhattan neighbors. True or not, he gets awards at Tribeca and Woodstock Film Festivals."

I whirled around and stared at Bob.

"Haiti? Manhattan?" I turned to stare at the howling man still on the ground enjoying his footbath of sorts. The same man who had talked about God working through a film project in Haiti. "Woodstock? It can't be."

"Yep," Bob said. "It's him."

I looked out the kitchen window in disbelief. In all my days traveling the state with Bob Hollywood, I had never seen him so starstruck. We'd interviewed the governor, lt. governor, and a legendary NASCAR driver, for goodness' sake. And he'd done little more than smile. To see him fawning over John Carter was disgusting.

"This is pathetic," I grumbled.

"Yeah, I know," Catty said. "Corn again." She reached over my corn silk–covered arms and grabbed two more ears of corn from the sink.

"No, not the corn. Them." I nodded toward John Carter and Bob walking toward the back door. Bob was still carrying that camera on his shoulder. If only this was an interview.

Just turn the camera back on, Bob.

Catty studied the two men for a minute and stretched her cute face into a cheesy grin. "That reminds me, Celine, could I have your autograph?"

I shook my head and groaned.

She giggled. "I know. Pathetic. Is Bob staying for dinner?"

"Beats me."

She shook silk from her arms and wiped her hands on her apron.

"I'll ask him. Hope he doesn't have any food allergies."

"Food allergies, my foot. The man can eat shoe leather."

She left me to tackle the mountain of corn by myself and went to talk with Bob and John Carter on the patio. Their conversation drifted in through the screen door.

I listened with one ear to their talk about food allergies as I reflected on the day. The sun twinkled like a blazing fire through the fanning tree branches. Birds twittered on the breeze. A cricket chirped somewhere in the kitchen. A child's giggle from the front porch made me smile. It was an idyllic summer afternoon, far removed from all hurt and harm.

Most of the other neighbors had left. Although the power was still off, the road and yard had been cleared thanks to their efforts. Smoke from the burning of leaves earlier barely lingered in the air.

I had decided that I would spend another night here if Catty didn't mind having me occupy her bed one more time, then I would visit Mom. And after that, back to Raleigh, whether I still had a job or not.

Abraham's voice drew me out of deep thought. "Things have changed. I'll be able to meet you tonight after all," he said.

From the sound of it, he was on the phone in his office. A door closed and I could only hear him in muffled tones.

I wiped my hands on a dish towel and tiptoed through an arching doorway connecting the kitchen to the dining room. With my back pressed against the facing wall, I could hear Abraham talking in the next room.

"No, Gerome will be gone. Nobody but me, sir," Abraham continued. "Don't worry, I'll have all of the money. Everything you asked for. You're welcome. Good-bye."

My mind raced. He was going somewhere without Buxton. What about the ankle bracelet? To whom was he giving money?

A senator? A member of the United Front? It could be anybody. Where was Buxton? He had to know.

The office door opened. I held my breath and scooted back into the kitchen. Buxton's voice echoed in from the front entry. I fished the last ears of corn out of the water and glanced over my shoulder and down the hall as I plucked at invisible silk. Buxton was leaving the office.

"I'll get your case ready, sir," he added before bounding up the stairs.

He'd been in the office the entire time. What was going on here? The implications made my skin crawl. Was Buxton on the take?

"Oh, Celine," Catty said, returning to the kitchen. The door banged behind her. "Sorry to leave you so long. The water's boiling on the grill. Can you help me take these out to the men?"

"Sure."

I wiped my hands and grabbed a plastic bowl full of corn on the cob. She stopped me with a hand on my arm. Her big brown eyes searched mine.

"Are you okay?"

"Yeah, sure."

"You just look funny. Kinda scared or worried."

"I'm fine, Catty. Thanks."

She gave my hand a squeeze and let me go.

"Okay. I'll get these burgers ready."

"Meat?"

"Thank Ms. Nichols. Contrary to what your friend Crazy Eddie has to say about her, she is plenty generous after a tornado."

The men were standing around the boiling pot on the grill, holding plastic cups of lukewarm soda and talking about life in third-world countries.

Any other time I would have joined in the fun, but I had other things on my mind. I placed the bowl of corn on the table beside Isaac and settled into a folding chair behind Bob. His camera put away, he chatted it up with John Carter about camera technique.

Once upon a time, back when I still had hopes of being

the next Barbara Walters, I'd been good at seeing through a lie to the truth. But that was all a bunch of starry-eyed college kid talk. I knew that now.

What was the truth concerning Abraham? Who was in with him? Isaac? John Carter? Which of them knew the whole picture? I looked around the small group standing before me.

Catty came out with a plate stacked with patties. She passed me a cup of soda and gave Isaac a pair of tongs. He used them to drop ears of corn into the bubbling pot. I smiled and thanked her for the drink.

What about Catty? Would she talk? She'd been so tight-lipped earlier. So guarded. I was sure she knew something. She worked so closely with Abraham. But getting it out of her would be difficult.

Like cracking a clam, no doubt.

My eyes went to the pot on the grill.

I've got to turn up the heat.

The happy couple stood side by side at the grill. Isaac bent his head to whisper something in her ear. Catty giggled and tapped her spatula against his tongs. I pushed down the jealousy that bubbled up. I sipped on my soda and looked away.

"And then, you know what the governor did?" Bob was telling one of his funny politician stories. I smiled and leaned forward. Catty and Isaac had turned around to listen. Bob was gesturing wildly, grappling with an imaginary set of bull's horns in the air.

Catty was giggling at all the right moments. Isaac was chuckling and nodding. I couldn't help smiling too, happy that Bob Hollywood was fitting in. Too bad there weren't any girls here his age.

I glanced at John Carter. He was looking at me. Not smiling or nodding or chuckling. He was looking straight at me, his forehead wrinkled and those magnetic brown eyes piercing me.

I struggled to even out my breathing and pulled my eyes away.

"It's a good thing that bull was as old as the hills," Bob added and waited for the laughter. He glanced at me. I smiled and gave him a thumbs-up. "Celine was rolling on the ground. I have it all on tape."

From the way Bob looked at me, I could tell he'd seen my silent exchange with the playwright. I looked away and mumbled, "Celine's most embarrassing moments."

"I'm sure it was pretty funny," John Carter added and went inside.

❀ ❀ ❀

At dinner, John Carter had the nerve to sit across from me and I'm sure his eyes never left me. Bob sat to one side of him and Isaac to the other.

Tight-lipped and distant, Abraham arrived late and sat at the head. I pushed away from the picnic table at his arrival. As Catty rose to serve the man, she whispered to me.

"Take it easy. Please, Celine."

So I stayed, eating with my back to Abraham and a doubtful eye on John Carter.

The preacher man, Trip Robertson, arrived just as the sun fell below the lower branches of the sycamores that bordered the house to the west. He had a pretty white woman on one arm, his wife, Frieda, he explained. In his left hand he carried a paper bag full of ice cream.

"A gift from Miss Emily's," he said, setting the bag on the picnic table.

Giggling, Catty took the bag and rushed inside to get bowls and spoons. Frieda followed.

Ice cream.

The thought of dessert made me smile. I hadn't had anything that resembled dessert in months. The camera always told the truth about how many ounces I'd gained. It never lied.

I wiggled my toes out of my shoes and stretched. How long had it been since I'd enjoyed a summer evening in the country? A decade? Too long.

Lightning bugs chased each other in the dark recesses of the branches swaying nearby. Far off, past the greenhouses, I spotted a young deer tipping through the brush.

Abraham, sitting at the head of the table, saw it too. "Look," he whispered and slowly lifted a finger. The others looked and gasped.

"A doe with a baby."

Yes, there was a baby. Forgetting for a moment about the deception and the destruction he represented, I smiled at him. Then I turned away only to see John Carter looking at me.

The corners of his mouth turned up and he asked, "Do you have an answer for me yet, Celine?"

Wide-eyed, I stared at him. What was he talking about? How happy he seemed with himself. The other men forgot about the deer in the woods and turned to look at me.

"What's that, Celine?" Bob asked, his eyes pleading, it seemed.

I laughed and played with the corner of a paper napkin. "You've got to be kidding."

Crossword puzzles were one thing but riddles were never my thing. I searched my memory for any mention of a riddle. My mind came up blank.

He smiled and lowered his chin. "Well now, shouldn't be a hard one to answer."

Trip and Isaac exchanged glances, grinning.

"Another one of John Carter's riddles," Isaac said.

"Must be a good one," Trip added.

Bob wet his lips, concern etched on his face. "It's a riddle?"

John Carter's smile widened. His pretty teeth flashing sarcasm. "Yes, a riddle. Come on, Celine, a harmless riddle."

"Yeah, right, harmless," Trip said. "Like Daniel-in-the-lions'-den harmless."

Standing with his son and Trip, Abraham chuckled and worked a toothpick through his teeth. John Carter leaned forward and placed his hand over mine. My already wide eyes grew wider. I was hot all over.

"It's not like I asked you to marry me."

Isaac, Trip, and Abraham fell together like bowling pins, laughing and slapping each other on the back. Bob, his face relaxed a little, smiled at me as I drew back my hand.

"What do you really want, Celine?" John Carter whispered.

Oh, for goodness' sake.

I rolled my eyes and opened my mouth to give him a piece of my mind. At that moment a commotion in the yard drew my attention away from the so-called riddle.

"What in the world," Trip exclaimed and followed Abraham and Isaac as they rushed to the edge of the patio.

John Carter stood and said, "Truth finds truth, Carla Celine," before he walked away into the gathering dusk.

✻ ✻ ✻

My mother arrived in a ball of dust. She was always known as a woman who arrived fashionably and late. Her fingernails would be done. A new hairdo would be catching the light. The handbag would match the shoes. But not tonight.

What seemed like dozens of cars and vans had arrived quickly and at once. Their headlights lit up the swirling dirt from the yard, making the people who walked toward the house look like zombies.

Leading the group was my mother. Smells of sweat engulfed me as she embraced me and kissed my neck. Her face was fuller than it was in the last photos she'd sent. The baggy, brown T-shirt she wore made her look old and tired.

"You look awful, Cee Cee," she said.

And you need a shower, Mama.

A man pushed a mic in my face. I recognized his face from the local NBC affiliate. The name escaped me.

Familiar faces stood out from the twenty or so people pressing close. They were more gray and pot-bellied now but there was no mistaking my old high school principal, the woman who delivered our mail, and my old boss, Dale.

Lord, help me get along with my mother and survive this night.

I looked to my mother. She cocked an eyebrow and smiled back. A bright light blinded me. I held up a hand to shield my eyes.

"Ms. Johnson, we're told you narrowly survived a horrendous storm earlier today. Tell us about that."

"Not right now, please," Mama addressed the TV guy and turned back to me. "Cee Cee, what have you done to your head? For goodness' sake."

"Mama." I expressed slight indignation.

"Let's get you inside. I brought a few changes of clothes."

A garment bag swayed over her arm. She had her hands

on my shoulders and was pushing me toward the kitchen door.

"What?" I said, still a bit indignant over the whole scene.

Another TV guy had pressed closer. The letters CBS stitched on his polo shirt.

"Ms. Johnson, what one word would you use to describe the twister that almost took your life?"

"Honey, you look a mess," Mama interrupted.

Honey?

My mom never called me honey unless I was in for a long talk. It had been a mighty long time since I'd received one of her long talks.

With all that had happened since she called, I'd forgotten to make myself look more presentable. Little did I know that she would arrive with the evening news crew.

If this was her way of paying me back for my years of negligence, then we were even. A certain man had recently accused me of being a shock jock. In my book, Melissa Johnson was the original Pettigrew shock jock.

I held up my hands and yelled, "Stop!"

The mass of people and equipment slowed but didn't completely stop. Like a hungry animal, it made its way into the kitchen and began putting down roots.

Okay, I was the news event of the week. By the look of the hardware being erected outside, I was going to be live on the late news. What good reporter wouldn't make me the news: LOCAL GIRL ESCAPES KILLER TWISTER. Sure. But at least let her do her hair first.

Chapter 16

I MASSAGED my temples and climbed onto a bar stool. The room fell quiet as I steadied myself on a rung of the stool and scanned the faces around me. With the camera lights flooding the dim kitchen, everyone looked like they were wearing latex masks.

How I wished this could be just a dress rehearsal. The director would call for a break and I could pretend to be someone else. Someone who could show her feelings. Someone who could be real.

"Listen, everyone. I need to change. I'll answer your questions and make a statement. But please allow me to make myself more presentable. Please excuse me."

"Hi, Celine. Good to see you," said the NBC guy to me as I climbed down from my perch.

What's his name?

"Hi, good to see you too. How's Katy?"

Great, I could remember his coworker's name but not his.

"Doing great. Delivered twins last week."

"Wow. Well, I'd better get ready."

"Yep, you're big news, girl." He winked and turned to his cameraman. "We're on in twenty."

I hid a scowl as I reached the floor. Girl?

Don't call me girl.

Bob was on one elbow, following me from the kitchen and down the hall. My mother was on the other. I glanced back. A reporter was talking to John Carter. He shook his head and walked away.

"Cee Cee, what size are you now?" Mama asked. "Four? Six? My goodness you've lost weight."

"I'll set up in the kitchen too," Bob said.

My mother was pinching the skin around my waist.

"Mama, please."

"Skin and bones, *honey.*"

I glared at her and turned back to Bob.

"The front steps." I pointed to the open front door as we passed it. "I prefer there. We need to control this situation if at all possible. We had no choice on the time but at least we can pick the place."

"So this is Bob." Mama offered her hand. Bob shook it. "Nice to meet you." She flashed him a smile but turned on me with raised eyebrows.

"Thank you, ma'am," he said and then left us continuing on to Catty's room.

With the door closed behind us, I threw my handbag on the bed and started pulling the sweatshirt off. My mother stood looking at me, her face blank.

Here it comes, Celine.

"Mama, please don't start. I have a really bad headache, and I know I've been too focused on work and not enough on you, and . . ."

She wrapped me in a hug, smoothed my wild hair, and kissed my cheek.

"Mama?"

I pulled back and looked her in the eye. She was crying. I caught my breath.

"Oh, Celine."

She pulled me back into her arms.

"Are you okay?" I asked.

"Hmm. I'm okay now. With you here in my arms, Cee Cee."

Tears clouded my eyes.

Oh, Mama.

"I'm sorry for not calling. Not checking in with you. What kind of daughter comes back home and doesn't call her mother."

"Shhh."

She held me for a minute or more, stroking my hair and talking softly. "You need to take some time off, child. God knows you work hard. You do good work. But it ain't about all that. You need to just take it easy for a while. God sent that storm, Cee Cee."

I nodded and cried. With her arms around me, it didn't matter what foolishness she said. All that mattered was that someone cared. I felt connected. This is what I'd been missing all along.

"You need to listen to the message from that storm. Your life is too crazy. You don't have no friends. You act like you don't have family. You need a man."

Enough Mama love.

"Mama, please."

I pulled away and unzipped the garment bag on the bed. The white denim pantsuit inside looked like one I'd sent her a few months back.

"Wasn't quite my style, Cee Cee. Here sit down and let me do something to that hair. You look a mess."

I sat on the ottoman and let her rub moisturizer through my unruly hair.

"That suit is too big for me."

"You can wear the jacket. Cinch it up in the back with a rubber band or safety pin to show off some curves. Too many donuts on them hips, Cee Cee."

"I don't eat donuts, Mama. Besides, I thought you said I was skin and bones."

She grunted and pulled a brush along the right side of my head. "Except for those hips. You've always had a nice shape. And I've got some of your old jeans in there."

"My old jeans? From high school?"

"Maybe you could squeeze into a pair. Size six?"

"Yeah, right."

Mama jerked my head around.

"Ouch. I'm not thirteen anymore, Mama."

"Don't give you right to sass me."

"Yes, ma'am."

She chuckled. "That's better, Cee Cee. And another thing. I'm glad I didn't lose your hardworking tail in that tornado but it doesn't mean I'm not mighty aggravated with you. You did a dumb thing going out in it in the first place."

"So who told you I went out in it?"

"Well, you were out in it, weren't you? I never was able to tell you girls nothing. Brother always minded his mama. But you and Tabby. Lord, help me. Turn your head."

I obeyed. Finished with her fierce brushing, she pulled my hair back and wrapped it with a rubber band.

"Now, do you want a wig or a scarf?"

"Neither one. I want to talk about Abraham, Mama."

I inspected my hair in the dresser mirror. She rooted through the bottom of the garment bag.

"Cee Cee," she chided. "Some earrings and makeup and you're ready."

"How much money did he give you? Was it like a certain amount every year?"

I waited for her answer as I smoothed my hair in place. The brushing had done wonders. A happy head is a . . .

"Mama, get out of my bag."

She had pulled out my tape recorder and scarves and was pushing things this way and that.

"Why? What's in here? Condoms?"

"Mama!"

I stuffed my things back in the bag as she wrapped a gigantic black silk scarf around my head. In a matter of seconds I looked like a bad Erykah Badu flashback.

"This isn't gonna work, Mama."

"Yes it will. Lipstick. You're darker than me but maybe you could still get by with mine. Slip into that jacket and a pair of pants while I find some makeup. Hmm. Earrings."

"I'm not interviewing you, Mama. I just need to know. You're having too much fun with this 'let's dress Cee Cee up' thing. What time is it?"

"Know what, Cee Cee?" She glanced at her watch. "Hank said twenty minutes."

I stopped short with a pair of red jeans halfway up my thighs. "Are you trying to bury me or what? They're gonna try to eat me alive."

"What doesn't kill you—" Her eyes twinkled.

"Thanks a lot."

"Make your mama proud. You always wanted to do local news. Now zip up. Turn around."

"I don't have a top to go under this jacket. When are you gonna answer my questions about Abraham?"

"No need for a top. Button it up about three-quarters of the way. Not too high. Show a little skin."

Shaking my head, I wiggled into the jacket.

"This ain't prom night, Mama."

"Well, we missed out on that whole thing, didn't we?"

"Don't start."

She bit her lip. "I'm sorry. I shouldn't have said that."

I hadn't attended my prom out of shame. No decent black boy had wanted to be my date. And I didn't want to go alone.

I shrugged and buttoned up the jacket. There was movement outside the room. "What time is it?"

"Here you go." Mama handed me a tube of lipstick.

"We don't have time for that."

She shoved the tube in my hand. With a huff, I took it and smeared it on.

"Very nice," Mama said.

I shook my head and groaned. She adjusted my head wrap from behind and gathered the jacket at the small of my back.

"There, much better," she said.

I shrugged. It did look better but I wasn't about to rave about it. My mother would not let me hear the end of it if I did. She slipped a pair of gold hoop earrings into my hand and we made for the door.

"Cee Cee," she said with a hand on the knob, "I have done my share of . . . um . . . not telling the truth . . . to you about Abraham Benson. Lord, help me." She cleared her throat and sighed. "So maybe that's why I've looked the other way all these years about your little lie. So please, just give me some time."

She looked me in the eye, a mixture of fire and sorrow on her face. "And don't you ever pull on me the kind of stunt that I've pulled on you tonight. You hear me?"

For the first time in my life, I didn't want the glare of the light. I didn't want to hear the sound of my own voice. The thrill was long gone. But my mama wasn't going to let that stand in her way.

"Yes, Mommy Dearest."

❊ ❊ ❊

My glorious moment under the spotlight of local news lasted all of ten minutes. Hank and his cronies packed up and drove away before I had time to work up enough energy to bask in the glamour of local fame. I was left feeling used.

It truly felt strange talking about the storm that had nearly swept me away less than twelve hours earlier. I mentioned John Carter's heroism, making sure I left out most of the how and what of his sacrifice. The sensation of his body on mine still disturbed me. Holding a bowl of ice cream, my hero resurfaced to wave good-bye to the TV crews.

Bob, bless his heart, kept rolling as the crowd thinned and the bright TV lights left. He'd set up every light we had in our puny arsenal. By the grimace of concentration on his face, he was in the zone and didn't care that the lighting was not the best.

I nodded to him and he followed my lead. We were a team. If I lost my job for what I'd done in Pettigrew so far, then this would be the last time we operated as such. I'd miss Bob Hollywood.

"Cee Cee, we have newspaper folks here," Mama said, approaching me with two young reporters in tow.

"I figured as much. I should hire you as my publicist, Mama."

My mother introduced the reporters to me. One was from

the *Elizabeth City Daily News* and the other was from my old employer, *The Finleigh Record.*

"Excuse me, everyone," I said, standing on the top step of the porch.

"I'd like to make a statement."

The sound of my heartbeat was deafening. I took a couple of breaths and opened my mouth. Nothing came out. The words felt like jagged chunks of ice lodged in the back of my throat.

My mother slipped a hand in mine and squeezed. Tears welled in my eyes.

"This has been a day I'll never forget."

I looked around at the faces surrounding me. A bright star was winking over the distant fields; I focused on it and continued.

"The events of this day have caused me to think hard about what's important. What's real. And what's true."

What do you really want, Celine?

"Coming back to Pettigrew has been hard because it meant facing an untruth. A lie."

My voice cracked. Tears rolled down my cheeks.

"I've told myself for years that it was only a little lie. What would it matter if I denied my birthplace and denied my parentage? Who really cared what little country town I was from?

"My deception has ruined my relationship with you. My people. I was ashamed of you then; I am ashamed of me now. Please find it in your heart to forgive me. To accept me as one of your own again.

"For I am a Pettigrew girl, born and bred."

The newspaper people snapped pictures and scribbled furiously in the dim light. My mother hugged me and pressed her own tearful face against mine.

"You did good," she said.

I needed to hear that. It was good having my mother at my side, despite our differences and the secrets I knew she kept about Abraham and possibly about my father. It was still good.

What would my father have done or said? It would have been negative. And it would have cut me to the heart.

Others approached with arms outstretched. I let them hug me and I responded to their comments and well wishes. All the while I could only think about how different this day would have ended if Quincy Johnson was there.

The townspeople left one by one, my mother and Abraham wishing them safe travels as they left. As Bob and I held dishes of ice-cream soup, I spied the two of them with their heads together just beyond the reach of the TV lights.

What's going on there?

"I'm heading back as soon as I pack up," Bob told me.

"I thought you'd stay the night."

"That was before I knew about your mom and stuff."

"My mom and stuff?"

"Uh oh." It was apparent that Bob was about to have a slip of the tongue.

"What about my mother?"

Bob watched himself make circles in his ice cream with a plastic spoon. "She had some damage."

"From the storm? And I'm the last to hear about it. Is she homeless or something? Talk to me, Bob."

Bob's face contorted into a little boy's "I dunno nothing" look. I handed him my bowl and marched past Catty and the others to where my mother stood whispering with Abraham. He shushed her and stepped back as I came near.

"Cee Cee," she said, her hands out like a traffic cop. "Slow your roll, child."

"Don't child me, Mama. What happened to the house?"

"A branch."

"A branch!"

"Mmm hmm."

She nodded and tried to step away. I placed my hand on her shoulder.

"Must have been a pretty big one for you to be homeless."

"I ain't homeless. Who told you that?" She frowned and glanced at Bob who was still stirring his melted ice cream. "I just don't want to sleep in a house with a broken window."

"A broken window? Who's looking after the house? Where are you staying tonight? Where are your bags?"

"My goodness. Don't worry yourself, Cee Cee. I've made arrangements. Now let me get my bags." With her hands on my shoulders, she pushed me aside and moved around me.

"Don't treat me like a child, Mama."

She lowered her chin and looked me in the eye.

"Well, then, don't act like a child. We are staying in the old Ross house tonight. That's all I have to say about that, Carla Celine."

All eyes were on me, I was sure of it. Except for the chirp of crickets, the porch was quiet. I glared at the white man hovering over us.

"Is that what he said?"

"Stop acting ugly," Mama said. "Go get your things; we're going over there now."

"No, we're not . . ."

"Cee Cee!"

My mother's fingers dug into the meat of my shoulder. I felt like a child in Sunday school. "Go, get our things. Bob will drive us over."

She gave Bob a knowing smile. He set his bowl aside and carried his camera and equipment bag to the van.

"I'm coming too," Catty said, her voice strained. "The generator works better over there. We'll have AC, hot water, and a working stove." She flipped on a flashlight and went about cleaning up the disposable bowls and spoons scattered around the porch. The others, except for my mother and Abraham, joined her.

And my mother, moving like she carried a crown of gold on her head, descended the steps and climbed into the van. Abraham rested a hip on the porch rail and gazed at the stars.

"Good night, Celine," Abraham said.

❋ ❋ ❋

The old Ross house reminded me of an old house in Raleigh. With its porch light bathing the wraparound porch in soft yellow light, the place looked quaint and inviting.

While Isaac, Buxton, and Trip attended to the generator in the backyard, Frieda and Catty unlocked the door and went inside. My mother followed, wearing her invisible crown. Bob followed with her luggage. I shook my head at the sight and he shrugged as he went into the house.

Pathetic.

Unfortunately, thoughts of Abraham came to mind as I slumped in a rocker at the far end of the porch. I remembered the phone call I'd overheard earlier. Whoever he'd been talking with was going to meet him tonight at Benson Ridge. If Special Agent Buxton stuck to the plan, Abraham would have no one to protect him. If he wanted to get killed tonight, that was his business.

I closed my eyes and rested my head against the back of

the rocker. The air was light. A breeze brought the scent of honeysuckle to me. Insects made night music with the distant hum of the generator. Sleep gnawed at the edges of my brain.

"I guess this is 'see you later' for real, this time."

I opened my eyes. Bob stood over me, wiping his forehead with the back of his hand.

"I figure if I don't leave now, your mom will have me moving more furniture and stuff."

"That woman. Take care, Bob."

"You're gonna be okay. You'll bounce back," he added.

"Yeah. You know me—a rubber ball."

He chuckled.

"I'll call in the morning. Oh that's right, the cell towers are down."

I sat up and stretched. "I'll call you. Tell my faithful housemate, Ming, what happened to me. It'll give you an excuse to call her. You drive safe, okay?"

He nodded and shuffled his feet a bit. "That was gutsy, what you did with the newspaper guys."

More like stupid.

"Thanks."

"Well, I guess I should go."

"Bye, Bob."

He nodded and left. As the van's headlights bounced along the dirt path leading back to the main road, a dark form separated itself from the trees in the yard.

From the familiar lope of the walk, I knew who it was, so I undid my head wrap and waited for him to cross the yard and climb the steps.

"How long were you there watching me, John Carter?"

He tossed his hair back and leaned forward, setting one foot in front of the other.

"Found something for you." He set a pair of low-heeled pumps on the porch rail. "They're a little dirty."

"You've been watching me like a hawk."

"You won't believe where I found them. One of those tornado mysteries. The kind you tell your children about."

"Do you think I'm going to kill somebody or something?"

"They were in the bed of my truck. Had to be yours since I don't make it a habit of picking up women or women's shoes."

The rocking chair banged the wall as I sat forward. "What is wrong with you?"

"That's a question I should be asking you, Celine."

"And that means what?"

"What was that speech to the newspaper guys about? You laid it on a bit thick."

"Why are you here?" I questioned.

"To bring those shoes back and to get an answer to my question."

"Your question!" I blew air. "I don't care about your question."

"I think that's obvious. You *should* care about my question. Make it your question, Celine. Your freedom depends on it."

"My freedom depends on it. So you're like some great sage. An oracle from God."

I was in his face now, pointing at his chest. "John Carter, I am so tired of you. Freaking me out with your staring. Pestering me with this cryptic question.

"Okay, let me answer your stupid question. This is what I really want in life. I want a super challenging, rewarding job that allows me to bring home the bacon and fry it up in a big ole, super frying pan for my super happy husband and our two and a half super lovely kids."

169

With each super, my voice had gone up a notch and I'd brought my index finger closer to his chest. He responded by grabbing the tip of my finger.

"That's a lot of supers, Celine." He pulled my hand down and wrapped his warm calloused fingers around it. "I'm sorry for making you uncomfortable. It wasn't my intent to antagonize you."

His chest rose and fell in short, shallow breaths. Even in the shadows of the porch, I saw the fire in his eyes. My stomach trembled with the intensity.

"I only wanted you to think about what you're doing. Really think about your future. Your father wanted me to ask you that question. It was what you argued about the last day you saw him alive. That day you visited . . . I was there."

I pulled my hand away. "What? Where?" I vaguely remembered that argument. What had we argued about? Had it been about my future? Maybe. But I had no idea anyone else had been putting ideas in his head, especially a young white man.

"I was behind the screen in his hospital room. He'd told me to stay. But he didn't know how you'd react seeing me there."

"Seeing you there? What are you getting at?"

"Nothing, Celine. Your dad was not the most perfect dad." I huffed.

"But he cared about you, especially as he got sicker. He wanted to make sure you would be okay."

What did Quincy Johnson know about me? He knew nothing about my career. Nothing about my beliefs. Nothing about the lump inside my breast that he'd probably caused. He didn't know me. I was glad that I'd shared none of me with him.

"After he warped me for life. Guilt, that's what that is. Not caring."

"Celine, listen to yourself."

"Yeah, yeah. Tell me about my paternal hate problem. Everybody else does." I threw up my hands and walked to the far end of the porch. "You know, I've had enough of this. Everybody's trying to fix me. I'm okay with me. Okay, I have a small diva issue."

John Carter followed, chuckling to himself. "Good for you. Confession is good for the soul."

"And you, John Carter Manning. Do you care to make your confession?"

He leaned against the porch rail and crossed his arms. A slice of light from the window covered one-half of his face. "Hmm. I guess I can be a little bit foolish at times."

"Ha!"

"Hey, I didn't chide you."

"Sorry."

"I want to show you the video I made of your father."

"I don't want to see it. Can we change the subject?" I looked at the starry heavens.

"No."

"I haven't seen the night sky in so long. I mean, really seen it. It's amazing, isn't it?"

"Celine."

"John Carter, please. No more."

"The DVD. Will you let me show it to you later? It's important."

I sighed. "Sure. Later."

In my next life.

"Can I ask you something?"

"Mmm hmm. Sure. Wow, there's the Big Dipper. Haven't

171

seen that in years." I leaned against the rail, my nose pointed skyward like a kid. The smell of moist earth filled my head. I felt like a little girl again. Setting out at night to dig worms for fishing.

"Did you see the twister?"

My smile faded.

"I think I want the foolish John Carter back."

"We came so close to leaving this world."

"Okay, if you're hinting around for a thank-you, then . . . thank you, John Carter Manning, for saving me from that durn tornado."

He leaned toward me. Light illuminated his entire face. His brown eyes glowed down on me.

"I was scared to death. I've never been so scared in all my life. I've been caught in the crossfire of gang shootouts in Brooklyn and almost kidnapped on the streets of Haiti. But I've never felt so close to my own end. But this morning . . . I held someone else's life in my hands. Yours."

He held his hands out, palms up. They trembled. "I'm sorry. Didn't mean to get so tragic on you. Too little sleep."

"I really am grateful for what you did. It's not like I have a death wish. You see those storms on TV but there's nothing like seeing a twister for real."

"And feeling its power down in your gut."

"Like it's gonna suck you inside out."

We sat quietly for a few moments until he spoke again. His words came out soft and slow. My pulse had quickened and my mouth was dry.

"Now that you know I'm a big chicken—"

"You're not. I mean, who wouldn't be ready to wet his or her pants clinging to dear life, literally, in a ditch with a tornado less than a mile away from you?"

172

"You scare me, Celine."

I looked him in the eye. There wasn't any fear there. Only a focused determination that scared *me*. I let out a nervous laugh.

"What are you talking about?"

"You're successful and—"

"Stop pulling my leg. You're the big-time movie director, playwright, superstar."

"Let me finish before I back out. It's complicated." He took a big breath. I gulped, searching for a way out. "You're successful and intense, and something tells me that you could be a real and easy person to be with. I like that."

Oh, Lord.

"I like that a lot."

"Oh."

"That's the scary part. I haven't felt this way about a woman for a long time. And never this quickly. You may think I'm crazy for telling you this since it's obvious you don't feel the same way."

His words had knocked the wind out of me. I wrapped my arms around my body and sat there biting my bottom lip and struggling for air.

"Are you in a relationship with Bob?"

Bob's confession of having feelings for me came back like a flash of light from an old-fashioned camera. Relationship? How had I become a magnet for white men?

Lord, help.

"What?" I managed to say.

"He seems so . . . into you."

"No, Bob and I are just friends," I gushed. "He's got that protective little brother thing going on."

173

"So, is it because I wrote this play about your dad or that I'm white?"

I wrung my hands in silence. "You don't beat around the bush, do you?"

"Like I said earlier, I'm not asking you to marry me. I just want to know if I could take this further. I don't know what to do with the way I feel about you. My gut says ignore the feelings. Getting involved with you may not be a safe, easy thing."

In shock, I asked, "Do you say that because I'm black?"

"No, not really. It's mostly because you're struggling with being the safe, easy person that's the real you."

"What do you mean by that?"

My mind raced. How was I supposed to respond to this man? Memories of Steven washed over me. I gripped the porch rail tight and fought the urge to run away.

I heard my mother's voice inside. She was talking to Catty. A television was on somewhere. A car door opened and closed far away. Men were laughing and talking loudly. Catty's giddy laugh joined them.

"John Carter, I'm not ready for this."

"I'll be honest with you. I'm not really ready for this either. But should we wait for ready? A year ago, I came out of a bad relationship in California. That's one of the reasons why I left it all. After that, I thought I'd never marry. But something tells me to not listen to my gut. To go with my heart."

I wanted to cover my ears. I didn't want to hear about any more of his heart or his gut feelings. Or his bad relationships or California.

"John Carter . . . "

"My heart says to go for the risky. For the not-so-easy. Like I said, it's complicated."

"John Carter, please. Stop."

"There's no guarantee of tomorrow, Celine. That tornado gave me a reality check. I know you just met me."

"Stop it."

"I might be a white man, Celine, but I'm not Steven. I will only go as far as you want to go."

I blinked at the tears forming in my eyes. How did he know about Steven? He had to be at least four years older than me. Had my father told him? Was that in this play he'd written?

"How far?" he asked.

"This is too far."

Chapter 17

JOHN CARTER hung his head and nodded once. "Okay." He stood and walked to the top of the porch steps. "Good-bye, Celine," he said without turning and stepped down.

The front door opened and out walked my mom.

"John Carter," Mom said. "I thought I heard your voice. Where are you headed?" She glanced at me.

"Back home."

"How did your house weather the storm?"

"Dunno."

Catty's head appeared over my mother's shoulder. "Hey, you guys. Didn't know you were out here. Such a beautiful night." She pushed a small black handbag up her shoulder and eased around my mother as she fished a key ring from the purse. A small Hello Kitty charm flashed in the light that spilled from the open door. "I'm going to check on the big guy over at Benson Ridge. You guys can start the movie and the popcorn. I'll be back in a few."

She turned and yelled at the men inside to close the back door and start the video. Then flashed us a smile and trotted to her car.

"Be safe," Mama called after her. But Mama's attention

was on me. Her dark face showed concern and suspicion. She looked from me back to John Carter.

"Stay here for a while, John Carter," she said. "No use going home now. Why be in that big house by yourself."

"Thank you, but I need to go, Miss Melissa."

Mama looked at me again.

"Good night, John Carter," Mama said.

"Good night, ma'am."

He walked across the yard and disappeared down the shadowy lane. The sound of the gravel crunching under his feet had faded before my mother spoke to me.

"Come inside, Cee Cee. I need to talk with you."

* * *

Cinnamon candles flickered on the nightstand. My mother patted a blue satin pillow against the headboard and invited me to sit down beside her.

The scented candles, the pillows on the bed, all said come and answer my questions. I wasn't in the mood. Talking to my mother did not come easily for me, especially when she was trying this hard. She was after something and I was in no mood to find out or go along quietly.

"Mama, I just want to lie down. Can we just talk later?" I threw my purse on the floor and flopped down beside it. "If this has to do with John Carter and what you may have over-heard just now, then it can wait."

"I wasn't listening in, Cee Cee. I heard your voices on the porch. That's all. It's not like I could make anything out. And it's none of my business what goes on between you and him."

"There's nothing between me and John Carter."

"Cee Cee, calm down. Like Brother says, 'get a grip.'" She laughed at her use of slang and shifted around pillows on the bed. "I want you to look at your father's video. The one John Carter recorded in the prison." She pointed to the TV on the dresser against the far wall. A dented DVD player sat beside it.

"I'll be out in the living room with the others. You can take your time." She slid from the bed and walked to the door. The light from the candles danced across the walls. Turning the knob, she opened the door a bit and spoke to me in low tones.

"Cee Cee, I haven't asked much of you since you left Pettigrew. I'm not trying to make you feel guilty about . . . about what you did."

"You mean about my lying."

"Cee Cee."

"Just say it, Mama. I lied by leading people to think I was not from Pettigrew and I let that lie live for years. I know it was bad, Mama. I apologized, remember."

"Cee Cee, it doesn't matter anymore."

"Well, then why are you still torturing me over it?"

"I'm not torturing you. You're torturing yourself. Yes, there are some folks in town who can't stand the sight of you. But they'll get over it. I pray you've learned your lesson."

I rolled my eyes and flopped back onto the carpet. "Mama, no sermons. Can I ask you something?"

She ignored me. "And I hope you'll be honest with yourself and others from now on."

"Others. Like John Carter?"

Lesson? That word reminded me of something I'd seen in Catty's room. In her drawer. The black-and-white speckled composition book marked "Betty's Wedding." What could my mother tell me about Catty's grandmother's death? Or even my own grandmother's untimely demise? It was time to press her a little further.

"I'm not trying to get into your love life, Cee Cee."

"Love life. Please, Mama, don't get so dramatic." I sat upright, an idea brewing. "I want to ask you about something I saw in Catty's room."

"What should I know about what that girl has in her room, Cee Cee?" She eased the door closed. "We've both been through a lot over the years. Don't drive a bigger wedge between us."

"Okay, Mama," I said as I climbed yawning onto the bed.

Wagging her head, she tossed a throw across my legs and turned to go.

"Wait. When did Grandmamma die? What year was it?"

"Cee Cee, no more of this."

"Please, humor me."

"Is this one of your story leads?"

"Something like that."

"She died in 1988. In the middle of May, I think."

I nodded, trying to ease her into the next question. "Did she know Catty's grandmother, Betty?"

"Most likely she did. But Catty's grandmother wasn't named Betty."

I let my head fall to one side. That made sense, in a way. The notebook hadn't been labeled "Grandma Betty." Just Betty. *Was Betty a friend?*

"Well, don't leave me hanging. Who's Betty?"

"Isaac's mother was named Betty. Betty Douglas. Very beautiful girl. Had eyes like Isaac. Although they were kind of gray. You know, there was a Betty Freeman who used to live over in the projects. But I doubt—"

"No. Stop. This Betty Douglas. Is she dead?"

180

"Yes. Died in a fire."

"When?"

She pursed her lips and stared at the ceiling. "Had to be later that same year."

"1988?" My mother gave a quick nod. I continued. "Was she married?"

"Betty Douglas?" She yawned and fluffed her fingers through her hair.

"Yes, Mama. Work with me here. Was Betty Douglas married?"

"Don't get all huffy, child. No, Betty Douglas wasn't married. Not that I know of. She came up from Florida with some Mexican migrants. Let's see, you were a baby then."

She was a migrant worker. I said it to myself, marveling that Isaac had left that part out of the story he'd told me. I chalked it up to embarrassment.

My mother went on.

"Her daddy died in the early eighties, I think. Then she moved into this house for a while. She and Olivia Ross were good friends. I never saw her much with any of the Bensons. Once or twice I heard she'd been caught riding in the same car with Fred Benson. Surprised me to no end to find out that she had shared a bed with Abraham, so to speak. Then when Abraham married Olivia in '89 . . . Good Lord, the rumors!"

She chuckled as she edged closer to the bed and started tucking the blanket around my legs.

"Shows me that a body shouldn't waste time listening to gossip. Messed me up. Nothing but lies," Mama went on.

I didn't remember anyone named Betty in Pettigrew. I would have been eight when she died. Isaac would have been four. Chances are if he stayed close to his mother, our paths would never have crossed, even in a small town like Pettigrew.

"Did Betty know Grandmamma?" I asked.

"Mmm hmm. That year I worked at the ice-cream parlor, she used to come over and help your grandmamma out around the house. Especially when Grandmamma felt bad. Isaac was a little thing. Maybe one or two years old. She'd bring him along."

Something wasn't adding up. In all the time I'd spent around my grandmother's house, I had no idea about Betty or Isaac. Betty and my grandmamma had both been killed in the same year. Both by those loyal to the Benson family.

According to Catty's notebook, Betty had married someone. Who? When? Had Abraham killed her husband and then taken advantage of her? Isaac had left out the part about his mother being dirt poor. What else had he left out? What was he trying to conceal?

Had Abraham killed her too? The possibility overwhelmed me. At least two women were dead because of this man. And he was going scot-free? Not on my watch.

I had to see that composition book. These questions weren't going to go away otherwise.

I just needed evidence to take back to Raleigh. I was sure I'd find plenty of evidence at Benson Ridge. Getting back into the house, though, would prove challenging.

"What are you trying to figure out, Cee Cee?"

"Don't know. Something's not adding up."

"You look like your daddy when you squeeze up your face like that."

I gave her my "Mama, please" look. She smiled and hunched her shoulders.

"I'm going to let you puzzle over this by yourself. I've got some popcorn to eat. You want me to put in the DVD so you can watch John Carter's interview?"

"No thanks, Mama."

My mother and I would never understand each other. That much I knew. What was the use in looking at the DVD? Putting myself through that made as much sense as sitting quietly and listening to Abraham read my father's letter. Or hearing John Carter tell me what my life depended upon.

Everyone had lost their mind. That much I also knew. I tugged the throw closer and let sleep take me away.

❅ ❅ ❅

Something wasn't quite right. The room was pitch-black. The air smelled of cinnamon and candle wax. My mind swirled around memories of the candles I'd burned the night after Steven attacked me. But then suddenly I awakened and remembered where I was.

I slipped from the bed to the floor where I found my bag. I sifted through the junk inside until I found my penlight. Though tiny, the strong light illuminated the room brighter than any candle.

Barefoot, I stepped into the hallway. The door across the hall was open, as was a door farther down. Heavy rhythmic breathing of sleeping people filled the house. On the living room sofa I found Buxton, snoring softly and curled up under a small blanket. Floorboards creaked under my feet as I followed my penlight into the kitchen. An oil lamp, set low, flickered on the table.

I switched off my penlight and closed the door softly behind me. A small purse lying sideways on the countertop caught my attention. Hello Kitty's two black eyes stared back at me. Catty's keys. I pulled them slowly out and slipped them into my pocket.

It wouldn't take me long to get to Benson Ridge on foot. I'd be there and back in under an hour.

I looked at the clock above the back door—4:15 a.m.

It would still be dark in an hour. I could slip Catty's keys back in and she'd never have to know.

Honesty, Celine.

"Okay, okay," I muttered.

After leaving a quick note on the back of a grocery receipt, I took my shoes from a basket by the door and tucked them under my arm before slipping quietly into the early morning darkness.

Taking it all in, the night air was light and warm. The sky twinkled with billions of stars. A now-lifeless generator sat like a big tank to one side of the back steps.

My sleep hadn't been fitful. But neither had it been restful. I had dreamt of my grandmother. She would know what to do. She'd sit me down on her front porch and pat my hand and tell me exactly what I needed to do.

She'd done just that in my dream. We were at church, standing outside with Bibles in our hands. She wore a wide-brimmed black hat that caught the sun like a crow's wing. She'd always been a hat-wearing woman. Gorgeous crowns of every color of the rainbow.

I stood there looking straight into her eyes. This was strange since she'd died when I was eight. She had been a short woman and I wasn't very tall at the time. So in a way, it seemed right to be looking at her eyes, searching for warmth and comfort there.

She was talking but she had no mouth. What had she said? She was reading from her Bible. But she had no hands. What had she read?

A man with paper-white skin came to us. From nowhere,

it seemed. His clear blue eyes sparkled like gems in the sunshine. He greeted me and placed a hand on my grandmother's shoulder.

And then, without another word, he dipped his head under the brim of Grandmamma's hat and kissed her on the lips.

Under the shadow of that hat, her smile glowed. "Blessings of grace to listen and learn and love," said the man—and he vanished. Within seconds, my grandmother was gone as well.

I'd woken confused and tired, searching for any recollection of her face in my mind. Why couldn't I remember what she looked like? What she sounded like?

And now I stood in the night, fighting tears. Pushing against those three words again. A million memories washed over me like hot grease. I turned my face heavenward and tried to pray.

"Lord, help," was all I managed.

What was I supposed to listen for? Who was I supposed to listen to or even learn from? It was all so tiring.

My public confession hadn't made everything all right like I'd thought. I still felt like a sham. Like everything I'd done was shaking, wobbling, on the verge of collapsing under me at any moment. And if I fell, where would I land? I probably no longer had a job at the station. That didn't upset me as much as knowing that there was nothing else to me and my so-called fabulous self.

I'd climbed up a ladder. Maybe I wasn't at the top yet. But I had spent many years getting to this stupid rung—and what for? I didn't even like this ladder. All I had to show for it was a lump in my breast and emptiness in my heart.

With trembling fingertips, I pressed the spot on my breast. The lump was still there. My heart sank.

Maybe I should just take some leave and stay here. Get some sleep for a change.

My thoughts scolded me. *That's why you have this lump in your breast. You don't eat right. You don't exercise. You don't know how to slow down and rest.*

I had been a terrible daughter. An awful sister and aunt. Nobody's real friend. A class-A liar. I deserved to get cancer. I hung my head and cried.

Oh, Lord, I'm sorry.

What if I had died in that tornado? What would I have left to the world? No children. No husband. Just a family that barely knew me anymore.

I didn't know me. I'd become someone else. Someone the camera liked. Someone that I no longer liked.

How can I find me *again?*

With closed eyes, I listened to the night sounds and tried to regain a few shreds of composure. The crickets, the breeze in the trees, the rumble of a lone big rig on the Highway 64 bypass a mile away.

After so much deep contemplation, with my shoes still tucked under my arm, I stepped down onto the dew-wet grass. The soft wet blades beneath my feet made me smile. I thought of many summer nights, walking with my grandmother, and I cried some more.

As I neared the edge of the yard where the grass coarsened into weeds, I put on my shoes and followed a shadowy path. The short path opened to a clearing. Several tombstones caught the light of the waning moon. Up ahead, a possum ambled across the path and disappeared into the woods.

The path, a narrow strip of gravel, led me around the small cemetery to a field. Corn stubs and stalks were scattered around. By the way they crackled underfoot, it seemed they were old. After a few uneven steps I stopped and looked out over the field.

Where was my grandmother's house? Could I get to it from here? What condition would I find it in?

Our old trailer park had been at the edge of a cornfield. But which one? Fields were everywhere. Corn and soybeans connected us all to the land, to each other. Which row would take me to Grandmamma's? Which row would take me home?

I bowed my head.

"Lord, I don't know what to do. Please help me sort out my feelings."

My mind went to John Carter. Tears coursed down my cheeks.

"Please help me hear what You want me to do about my so-called career. This is really hard, Lord Jesus. I stand here and confess my selfishness. My bent for doing things my way. Please forgive me. Direct me. Help me to listen."

Sobbing, I covered my mouth with my hands and tried to focus my heart on what the Lord might share. In college, He had directed me so clearly. But when was the last time I'd listened?

Chapter 18

LISTEN. LISTEN. LISTEN.

The tears had stopped and my heart had settled a bit and then I heard, "Go."

Or at least I thought I did. My eyes flew open and I spun around. Was someone behind me? Or had it been God?

"If this is You, Lord. Protect me."

My feet snugly in Catty's flip-flops, I put one foot in front of the other and crossed the cornfields. A trek I'd made countless times as a child but never with so much fear.

* * *

The back door of the Benson Ridge farmhouse creaked as I opened it. After pocketing the keys and pulling the door shut, I tiptoed in.

Faint smells of cigar smoke and burnt bread met me. Printouts and maps littered the kitchen table. An unlit hurricane lamp stood in the middle. Three empty glasses and a full metal ashtray were pushed to one side. Boxes of cookies and crackers stood open on the bar.

Next to the snack boxes, like chess pieces on a board, sat

six or seven gold finger rings. By the thickness of the bands, I figured they were men's rings.

Someone had been here with Abraham. Maybe they still were. I'd entered the house from the rear and hadn't seen any cars. I hadn't bothered to look for cars in the front. How slack could I be? I held my breath and listened for movement. All I heard was my own heartbeat.

I bit my lip and walked on past the closed door of Abraham's office and down the hall to Catty's room.

Traces of aftershave met me as I entered Catty's haven of lace. Despite the churning fear in my stomach, I smiled and flashed the penlight around. I closed the door softly and locked it.

The notebook wasn't where I'd left it. The headache medicine was gone. Neither thing was a good sign.

I fished around until I uncovered the notebook and slipped the rubber band off, leaving it and the photo of Catty's grandmother to lay among the underwear. With the notebook in hand, I went inside Catty's closet and closed the door behind me.

Wedging the penlight in a stack of sweaters, I opened the book. The flawless brown face of a woman with gray eyes stared at me from a 5 x 7 glossy. It was a school photo like the one I remember seeing of my mother. The kind high school senior girls used to take—a black velvet drape slung low over the shoulders.

This was Betty Douglas. There was no smile on her face but she looked friendly. Something in the tilt of her finely styled head or the set of her jaw made me think she could get her way if she wanted. I could see Isaac in the set of the mouth and eyes.

The next several pages were blank. Even in the waning

glow of the penlight, I could tell that something had been taped to at least ten pages. Who had taken the pictures? And why?

As I shifted the book to get a closer look at something written in the margin, a card fell onto my lap. It was a postcard. The front displayed an azalea garden in full bloom. The back copy read, "WRAL-TV Gardens in full splendor." Someone had scribbled a date along the edge: May 21, 1984.

Only a short drive from my home in Raleigh, I knew the area well. The gardens were now closed but years ago they were used frequently for weddings. Why would a WRAL Gardens postcard be in this book? I could think of only one reason.

With one last look at Betty Douglas's lovely face, I tucked the composition book and postcard back into the dresser drawer.

On one hand my little bit of breaking and entering had produced nothing. But on the other hand I did have a good lead. Bob could help me fill in the rest.

The faint scent of smoke arrested me as I made my way slowly down the hallway. It wasn't cigar smoke but the smell of wood burning. I flashed the penlight's beam down the passageway. Fingers of smoke were curling from beneath Abraham's office door. The knob turned. I gasped and turned my light off.

A door opened and someone moaned. Something metallic hit the floor followed by the thud that could have only come from a heavy body hitting the ground.

Suddenly my feet were heavier than cinder blocks and I couldn't seem to move fast enough.

Crouching low, I scrambled forward—the growing fire in the office illuminating the man lying facedown in the entryway. At the foot of the stairs I tripped on something and went skidding across the tile floor. Gagging from the thickening smoke, I rammed headfirst into the man. He grunted and lifted his head a few inches before collapsing again.

Abraham!

The front door was only a couple steps away. Just a few steps to fresh air, safety, and freedom.

I could run from this house and be free from the tyranny of this man and all he stood for. He had most likely killed my grandmother by fire. He had killed Betty Douglas. Didn't he deserve the same fate?

Why did the idea of leaving him here disturb me so?

I braced my feet against the wall and rolled him over. His moan sounded like a protest. As I hooked my arms under him, his right arm came down like a lead pipe across my head.

Gagging, I let him fall back to the floor and turned my attention to opening the front door. I stumbled across the porch, gulping the rush of fresh air. Movement across the yard caught my attention.

I started when I realized it was a man dressed in dark clothes running toward the road. With each swift step he took, I knew he was a black man. Was he a looter? He wasn't carrying anything. Maybe Abraham had caught him in the act.

Had this mysterious man set the fire? I hoped not because as I watched his soundless escape across the dewy grass, I felt I knew him.

As my lungs filled with air, I yelled, "Hey! Stop!"

He slowed and turned his head a little. My heart sank.

Not Brother!

I hadn't seen my brother in years but I knew it was him, Quincy Johnson Jr. He'd grown up to look so much like my father. I opened my mouth to call out again but he leapt into a waiting car. Without bothering to look back or even turn on headlights, he raced away.

"Why, Brother?" I asked myself.

I pulled the sweatshirt collar over my mouth and nose and reentered the house. The fire in the office had spread over more than half the room. Flames crawled along the ceiling. Thick smoke filled the entryway. My eyes watered. And Abraham was nowhere to be found.

"Abraham!"

No answer. Did the man have a death wish?

Hacking, I returned to the porch to gulp air before dropping to my knees and crawling in again. I screamed at the touch on my ankle. Turning, I looked into a set of familiar eyes.

"John Carter!"

"What are you doing, Celine?" He jerked my leg. "Come out!"

I rolled onto my side and out of his grasp. He nearly pounced on me.

"Why are you here?" I asked.

"I saw the flames."

"What?"

"Get outta here, woman!"

I ignored his insensitive tone. "Abraham's inside." I turned away and tried crawling back inside. He yanked me back. I fell on my face.

"Stop that!"

He pulled me to my feet and dragged me outside. "Why don't you stop? And stay in the yard. I'll get Abraham."

The fire had engulfed the wooden frame of the office door. Parts of the burning frame crumbled away. The chandelier shuddered and splintered across the floor.

John Carter pulled me into the yard.

"I'm going around back," he said. "Go to your mother's and call for help."

He was running toward the rear of the house. I followed. "My mother's?"

"Her phone is working." He jabbed a finger toward a distant yellow light across the vast darkness of the fields to the south and west of Abraham's land.

"How would you know that?"

He turned around and shook me by the shoulders. "There's no time for all this, Celine. Just go!"

Then the anger in his voice had melted. He released me with a gentle push. "I don't want you to get hurt. So please go."

My stomach churned with emotion. "You'll need these," was all I could manage to say before handing him Catty's key ring and my penlight and running away.

※ ※ ※

My feet were muddy by the time I reached my mother's front door. I'd left the flip-flops behind long before I plunged through the line of pines and crossed the shallow ditch separating my mother's land from Abraham's.

Half the old pecan tree where Brother and I used to play pirates was gone. Much of the missing part had most likely been scattered across the surrounding fields. One large branch the size of a man's torso lay across the roof of her house.

My mother had a gift for understatement.

I glanced back toward Benson Ridge Farms. Flames leapt high above the tree line, casting a red hue across the sky.

John Carter's truck sat to the right of the front door, the driver's door hanging open, the radio murmuring softly to itself, two moths beating their bodies against his dome light. I closed the door.

By the look of things, he hadn't been in the house. I wiped dirt and gravel from my feet on the coarse doormat and tried my mother's doorknob.

Locked.

On a whim, I overturned the fifth stone in the edging around her flower bed. The spot she'd always kept a key.

"Bingo."

I wiped the key across my cuff, opened the door, and stepped back in time. Like I'd just walked in from a late night out with my high school buddies. I found the phone just where it had been more than a decade earlier.

The smells were the same—black licorice mixed with disinfectant spray, that's how Tabby had described it.

As I stood in the darkness waiting for the 911 call to connect, I imagined the same faded pictures on the wall, the same place mats on the table in the eat-in kitchen.

So many things had changed though. Things and people that I wished had stayed the same.

Where was Brother now? What had happened to him that he would try to kill a man tonight?

I remembered my own rage-filled moment, facing the truth about Grandmamma's death. For a flash of a second I had wanted Abraham dead. But following through with it . . .

"Yes, I'd like to report a fire."

Hearing my calm voice felt like I was listening to someone else. I relayed the details to the operator. I replaced the key and stumbled back into the night.

In the distance, the fire seemed higher, defiant almost.

"Lord, please protect them. Save them," I whispered.

Weary at even the thought of returning to Benson Ridge,

I locked my mother's door and sat on the edge of John Carter's tailgate, pulling my knees close. Like the far-off whine of a mosquito, I heard the town's fire siren. It grew louder. In seconds, I saw the flash of red lights across the dark landscape.

The crunch of gravel at my mother's front door startled me. I turned to see a dark silhouette stooping over her flower bed. I knew it was my brother even before he stood.

"Brother."

He swiveled around toward the sound of my voice.

"It's me. Cee Cee."

It felt strange calling myself by that old nickname. I hadn't been that woman for so long. The simplicity and sincerity of her came rushing back to me.

I slipped from the tailgate and walked into the open. We stood facing each other, no more than three steps apart, for several moments.

Red lights from the fire engines miles away strobed across his dark face. Shouts from the firemen drifted across the land.

"Why did you do it, Brother?"

"You don't know nothing."

His arrogant tone soured my stomach.

"I know what I saw."

"You didn't see nothing."

"Yeah, nothing. Just a man who looked like my brother running from a burning house."

"Go on back to Raleigh, Cee Cee. Forget about us for another ten, twelve years. Shouldn't be too hard. By then you should be just like Oprah."

"Abraham did a lot of bad mess, Brother. I'll give you that. But don't let what he did ruin you."

"Isn't that what you want, Cee Cee? Be like Oprah. Nappy headed, dirt-poor girl makes it filthy big."

He stepped toward me. I fought the urge to step back.

"You probably know that he killed Grandmamma. I think he killed someone else too," I told him.

"Don't worry about us here in Pettigrew. We're not your home folks anyway. Just send your billions to help the impoverished millions around the world."

Ignoring his scornful comments, I continued. "I aim to make sure Abraham pays for those murders. In the court of law. He'll be in prison for the rest of his life."

"That's right, Cee Cee. Just send all the poor little darkies your love. That way you won't get dirty."

I stepped toward him. "Why don't you just shut up, Brother."

"I was thinking the same about you."

"What happened to you?"

"Ditto."

He let out a short laugh and turned back toward the house. Without another word, he let himself in with the spare key.

"Brother, listen to me."

I rushed forward.

"Good-bye, Oprah."

Without even a glance my way, my brother closed the door behind him and locked it.

❋ ❋ ❋

"They can't find John Carter?" The scene was grim when I returned to the Benson farmhouse.

My mother clutched Catty to her chest and smoothed her hair. Tears streamed down their faces.

"Isaac went in the copter," my mother managed.

The *chop-chop* sound of the medevac copter carrying Abraham had faded. Special Agent Buxton stood a few feet away talking quietly into a satellite phone.

"Yes, sir," Buxton said, "someone from the Greenville RA will meet the copter at Pitt Memorial. I'll be there within the next two hours."

"Mama," I said, shaking her shoulder. "What do you mean, they can't find John Carter?"

Men in turnout gear stood in the now-muddy yard, spraying water on the blackened timbers that was once Abraham's office.

Two firemen carrying hooked poles went jogging by. Another, carrying an axe, followed them through the back door.

My mother had started humming a hymn. Its mournful tune was muffled by the swoosh of water along with the chopping and crashing inside the house. The smell of burning wood soured my stomach. I couldn't bear the thought of John Carter being trapped inside.

"Mama." I shook her shoulder.

"They've been searching for a while now," Buxton said. "Got caught under a beam, maybe."

In the red lights from the fire engines, Buxton looked older and younger at the same time. He pocketed the sat phone and placed a hand on my mother's shoulder.

"We'd better go, ladies. I'll take you back to the house and then to the hospital if you like."

"But what about . . . " I said, glancing toward the burnt-out structure behind us.

"I'm sure the firemen will do their best," Buxton said. "My car is this way."

My mother nodded and ushered Catty along. Buxton

followed, his fingertips resting on both ladies' shoulders.

"No. No," I said. "We can't leave him."

Buxton stopped, whispered something to my mother and turned to face me. My mother escorted Catty to a dark car idling several feet away with a pulsing red light on the dash.

"Ms. Johnson," Buxton said, keeping his voice low. "I'm gonna be blunt with you, so forgive me. Two top-level FBI agents died in that fire tonight. One was my brother-in-law. So I hope you'll understand my not feeling so strongly about Mr. Manning. Okay?"

Tears glistened in his eyes. I gasped.

"I'm sorry; I'm so very sorry. I didn't know."

"There was no way you could have known. Now, if you'd like to come to the hospital. We're leaving now."

"Well . . . um . . ."

He ran a hand across his wet face and left me standing there.

"Hey, we've got a man down over here," a fireman shouted.

A man down?

My heart stopped.

I ran toward the fireman crouching beside a pile of deck furniture. What looked like two boots protruded from one side.

"Oh, my goodness! John Carter!" I shouted.

An arm held me fast and turned me around. A man's wide face loomed over me. His thin lips moved but the words made no sense.

"John Carter!" I screamed, turning away.

Two strong hands gripped me and shook once.

"Miss, you have to stand back."

"What? No."

"Stand back."

I was being pulled away, flailing and screaming, by this strong man. "No, no. You don't understand. He saved my life. I have to help him."

He lifted me, carried me to the dark sedan with a flashing red light, and closed the door. The locks clicked down and the car pulled away. Tears were clouding my eyes. My throat burned.

"Wait. No," I sobbed.

"Cee Cee," my mother said from the front seat. "Everything's going to be all right."

I banged on the window but the man never turned around. He ran to join the EMTs who were now gathering around John Carter. I strained to see but Buxton sped across the yard and onto the pavement.

"No," I uttered helplessly.

My mind swam with images. Brother running. My mother rocking and humming. John Carter dead.

Chapter 19

AS I DRIFTED OFF, horrible thoughts of my brother invaded my sleep. Hooded and gargantuan, Brother ran through my dream with fire shooting from his fingertips, blood dripping from his fangs. Charred body parts of John Carter swam in black puddles at his feet.

I woke shaking from the fright of that intensely disturbing dream. Brother had killed two people, maybe a third. Word about John Carter hadn't reached us yet.

Lord, please spare his life. I'm sorry for how I treated him. Please, Lord. A miracle. Please.

"Glad to see you awake," Mama said. She slid into a blue plaid chair beside me and handed me a cup. I stared down at the dark brown swirling contents and shook my head.

We were in a waiting room at Pitt Memorial Hospital. Catty and Isaac sat across from us, arms wrapped around one another, staring into space.

Abraham was alive. We had been told only moments after arriving an hour earlier. But his life was still in danger. He'd inhaled a lot of smoke and suffered some nasty burns trying to rescue the FBI agents.

Questions about their meeting circled in my mind. Why

wasn't Special Agent Buxton invited? Who were these two other agents? What was the meeting about? Was Brother an invited guest? There had been three glasses in the kitchen. Why not four?

Sighing, I tabled the questions. Surprisingly, I was happy that Abraham was alive—Isaac still had a father. I was happy for that fact and happy for Catty, that she would have someone to give her away.

But I was also happy that Brother hadn't killed Abraham. Had the Benson patriarch been his target? Most likely. Would he try again? I pushed that thought aside.

Too many worries.

"Cee Cee, take the coffee. You look dead tired."

"Mama, I don't want any coffee. You know that." I tried to avoid caffeine as much as possible and for that reason had worked hard to eliminate coffee and chocolate from my diet.

"Well, you need to have some. You're going to need to stay awake, child. See that man next to Agent Buxton?" She nodded toward the men.

Buxton stood facing the room. Hands clasped in front, chin tipped low as he listened to the shorter white man talking to him. The man wore a brown houndstooth jacket over khakis. He was a redhead and talked with his hands and shoulders.

"That man came asking for you after you fell asleep. I told him to let you rest. He's another agent. Feld-something-something. Top FBI guy around these parts."

What would they ask me about? The fire? My brother?

"Thanks for the informed heads-up, Mama."

"Drink this."

She shoved the cup at me again.

"What's in it? Truth serum?"

Mama rolled her eyes. "You haven't had anything to eat or drink for hours, Cee Cee. Please drink a little."

I took the cup and swallowed a little of the lukewarm contents. "Yuck."

A shadow fell across my lap. I looked up into Buxton's face. The shorter red-haired man still stood by the doorway.

"Ms. Johnson. Could you come with me?"

His voice was firm. His manner calm. But sadness pulled at the corners of his mouth and eyes. I felt sorry for him.

I slid to the edge of my seat and slipped my feet into a pair of blue sneaker mules, shoes from my luggage Bob had dropped off the night before. It felt good to finally be in my own clothes again. If only I felt like my old self again.

"Give me a moment."

I gathered my bag, gulped the rest of the coffee with a grimace, and followed the men into the hall.

"This is Shelton Fesperman, special agent over the FBI's regional office here in Greenville," Buxton said.

Special Agent Fesperman extended a freckled hand. I shook it. "Folks call me Skelly," he said, waving a hand like he'd made a great point.

"Good to meet you," I said.

"Listen, Ms. Johnson. We'd like to ask you a few questions about what happened at the Benson Ridge Farms. Just a few . . . formality . . . run-of-the-mill questions. You know."

"Skelly," Buxton interrupted. "Could we possibly sit over there?" He pointed across the bustling common area to a cluster of three white rocking chairs set back behind a ficus tree screen.

This was part of their plan, I figured. Give me permission to use his nickname. Offer a relaxing venue. Get me to talk. But it almost felt natural.

Tell the truth, Celine. Lord, help me to tell the truth.

"That's fine."

I followed them. They allowed me time to sit first. The good cop, Buxton, sat next. The bad cop sat last, making a big show of pulling up his khakis by the pleats before resting himself on the cushion.

"Now, Ms. Johnson, I know this is a difficult time. Buxton here has told me about the tornado and the power outage. I'm sorry that you've had to endure all this. I truly am."

"But, Ms. Johnson," Buxton, the good, spoke. Skelly rested his hands for a minute to let his alter ego interrupt. "You can imagine how we feel knowing that the fire took two of our comrades down. We're distraught. Much the same way you were when you saw Mr. Manning after he was rescued earlier. But we've got a job to do."

John Carter.

Did he know something? Why was he talking about him this way? Was he dead?

"We are distraught," Skelly interjected. "Extremely so. And like Buxton said, two of our men are down. Finding out who did that is our priority now."

A brief thought flashed across my mind. John Carter had appeared so quickly after the fire started. *Had he set it? Would he have risked his life if that were the case? Could it have been John Carter's fault all along and not my brother's?*

Lord, help.

"Is he dead?" I said. The question slipped out before I could pull it back.

"Who?" Skelly asked, leaning forward.

"John Carter."

Skelly glanced at Buxton, his red-brown eyebrows drawn together.

"That's Mr. Manning, Skelly. We don't know, Ms. Johnson. I'll look into that, if you'd like."

Buxton's words were void of emotion. His eyes, though, had narrowed as he rose from his seat. Did I see disappointment there? Disapproval?

"Well, um . . . "

"I don't mind." He glanced at Agent Skelly.

"I don't mind either," Skelly added. "We'll need to talk with him as well."

Buxton adjusted his face, nodded once toward me, and left. Skelly leaned in again, the rocker creaking loudly as he did so. He looked at me for several moments, rocking ever so slightly in his chair. I played a game of connect-the-freckles on his face.

"Did you meet John Carter at the house before the fire?"

"No, sir."

"Skelly, please. So you saw him when?"

"After I saw the fire. I was trying to move Abraham after the fire broke out in his office."

"Move Abraham?" He took a small notebook from his coat pocket and started scribbling with a pen more suited for a little girl. Pink sparkles danced around inside the see-through top. "You'd better start from the beginning."

My thoughts exactly.

"Why did you go to the house in the first place? After 4 a.m. What business did you have at Benson Ridge Farms at that hour?"

"I wanted to take another look at a photo album that I'd run across earlier."

"A photo album?" He twirled his sparkly pen around in a slow circle.

I continued. "It was of Betty Douglas's wedding. Or so I believed."

"Betty Douglas was Isaac Hunt's mother by birth. What interest did you have in her wedding? Are you related?"

"No, sir."

"Skelly."

"I am a reporter."

His eyebrows met in a give-me-more expression.

"For Public TV. WCNC-TV. I thought maybe Isaac's story might lend itself to a feature on our weekly newsmagazine."

It was all a lie. My stomach fell like a big, cold rock. Skelly scribbled on his pad.

"That isn't true," I said, looking at the tip of his pen and feeling my insides melt into a pool around my ankles.

"The part about you being a reporter or the feature story?"

Didn't he know who I was? Apparently the man didn't watch much TV.

"I do work for WCNC. I wasn't fishing for a feature."

I took a deep breath and told the man the truth. How I was searching for evidence to bring Abraham down. How he'd killed my grandmother and possibly killed Betty Douglas. He was going to pay for those crimes if I had anything to say about it.

"Do you hate Abraham Benson?"

I drew a quick breath.

Hate? It was such a strong word.

"Yes."

"Do you want him dead?"

Frowning, I looked the FBI agent in the eye. "I don't know."

"You went into a burning house to save a man you hate."

How was I supposed to respond to that? He scribbled. I stared at that pen.

"What is your relationship with John Carter Manning?"

206

Relationship?

"I met him yesterday."

Just yesterday. So much had happened in so little time. John Carter's words came back to me.

"You scare me, Celine," he had said.

His eyes. His scent. His nearness. My breathing quickened at the thought of him.

"You're successful and intense, and something tells me that you could be a real and easy person to be with. I like that."

This is what he had said of me.

And now he was gone. Just like that. That foolish white man. What had he done to me?

"Ms. Johnson. Excuse me. Can you answer the question?"

"Question?"

I had been so lost in my thoughts that I hadn't heard a thing.

"Yes. When was the last time you saw Mr. Manning? Before seeing him during the fire, that is."

"He went in to save the others."

"I know that. I'm just trying to establish a time line. Strictly routine. See?"

"You're successful and intense, and something tells me that you could be a real and easy person to be with. I like that."

I couldn't help but remember those words.

His eyes had burned with such intensity. Such passion.

"We talked for about half an hour last night."

"Just the two of you? Any witnesses?"

"Yes. My mother and Catty Wright."

"Ms. Wright, the domestic?"

I nodded.

"What did you talk about?"

Buxton had returned. Bullets of sweat were forming on

the back of my neck. I took a deep breath and glanced up at his blank expression. Special Agent Skelly stood and conferred with Buxton. Their exchange was brief and quiet.

"Ms. Johnson," Skelly said, sitting again. "What did you talk about with Mr. Manning?"

I giggled. The stone in my stomach had risen like a rocket to my throat. "We didn't discuss setting a fire."

Buxton, the not-so-good cop now, sat down and needled me with his eyes.

"What exactly did you talk about?" Skelly asked.

The truth.

"You scare me, Celine." John Carter's words kept coming back to me.

"He . . . um . . . expressed feelings for me." I stole a glance at Buxton. He looked away.

"Romantic feelings? I see. Pardon me for intruding. When was that conversation over?"

I looked again at Buxton. What had he discovered about John Carter? Was I going to be told or made to suffer for my indiscretion?

"Around 9 p.m.; I went to bed shortly after that. My mother can vouch for me. And Special Agent Buxton here can as well, I suppose."

The big guy had turned his face away from me again. He fussed with one of the studs in his earlobes.

"When was the last time you saw your brother?"

Red flags as big as Texas flashed before my eyes.

"My brother? What does he have to do with this?"

"We want to talk with him. Strictly routine. See? When did you see him last?"

"This morning."

I paused and looked at both men. Blank faces stared back

at me. I continued. "After I tried to move Abraham away from the fire in his office."

"So here we are back to Abraham now," Skelly interrupted. "You were in the house looking for this photo album. You saw the fire. Then you saw Abraham passed out on the floor in his office. Is that correct?"

"The fire was in his office but he was in the entry. Passed out on the floor there. I tried to move him. The smoke overwhelmed me. I went outside. Saw my brother. Then I saw John Carter."

"How did you know it was your brother? It was dark. Not much moonlight. He's about Buxton's complexion. Correct? Did you speak with your brother?"

"Yes, I yelled at him. He didn't say anything but I could tell. He has a distinctive way of moving."

"I see."

Scribbling with the pink pen.

"And where did he go from there? After you yelled at him in the dark?"

I fought the urge to clench my teeth.

The truth.

"He . . . um . . . ran to a car parked alongside the road."

"In front of Benson Ridge Farms? I see. And you made the 911 call reporting the fire. From, let's see . . ." He flipped to an earlier page in his notebook and then gave my mother's address. "Is that correct?"

"Yes."

What else did these guys know? What else did they want to know? Sweat was running down my back.

Skelly wrote some more in his book, whispered with Buxton, and then he stood up. "That will be all for now, Ms. Johnson. Don't go far."

Chapter 20

GEROME BUXTON couldn't have given me a colder shoulder if I had iced it myself. Leaving Special Agent Skelly Fesperman to pore over his notes alone, Buxton had led me across the lobby and down a flight of stairs to the trauma ward.

My questions about our destination went unanswered until we stood in front of a door guarded by a uniformed policeman.

"Your friend is in there."

My heart leapt. Did I understand Buxton correctly? John Carter was alive? I couldn't breathe; my senses had taken a vacation.

What is wrong with me?

"I'm sorry. Who—?"

The man looked down at me and rolled his eyes. "Who do you think, Ms. Johnson?" He gave instructions for the guard to watch me like a hawk and marched off.

There were eight beds in the windowless large room. Four on one side and four on the other. Four men and three women, wrapped in bandages and casts of all descriptions, watched me enter. The last bed on the left was surrounded by a curtain.

"Hey, lady." A man with an eye patch and a chest dressing put down his cell phone and addressed me. "Who you looking for?"

I heard John Carter's voice, loud and raw. "Ow! What in the world did you do that for? Get away from me, you idiot!"

"Him," I said. After taking a deep breath, I walked toward the curtain. As I approached, a woman in scrubs pulled the curtain away.

"He's all yours, honey," she said, shaking her yellow bangs from her eyes. After gathering needles, gauze, and used latex gloves, she approached me.

"Keep him awake for me, will you? Head injury. The nurse will be in soon."

With that she left me to face John Carter alone.

A cervical collar surrounded his neck; his still-clothed body was stretched out and strapped to a long plastic board resting on the hospital bed. His head was strapped firmly down by the chin and forehead. The only thing that could have moved was his eyes.

Machines monitoring his heart and respiration buzzed nearby. Hair had been shaved from the right side of his head. A bandage was taped to half his forehead. His wrists were tethered to the bed. His right hand was wrapped in a gauze mitt. He kept his eyes turned to the ceiling, away from me.

Blinking back tears, I stood watching the thin green line pulse across the screen. I knew that I couldn't leave, yet I didn't know what to say or do.

I thought of my brother. A new hatred stirred inside me. *Oh, God. Please help me stop it. No more hate.*

"She is an idiot," John Carter finally said, still not looking at me. "Stupid woman couldn't find a vein if it asked her for a date. Why are you here?"

212

Lord, help me. No, not me. Help John Carter. Please, heal him.

I took another deep breath, wiped the tears away, and pulled a metal chair from the foot of a bed across the room. His eyes were on me when I turned around but then he snapped them shut.

"Hard of hearing, Celine?"

I placed the chair to the left of his bed and sat without a word.

"I asked you a question," he said. His voice was low and harsh.

I bit my lip and swallowed hard. "I'm keeping you awake, like that lady wanted." I wiped my sweaty palm on my knee and rested my hand on the metal rail running along the side of the bed.

Dear, Lord. Work in every tendon and muscle. Bring complete healing, in Jesus' name. Amen.

He took a sharp breath. The hard edges of his jaw softened but he kept his eyes turned upward. I reached under the bar and wrapped my fingers around his cold hand. He bit his bottom lip and closed his eyes. I squeezed his hand; slowly, he wrapped his fingers around mine and a tear slid down his face.

＊ ＊ ＊

The coffee my mother had given me had been nasty, and it must have been caffeine-free. Not the thing I needed after a sleepless night.

I slipped my feet from my mules, letting my bare feet touch the icy floor. I bit the inside of my cheek and dug the nails of my free hand into my palm. My eyelids just got heavier.

John Carter's fingers around my hand were strong and comforting. He wasn't asleep although his eyes were still shut.

"John Carter?"

We'd been sitting in silence for more than half an hour. The other patients, just as startled as he was at first by my gesture of compassion, had gone back to their cell phones, lime Jell-O, and crumpled magazines.

I whispered his name again. No response except the firm grip on my fingers. My eyes grew heavier.

"I want to thank you. You didn't have to go back into the house. But you did, and now look . . . why did you do it?"

"I'm nobody's hero, Celine."

His lips had barely moved.

"You didn't think about yourself. You just went in. In my book, that's a hero."

"If you came here to show pity, then you can leave me."

He released my hand and pulled his fingers as far away as the restraints would let him. I rested my fingertips on his bruised knuckles.

"I'm sorry, John Carter."

"Don't be." His face turned hard again. "Just leave. You don't belong in Pettigrew anymore. Everyone's changed. You've changed. You know it."

"No, I haven't."

I reached for his hand again. He pulled his fingers into a tight fist.

"Go back to Raleigh."

"Stop this, right now, John Carter. You're in a lot of pain. You're just talking out of your pain."

"Why are you still here?"

I stood and leaned against the rail. Looking down on him, I whispered, "I don't know what's going on."

He opened his eyes and looked at me. My eyes welled up.

"Trying to get you to leave me alone."

"No, you don't understand. I mean, what's going on in *here*." I laid my hand across my heart. His frown deepened. "Last night you shared your heart. But my heart was so bound up with hate and fear I didn't know what to do with it all. There wasn't any room for anything else. Certainly not . . . love.

"God keeps telling me to listen and learn and love. But I don't know what to be listening for or learning. And the love part—it's so hard. Every time I try to get close to a man, I think of Steven. I feel his hands . . . up my leg. And his fingers . . . tearing at me. His mouth. His teeth. All over me. Pushing and clawing and biting . . ."

I'd never told anyone about that night. Just thinking about it brought up the strong taste of bile.

"It's just so hard. How can I love?"

My voice cracked on the last word. His beautiful eyes flashed with compassion, but only for a moment. They quickly hardened again. But I continued.

"When I thought you were dead, John Carter, I didn't know what to do. I knew I didn't want you to be dead. Part of me went wild, or maybe woke up—I don't know. It was a feeling that I hadn't felt in a long time.

"So many men have let me down. They used me and slapped me around. Trampled me and treated me like dirt. I guess lots of women have been through that with men and come out with their hearts still soft and intact. But for some reason, mine . . . mine isn't. It's hard and broken. Broken into a million angry, hateful, lying pieces.

"I didn't know how to put it all back together and be happy. I thought a career was it but now I know it isn't. Until you shouldered your way into my life. You . . . you crazy, staring, deep probing, foolish man . . . and forced me to think. You're not Steven and you're not my father or Abraham either.

"It's not because you're white. That's not it at all. It's because you're asking more than I know how to give right now."

Sobbing, I lowered my head and placed my tear-slick cheek against his. "I want to care for you. I really do. I just don't know exactly how right now. Please give me time. Don't shut me out—not yet. Give me time."

I stood back and looked at him. He'd closed his eyes again and set his lips in a rigid line.

Two young men in blue scrubs approached. An older man wearing a white lab coat, Dr. Jones, according to his shiny nameplate, followed them.

"Miss, excuse me," the doctor said, "are you family?"

Wiping tears on my sleeve, I shook my head and stumbled away from the bed. Without so much as looking at me, he told me to leave. I collected my bag and my shoes and moved to the side.

One of the men in scrubs pulled the curtain around the bed as the doctor spoke with John Carter.

"Is she a friend, Mr. Manning?"

"No," John Carter said, "not anymore."

I turned and ran out. I ran through the slick linoleum hallways that smelled of disinfectant. I ran through waiting rooms and down wide-carpeted stairways and through sliding doors. I stopped when the sun warmed my skin and the breeze brushed my face.

I was in a small empty courtyard. A fountain stood babbling in the center. Several slatted benches stood in groups of twos and threes here and there. The air smelled of fresh dirt and gardenias. One little bush, its white blossoms trembling in the breeze, caught my eye. I sat on a bench near that bush, buried my head in my lap, and wept.

I'd put my heart in John Carter's hands and he had crushed it. Why? I thought he was different. But he was no better than Steven or my father. They'd crushed me too. Used me for their purposes. Why had John Carter told me those things last night? I'd never know. I would never let him close enough again.

Never.

I dried my face and sat up. John Carter was a part of the past, but Abraham Benson was not. Neither was my brother. I needed to find out more about the missing photos in that composition book. And I needed to find out what Brother was up to.

First, the composition book. The WRAL Gardens postcard had me thinking that the key was Raleigh. Bob could help me out with that hunch.

I fished out my cell phone and punched in Bob's number.

"Hey, Celine," Bob said, sounding like he was talking to me from the inside of a closet. I hoped I didn't sound like I'd been crying my eyes out.

"Hey, Bob. Where are you?"

"In a very large box. Don't ask. How are you?"

"Not too good. Don't ask. I've got a favor to ask you. I need a little detective work done. Got a pen and paper? I need to find out when someone was married."

"Huh?"

"It's for a story I'm working on."

"What story? Coulton didn't like it when I told him you were staying behind for a little while. Sharon's still chewing on my tail and stuff for not getting *real* footage."

I cringed.

"Okay, I lied. I'm not working on a story. It's more like a lead to an exposé. Something big on our Abraham Benson. Something I can take to Bev or Harvey at WRAL."

I thought by throwing around the names of some heavy-weights Bob might jump on board.

"What are you getting at?"

"It could open a door for us. I've been thinking I don't want to stay with WCNC forever. If I leave, I'd like you to go with me. If you want to leave, that is."

"Celine, why are you working me like an out-of-tune fiddle?"

"Where'd you get that one?"

"Coulton."

We laughed.

"Look, Bob. I really need to know about this wedding. Can you please try and carve a little time out for me?"

"Would you really get me a spot at R-A-L?"

I could hear the smile in his voice.

"If I stay in TV, I'd love for you to be my cameraman, Bob Hollywood. You make me look good."

"All right, enough schmoozing. What was the date of the wedding?"

I heard the rustle of paper on the other end of the line.

"May 21, 1984. The bride's name is Betty Douglas. Also try Betsy or Beatrice. Not sure if there's a middle name. She was most likely married in Raleigh."

"Got it. I'll call you after four."

"Thanks, Bob. You're good people."

"So they tell me."

A thought crossed my mind. *Had Bob thought of me since that day he tried to kiss me?*

218

"Bob, how are things with you and Ming these days?"

"Where are you going with this?"

"Just making conversation."

"No you're not. I'm not your project, Celine. I know everything you touch is golden and stuff, but I'm not in the market for golden right now."

"I didn't mean to offend you."

The man cut me off.

"And I'm not pining away for you."

"What?"

"Nobly pushing my real feelings aside. Hoping that you'll notice me. Blah, blah, blah. I've got my pride, Celine. And I've got principles. I said what I had to say earlier. As you say, I'm not studying ya."

I covered the laugh by clearing my throat.

"Bob, okay, I get the picture. I'm sorry."

"You want to know what they call you around the office?"

"No," I cut him off. "I do not want to know. Just call me when you get that information about Betty Douglas." I hung up and tossed the phone in my bag.

❋ ❋ ❋

Catty was asleep on her beloved's shoulder by the time I found the way back to the waiting room I'd left hours earlier. With eyes closed, Isaac was stroking her hair, tucking stray tufts under her pink paisley bandana.

When I sat down, he opened his eyes and gave me a little smile.

"Your mother went to look for lunch and you. You okay?"

"I'm fine. Thanks."

I studied a scuff on my shoe, hoping the water I'd

splashed on my face had covered all traces of my crying fit in the courtyard.

Isaac's blue eyes were disconcerting. It seemed he knew what I'd done, and not done. In his eyes, I saw Abraham's judgmental glare.

"Did you hear about John Carter?" he asked.

New tears threatened to form. "Yeah, I saw him."

"It's great that he's going to be okay. He'll walk again. An answered prayer, for sure."

Walk again!

"I had no idea," I said, more to myself than to him.

But now, looking back to him strapped onto the body board, it made sense. Why hadn't I seen it before? I placed my head in my hands. New tears dotted my lap.

"I want you to leave my father alone, Celine."

Isaac's voice had deepened into a husky whisper. I looked up into his anger-darkened eyes.

"What did you say?"

"I said, leave my father alone."

"So, he's fine. He's going to be okay?"

"Yeah. If you call being in critical condition okay. But I don't think any of that would matter to you, would it? You'd still be going after him like he was a criminal even if he was hanging on by the last thread of his life. He could be drawing his last breath and you'd stab him in the heart. Wouldn't you?"

"Isaac, what are you talking about?"

"Why'd you go back to the house?"

"I didn't start the fire."

"I'm not accusing you of starting the fire. The man who started the fire has got his due."

The man?

"You know who—"

"I don't know what you're searching for, but I want you to know it's not worth it. Trying to kill Abraham Benson will only leave you frustrated and empty. Been there. Done that."

My mind went back to the story he told me in Catty's bedroom. A story with obvious holes. I yearned to fill them. What was he holding back? And why?

"After this is all over, Abraham goes to prison."

"To prison?"

"It's the arrangement he made. When he's done testifying, he'll go to a federal prison in California. For life. So you see, what you're doing, or rather trying to do to him, is already done. What more do you want? He's a dead man, Celine. Can't get any more dead than dead. Would it make you feel better if you killed him yourself?"

His icy blue eyes had grown colder. I shifted in my seat and looked away.

"Don't be ridiculous," I said.

"Am I? It's all over. You can go home now."

"So your father's going to prison, what will happen to you? Your younger brother?"

"I'm not answering any of your questions, Celine. I'm not your story. If there's any story here. It's yours."

Mine?

I ignored the pain and confusion churning inside me. My questions needed answers. I pressed further. If I could get him to talk about his brother, maybe he would talk about the fire. Who was this man he spoke of?

"Your younger brother? His name is Patrick, right? Is he in a witness protection program somewhere?"

"You know, I have this theory," he said.

Catty's eyes fluttered and opened. She stretched and yawned. Isaac kissed her forehead and continued.

221

"My lovely Catty here says I'm always theorizing about something."

They smiled at each other.

"Too much hypothesizing," Catty said, sitting upright and stretching again, "only leads to a lot of gray hair. What's this new theory about, sweet?"

His smile faded as he looked at me. "It's about the human heart."

"Another one about the heart?"

"Well, this one's different. I think the heart can only hold so much hate."

His eyes pierced me. I studied my clasped hands. Isaac continued.

"After it reaches its capacity, it still enlarges. To the point of pain. But we ignore it, convincing ourselves that it's normal, comfortable even. Meanwhile, nothing else gets in. No happiness. No joy. No love."

He stood and held out his arm, his clenched fist inches from my face. He leaned over and whispered in my ear.

"Open it up just a little and a miracle occurs. The hate dries up. Blows away. Love pours in."

He sat back down and looked me in the eye.

"Are you afraid, Celine? Afraid of what might happen between you and John Carter?"

Wide-eyed, I looked away. I felt Catty's eyes on me. Could the woman dabbing at her eyes across the waiting room hear us? *Where had my mother gone?*

"Leave that up to God. You've got other things to worry about. My father. Your father. Your brother."

Our eyes met again.

"What do you know about my brother?"

"Deal with the hate first."

"What do you know about hate?" I asked him.

I no longer cared about what Catty thought or my mother walking in on us. A fire was growing inside me. With my fists in front of me, I turned the heat on Isaac and his simplistic solutions.

"You don't know me," I told him. "You don't know what I've been through. How can you just say, 'let it go' like it's just a little bird sitting on my thumb?"

"No, I don't know you, Celine. But it doesn't come down to me knowing you or not. I don't have to know you personally to know the depths of hate. Hate that hounds you until you can't sleep or eat until someone else is hurting more than you. But it never stops. It just wants more. Just hurting people isn't enough after a while. It wants people dead."

"What are you talking about? I don't want anybody dead."

"Not yet. Your brother does."

"What do you know about my brother?"

"Your father found a way out, though. And so did my father."

"Tell me what you know about my brother."

Isaac drew a breath and studied my feet for a few seconds.

"Your brother came to me about a week ago. Threatened to kill me." Isaac glanced at Catty. She shook her head and looked away.

"And he said he'd kill my father and girlfriend too. He's been watching us. I'm sure he saw you when you came to Benson Ridge.

"Gerome has found evidence of him in the woods around the house. It was like he wanted us to know he was doing these things. He was terrorizing us. But there was no reason to be concerned about his threats until now. He's a wanted man now, Celine. His life is ruined. I remember seeing a wedding band on his finger. Do you know where his wife is? Does he have children?"

This had gone further than I'd imagined. Brother had threatened Isaac to his face. He didn't care anymore. Was it too late for him to turn around? I couldn't believe that. I would talk to him. Get him to turn himself in.

"You don't know Brother like I do."

It felt silly using a pet name for a grown man. But I couldn't bring myself to call him Quincy. Quincy was my father's name. Just the thought of that name brought back feelings I didn't want to deal with.

"There's one thing that can turn him around. Love."

"I love my brother."

Isaac lifted a hand.

"Wait a minute. I'm not talking about just loving your brother."

"Well, who then? John Carter? Don't go there again."

He lifted both hands like a traffic cop. I gripped the edge of the seat and pushed forward. It was time to go.

"Celine, just wait a minute. Hear me out. Please. I know you want to help your brother. But you can't help him, really help him, until you let go of what's inside of you right now. This hate for my father. The feelings you have toward your father. You've got to let it go. Find a way to forgive them. To love *them* first.

"If you go to your brother now with this still bottled up inside, it'll only grow deeper. How can you show him out of the dark if you're blindfolded yourself?"

He glanced at Catty who nodded, her big eyes piercing me.

"I know this is hard, Celine," she whispered. "But please find a way. Let it go."

I drew a long breath and studied my trembling hands. They were right. I knew it. I just didn't want to hear it. I didn't want the feelings that were crowding my heart.

"You don't know me," I said, my head still down. "You don't know what I've been through. Please leave me alone."

"Please stay," Catty said. "Just stay and listen to what Isaac is saying. Just listen."

Listen. Learn. Love.

God was driving me crazy with those three words. I grabbed my bag and stood up. "No! I don't want to listen."

"Cee Cee, we love you." My mother's voice over my shoulder startled me. I turned to face her. How long had she been there?

"Mama, I just want to go home."

"I love you."

I closed my eyes against the tears. Never had I heard her say that. Never. My heart was beating so hard that I was sure they could see it banging against my rib cage. She walked around the chair and took my hands in hers. My eyes settled on her shoes, her belt, her hands—but not on her face.

"I love you and I want the best for you. I know I haven't been the best mother. Always nagging you about something or another. But I do love you."

The tears were running down her face. I could no longer hold back my tears. Shoving my bag up my arm, I brushed past her. She held my arm fast.

"I'm sorry," she continued, "for not being that shoulder you needed when your daddy treated you so badly. Can you forgive me, Cee Cee?"

"Mama, please. Not now. Not here. I just want to go." I pulled away from her. Buxton, straddling the doorway across the room, caught my eye. "Agent Buxton, can you take me back to Pettigrew?"

He dipped his chin in a slow nod. "Will anyone else be coming along?"

"Cee Cee. No, please stay. We can get lunch. Talk things through. Just you and me. Please."

"No, Mama. I need some time."

Buxton was waiting for me at the elevator on the other side of the nurses station. I turned to Catty.

"My things are at the Ross house. Could I have the key?"

"It's not locked," she said with a shrug. "Please don't go. You don't need to be by yourself."

She couldn't have been more wrong. Being here with them was crowding my mind. They all wanted me to come along nicely; it was the right thing to do. That's what my head told me, but my heart . . . it was saying something different. I just couldn't figure out what it was. I only knew it was different. There was something there. Time and solitude would help me find it, not more talk.

"I need to go, Catty. Please understand."

Her small face contorted with agony, she stood and pulled me into a hug. I felt my mother's hand on my shoulder.

"God's grace, Cee Cee," she said. I stepped out of the hug without looking back and I left.

Chapter 21

SPECIAL AGENT Buxton's manners hadn't returned to him since the last time we talked. He was still cold and distant. For that I was grateful. As he pulled onto Highway 64 and pointed his shiny black government-issue sedan eastward, I closed my eyes and leaned my head against the window.

For the first time in what seemed like forever, I slept. But the fitful sleep was littered with dreams of my brother running through fields. Cornfields. Wheat fields. Minefields. He was running. And I was chasing him, yelling after him. Frantic. Fearful. Crying.

I woke with a start. Buxton was on his cell phone. He glanced at me and went back to his hushed conversation.

My dream had been so real that I could still feel the lashes from the tall grasses on my legs. Like so many times that I had run in the fields around Pettigrew in real life. *Trying to escape the confusion at home.*

On one occasion shortly before the fatal trailer park fire, I had wandered away from the trailer. Running away from home was always in the back of my mind. But that day I was just wandering, trying to forget my parents' argument.

I had wandered into the woods and near Lake Finleigh I

figured, because the air was cooler. I found myself in a field of high grass. It was thick and feathery. Up to my ears. Whispering to me. Brushing all over me. Like lots of soft hands.

I knelt down on the dry grass and could almost hear it brushing past my ears. I remember feeling like I was floating. Like in water or air. I closed my eyes and imagined that the grass was washing me. Cleaning all the anger away. All my father's talk against Christianity. All the dirty looks and gossip from people in town about his crazy attitude.

What did I know or care about my father's personal beliefs? They were strange and dark and angry. Why did I have to answer for his bizarre rages or lengthy disappearances?

But there in that field all the confusion and dirty feelings were gone. If only for a moment. Then, like something out of a Stephen King novel, a hand touched me. I opened my eyes and nobody was there.

And then, no louder than a whisper in an empty room, I heard someone say three words, "Listen. Learn. Love."

I was so scared I just jumped to my feet and ran straight home.

Later that night I told my grandmamma. She said it was the hand and voice of God. She was like that. She'd said that He wanted to clean me and talk with me; come inside me and wash me. He wanted to wash me with His blood. He wanted me to listen and learn and love like nobody's business.

Grandmamma was that way. Everything was God Almighty. She was like day compared with her son Quincy's night. And now they were both gone.

Gone. Forever.

Never again to hinder me. Or help me.

The digital clock on Buxton's dashboard read 1:25 p.m. Tall pines, lined in neat rows, bordered either side of the four-lane road. A hawk circled the clear skies above.

I guessed we were probably nearing Finleigh. Minutes later, a green road sign confirmed my guess.

Finleigh: 15 miles. And twenty-five miles beyond Finleigh, we would be in Pettigrew.

Would I find Brother still squatting at Mama's house? I closed my eyes and prayed that I would.

Sleep enveloped me again and I woke to the smell of fries.

"You eat beef or chicken?" Buxton asked as he maneuvered the car out of the McDonald's drive-thru.

I sat up and rubbed the sleep from my eyes. My neck hurt and my stomach was growling.

"What?"

"Are you vegetarian?"

"No." My mouth was watering. I smelled cheese. Greasy cheese. I could have eaten cardboard if it had cheese on it. I hadn't eaten cheese in months. "Do you have a cheeseburger?"

"Yeah. It's on the bottom." He shoved the bag over and made a right turn. "No onions."

Salty, hot french fries tumbled over my hand as I lifted the burger from the bag. Specks of salt looked like tiny little snowflakes on my skin. It felt like snow on Christmas. I licked the salt from my knuckles. It tasted better than any snow I'd ever let land on my tongue. Eyes closed, I held the wrapped burger to my nose and inhaled.

When I opened my eyes, Buxton was looking at me.

"Don't hurt yourself, Ms. Johnson." He chuckled and rummaged through the bag. "You want fries and a Sprite with that?" He pointed to a cup of soda in the drink holder between the seats.

Cheeks bulging, I smiled and nodded. How could grease taste so good? It was illegal. And I get to have a carbonated beverage to boot. I'd died and gone to heaven.

Wait a minute.

"Are you trying to butter me up?" I asked the large black man smiling in the driver's seat.

"Butter. Grease. Same difference. Is it working?"

"No, not really." I crumbled a paper napkin and wiped ketchup from my chin. "I don't know anything about my brother."

"Who said I was working you for information about your brother?"

I pulled a fry from the bag. "But you are working me? Even though you'd rather dump me on the side of the road."

"Now you're jumping to conclusions." He finished his chicken wrap in a couple of bites.

"You comforted me."

"What?"

"In Abraham's pantry the night we met. I cried on your shoulder. Remember?"

"Yeah. What about it? Pretty women cry on my shoulder all the time."

"A compliment like that from you goes a long way, Special Agent Buxton."

"And they call me complicated? What's your game, Ms. Johnson? Alienating the FBI agent doesn't sound like a safe move—especially with you being a suspect."

"And a love interest." I nibbled at two fries I held together.

"A what! Woman, don't kid yourself. You and that white guy . . ." He stopped short and glared at me. "Hey, wait a minute. You're playing me like a beat-down fiddle, aren't you?"

I nodded. "But you're smarter than you look."

"Thanks," he said with a cocked eyebrow. "Simple fact is

230

I have a job to do. There's been a double homicide. I've lost a brother-in-law. And you and your brother are suspects. This is real life. Not Hollywood. No FBI romance going on here. Am I clear?"

"Yes, sir."

We settled into an uncomfortable silence for several miles. He was watching me but not watching me. It made me uneasy; but, for a few seconds, I'd unsettled him. That had to count for something.

Sure, he was on duty 24/7, but he was a man too. He'd get sleepy or distracted. Then I'd have a chance to slip away and find Brother.

Finally, the first exit marked Pettigrew appeared in the distance. Three more miles, I estimated. Buxton signaled and slowed for the exit marked Old Pettigrew Road. I'd never heard of the road.

I glanced at him and then at the Pettigrew exits up ahead.

"Shortcut," he said and slipped on a pair of shades.

The winding road took us past the migrant camp and intersected with Benson Ridge Road.

"Voila," he said, sweeping his hand across the cornfields spreading on both sides of the road.

Seconds later we were riding past the remains of Benson Ridge itself. Charred and broken, the house brought heaviness to my heart. Two black cars stood in the driveway. One was a hearse. The other, I gathered, was a government issue as was the dark-suited man who stood cross-armed beside it.

As we neared the Ross house, a red sedan marked "Fire Chief" passed us. No doubt, heading for the burnt-out farmhouse.

Buxton's phone rang as he pulled into the Ross house driveway. He killed the engine and sighed.

"Please excuse me, Ms. Johnson."

I nodded and got out, taking the fast-food trash with me. The house was open just as Catty had said. I righted a potted plant at the door, probably upset during last night's excitement.

The air inside the house was stuffy. By the sound of the refrigerator, the power was back on. I'd search later for the AC controls.

After dumping the crumpled paper bag in the kitchen, I helped myself to an apple in the wire basket hanging over the sink.

A noise in the bedroom made me jump. Had Buxton come in? I hadn't heard the front door open.

I heard a sliding noise and someone grunting. Was he opening a window? More grunting, followed by a *whoosh* and a muffled curse.

Brother!

I tossed the apple aside and rushed toward the bedrooms. A cool rush of air led me to the room I'd spent part of the night in. I pushed the door completely open and saw my brother looking back at me.

The bedclothes were just as I'd left them the night before. The window was partially open. Clumps of dirt littered the bloodied windowsill. He held a bloody right hand in the tail of his yellow T-shirt. There, to the right of his navel, was the scar from when we were kids. Frowning and breathless, we stared at each other for several seconds.

"What do you think you're doing here? They're looking for you, Brother."

"Come on out, Tab. It's Cee Cee."

The bed skirt shifted and two arms reached out. Brother stooped, his right hand still folded in his shirt, and pulled one of the hands with his left.

232

A woman with my mother's coloring and eyes peered up at me. Other than a few fine wrinkles creasing her forehead, she looked the same as she had the last time I'd seen her.

"Tabby!"

Chapter 22

"HI, SIS," my older sister said, tipping her head to me as though being pulled from under a bed was as natural as passing the salt. Clumps of dust clung to her head scarf and shoulders. I knelt to help pull her out farther.

"What are you doing here? You could get in serious trouble, Tabby. Where are the kids?"

She stood up and looked at her reflection in the mirror behind me.

"Don't be fussing at me, Cee Cee. I'm a grown woman. What's up with your hair, anyway?"

My hand went to my unruly coif before I could stop myself. I eyed the black hat on the bed. Was it Brother's?

"Never mind my hair. You are a grown woman with children."

"And? It ain't like you've given a care about my kids. When was the last time you saw them? Huh? They were babies, if I recall correctly."

"This isn't the time or place, Tabby."

She reached for the hat and pressed it on my head before continuing. "But from the looks of things, you've got it all figured out. Don't you?" She turned the brim up and gave me an approving look. "You see me in here with our fugitive brother and figure I'm up to something."

Brother looked up from his injured hand to roll his eyes at our older sister. "I ain't no fugitive, Tab."

As she wagged her finger at him, I turned my attention to the hat she'd fobbed off on me. By the size of it and the strong scent of oil sheen it gave off, I figured it was my sister's. Edging her to one side, I looked at myself in the mirror. *Not half bad.*

Tabby continued to talk. "What you don't know is gonna kill you, Cee Cee. Mama called me from the hospital about an hour ago."

"How do I look?" I asked.

"Not too shabby. Where's that wig you used to wear on the show?"

"Lost it. Long story. Thanks for the hat."

"I'm letting you borrow it. So that you don't shame the family. Anyway, Mama told me to come and look at this DVD of Daddy in the prison. She's been pestering me for weeks. Like I can just drop everything and come over to her house and watch this durn DVD."

She motioned to the TV in the corner. I followed her finger to the dresser across the room and discovered that the TV was already on. My father's smiling face startled me. The picture had been paused but his eyes seemed to pierce me. I looked away, hoping that Tabby hadn't seen the shock that flashed across my face.

"My children are with their daddy. And if you must know, baby sister, I will tell you what I was doing here. I was sitting here, watching Daddy, trying not to lose it. Crying. Then, in walks Brother. How's your hand, Brother? The bleeding's stopped? Have you been taking your medication?"

Looking down at his arm wrapped in the bloody shirttail, he nodded. "Yeah. Got new medication. Mama helped me find a good doctor. Least she still cares about me. And I ain't no fugitive."

"Whatever, child. Where was I? Oh yeah. For a split second I lose it when Brother comes in and I slip under this high-tail bed. I'm so glad I can still squeeze under a bed."

Pushing the rumpled comforter aside, Tabby chuckled and sat on the bed. The way she moved her head and hands when she talked made me think of Mama. They were so much alike. I was so different. She glanced at Brother and went on.

"And you, little brother, I thought you were up in Elizabeth City. The last place I expected to see you is here. And then when you told me you needed money and you needed to leave Pettigrew fast . . . yada, yada, yada. I figured I needed to get out of here. That's when we heard you."

She pointed at me.

"Course, I didn't know it was you at first. All I knew is I didn't want to be involved with the mess our little brother is in. So I hid my big brown behind under the bed. I'm a grown woman with children *and* I'm Cee Cee Johnson's big sister. That's what I told myself."

I shook my head at her silliness.

"Very cute, Tab," I said. "I'm sorry for jumping to conclusions. There's an FBI agent outside. And this little family meeting doesn't look good. Brother is a suspect in a murder. Truth be told, so am I."

"Do tell." Tabby smirked and crossed her legs. "So, should I just tie y'all up now and turn you over to the authorities? 'Cause I ain't doing time."

She wagged a finger at the screen.

"I don't need none of what Daddy got. I mean, I love you both. Yada. Yada. But it don't take all this. Brother, come on. You know this ain't right. Go back to your wife. Turn yourself in to the law. Do the right thing. Please."

Tabby stood and reached for him, casting a pleading eye my way. Brother jerked away and glanced out the window.

He was my only brother and I wanted the best for him. I could still hear him squealing like a little girl when Tabby pushed him too high in the tire swing we'd rigged at our hideout in the woods. And the scar on his belly. A cut from the day he played with Grandmamma's collard-cutting knife. I'd stopped it from bleeding.

Please, do the right thing, Brother.

My little brother wet his lips and then pulled them back in a snarl. "You don't know what I've been through. Neither one of y'all."

"Well, tell us. Please, Brother," Tabby said.

"You wouldn't understand."

"Is this about Abraham Benson?" I ventured.

Our eyes met for a brief moment. Fear flashed across his face before he narrowed his eyes and looked out of the window again. Was he waiting for someone to appear in the thicket or merely avoiding my gaze?

"Brother. Are you trying to kill him?"

Tabby gasped. "Kill him?"

We started at the sound of the front door opening.

"Ms. Johnson?" Buxton called out. His heavy footsteps seemed to shake the house.

Brother was breathing hard and he had yet to take a step.

"Turn yourself in, Brother," Tabby urged, her voice lowered to a whisper.

His eyes went to the bed skirt.

"No, don't," I hissed and stood in front of him.

He lunged for the open window and shoved it with his left hand. The window moved a few inches. He cursed under his breath and lowered his upper body through the narrow opening. Under the force of his weight, the window flew open all the way.

"No," Tabby and I said, grasping for him. He wriggled out of our grasp and fell to the ground below.

The bedroom door burst open. Buxton stood in the hallway with his gun drawn.

"FBI, stop!" he yelled, adding a string of four-letter words at the sight of Brother running full tilt toward a row of pine trees behind the house.

"No, wait!" I yelled, pressing my hands against the rock solid chest of the advancing FBI agent.

"Ms. Johnson!" he growled and shoved me back. I fell backward onto the bed.

Tabby had knelt beside the window. She was yelling for Brother to return. "Don't make this harder than it needs to be, Brother. Come back here right now. Do you hear me?"

Buxton knelt before the open window and leveled his gun. "Move aside, ma'am."

Eyes wide, Tabby leaned back. Buxton fired a round into the trees. Chunks of wood showered to the ground. Several birds took flight. A flash of yellow streaked through the underbrush. Buxton fired again.

"No!" I screamed and rolled from the bed onto Buxton. He buckled to the floor under me. His gun fell to the floor.

"Woman!" he said, pushing me off his back. "What is wrong with you? I'm not squirting water here!"

"You were going to shoot my brother."

"No, he wasn't," Tabby volunteered. "The bullets were hitting the trees high."

I glared at my sister.

"You interfere again and you'll have an obstruction of justice charge slapped on you so fast . . . But maybe aiding and abetting, or even accessory to murder would suit you more." He snatched up his gun and stood. The phone on his hip buzzed. "Don't push me, Ms. Johnson. Stay put—both of you."

He stalked from the room, answering his phone with a gruff voice.

I sat on the floor trembling. Tabby stood over me shaking her head.

"You are crazy," she said. She lifted her hands like someone surrendering and shook them in the air. "What is going on with my family, Lord?"

My mind was on Brother. Where was he headed?

From the window I watched Buxton. With his gun drawn, he greeted four armed men in camouflage emerging from the woods. They talked briefly. Buxton pointed to the left and right. The men, two by two, trotted off in the directions Buxton gave.

Buxton turned and barked at me, "Close and lock that window. Now!"

Tabby complied. He holstered his gun and walked toward the house. I heard the back door open and Buxton's heavy footfalls again coming down the hall.

"He's gonna get caught," I said, kneeling at the window. My breath made a small circle of moisture on the glass. I wiped it away.

Where was Brother going?

Lord, help.

"Don't make that your problem, Cee Cee. We've got bigger fish to fry right this minute."

Buxton stood in the doorway and glared down at me.

"Draw those curtains."

Tabby nudged me aside and pulled the curtains together.

"Thank you, ma'am. And you are?"

"I'm Cee Cee's older sister. Tabitha Johnson."

"I see. Well, until this situation is contained, I'm going to have you ladies wait in this room. I've called for assistance from the sheriff's office. Until they arrive I will be right here. Behave yourselves."

He jabbed a finger at the threshold. I was well accustomed to seeing Buxton's broad back. He turned it to us and crossed his arms.

Tabby stepped forward. "Excuse me, sir."

"Move back, please, Ms. Johnson," Buxton said without turning around.

Shocked, Tabby faltered. "But wait . . . see I'm not involved in this. I was here viewing my mother's DVD. Then my brother and sister came in and all this craziness breaks out. I'm not involved with—"

"That's enough," Buxton growled over his shoulder.

"But I have small children. Their father is coming by in an hour with them." She was all smiles and soft words. Buxton turned around. With one eyebrow cocked, he looked her in the eye and spoke slowly.

"When the deputy gets here, he'll take you where you need to go and wait with you until someone from the Bureau can take your statement. He should be here within the hour. You may use the phone to make arrangements for your children. Sorry for the inconvenience."

Tabby huffed and thanked the man. I eased onto the bed.

241

She flopped down beside me and pulled a cell phone from her pocket.

"You're a crazy black woman, Cee Cee." She punched numbers on her phone. "All you had to do was hold Brother."

"Me? You had his belt."

"No, I didn't. Excuse me." She spoke with her ex for a few minutes, all soft words and smiles again, and hung up.

Buxton reached over and confiscated her phone, explaining that it would be returned later. Tabby curled up her lips and opened her mouth to protest. A diversion was in order, before she got into trouble.

"Tab, how are the girls?" I asked.

"Fine. So it's my fault that your crazy brother got away."

"Everybody's crazy but you, Tab."

She glanced at the big man filling the doorway.

"Brother never could run. Could he?"

"What?"

She chuckled.

"He would always run in circles. Screaming his little nappy head off. Mama would come after him with the belt and he'd lose it. He'd dart this way and that like a little scared bunny."

She stretched her eyes wide and pushed her top teeth forward. "Which way do I go? Which way do I go?"

I smiled. "What went wrong, Tabby?"

"With Brother? I don't know. It's water under the bridge."

"No it's not. He's our brother. How can you say that? You're the big sister for goodness' sake."

"Everybody's got to account for their own grown-up mistakes after a while, Cee Cee. He's my baby brother, for sure. But he's not my child. I'm not responsible for him. At least, not in that way.

242

"A lot of bad things happened to us when we were kids. And we made it through. By God's grace. And to some degree by helping each other. But mostly by God's grace. I've done all I can for Brother. No more. You haven't been here for a long time. It's time to let Brother go. Like Mama did with Daddy. God brought him back around."

I looked at the drawn curtains. Where was he going?

I can't let him go.

Brother wasn't Daddy. Daddy had real issues. Alcohol abuse. Maybe drug addiction. And all manner of illegal involvement with the Bensons. Brother just needed someone to talk to. Someone to believe in him.

Chapter 23

"YOU KNOW what I wish," Brother said, letting my porch swing carry him to and fro. "I just wish we'd had a chance to say good-bye."

It was the summer of 2000. Brother had come to visit me in Raleigh. I'd opened my back door to toss out trash and there he was. Sitting by my privacy fence in an old lawn chair that I kept forgetting to throw out.

It pained me to see the thin mustache over his lips. It reminded me of the father I was trying to forget. He wore a white starched shirt over dark brown slacks. A rolled up tie bulged from his back pocket. I hadn't pressed him about his strange appearance. My question about his new bride had been met with little more than a grunt. So I had invited him in for a late breakfast, which he wanted to eat on my front porch.

"I miss Grandmamma too," I had said, pouring a little more orangeade into his glass. "When someone dies suddenly it tears you up."

I poured myself another glass and placed the pitcher on a little wooden table in the corner before I sat next to him.

"You know what I miss the most?" he started. "I miss holding her finger."

"Holding her finger?"

"I know it's stupid. But you remember when we would walk down the road with her and she would let you hold her index finger." Smiling, he wrapped his right hand around his left index finger. "Not her entire hand but just that one finger."

"I don't remember that, Brother. I'm thinking she just did that for you. You being the baby and all. She was sweet on you. That's what I'm thinking. What was it she used to call you? Booky. You were special, Booky."

He laughed.

"Yeah, well. Don't be telling nobody 'bout that. I got a reputation to uphold."

We both laughed.

"Something's been bothering me, Cee Cee. About the fire. I've been wanting to talk to somebody about it for years."

I gulped and played with the frayed corner on my tunic.

"I went to see Daddy earlier today."

I held my breath.

"Why don't you go see him?"

"I get busy, Brother."

"Anyway, I asked him about that day. He didn't tell me much really. Doesn't want to talk about it. 'Leave the past alone,' he says.

"But all I want to know is how it got out of hand. I mean, he was just burning stuff in the barrel. How could the whole place burn down?"

I shrugged. "The fire was high. Too close to the trees. I don't know, Brother."

"Yeah, you're probably right. I just don't remember a whole lot."

"You were little. It's okay to be curious about it. It's natural to want to put the pieces of your past together."

"You know, sometimes I pretend that I'm adopted."

"Adopted?"

"Yeah, you know. Like I had different parents. Good people, you know. But Quincy and Melissa stole me from them when I was young. Three years old or something. It was so traumatic that I can't remember 'em. But then I look in the mirror."

He laughed out loud. I smiled, worry creeping in.

"It's hard, Cee Cee. Being his son."

"Tell me about it. But we've risen above. We've done okay for ourselves. In spite of all the mess in our past. Life is good."

"Yeah, well. Could have been better."

We chatted a little longer, mostly about the GED he was studying for. He hugged me and walked down Glenwood, disappearing around Hayes Barton Memorial.

Why had he come to visit? To see his successful sister? Hardly. He had only wanted to talk. I wish we had talked more.

* * *

Tabby's voice brought me back to the present. "What is this about Abraham Benson?"

I gave her a questioning look.

"Abraham and Brother? He tried to kill the man?"

I glanced at Buxton. I figured it didn't matter what I said. He knew it all anyway.

"Abraham killed Grandmamma."

"What? That's not what he told me."

"You've talked with him?"

"I used to clean for him before Henry Wright's daughter came on. I needed something that could support me and my girls."

My jaw went slack. I had no idea my own sister had any connection with the Bensons as well. That could explain her detachment. What else was going on? Had she been paid off?

"You worked for him? In his house?"

"This grown woman with children needed a J. O. B. For sure. Don't be so high and mighty, Miss Celine 'I'm from Finleigh' Johnson."

"Let's not go there. Well, what did Abraham say to you?"

"Oh, you are not going to believe it, Cee Cee. This was back when his wife was in and out of the hospital. Getting sicker all the time. His little boy Patrick was still around too. His wife was dying but they all looked like death. It was sad."

"Tabitha."

"Don't *Tabitha* me. I'm getting to it. Give me a minute. You're the one who always liked telling stories. Let me tell one for a change. Goodness!"

She gathered her legs under her and sat Indian style on the bed. I rolled my eyes.

"Most of the time I would clean during the day while the girls were at school. But one time I had to clean at night. I took the girls. He said he didn't mind.

"That was the first time I took them there. The first time he met them. When he saw them he got all sadlike. I mean he was already sad over his wife but he got even sadder. He was crying but he was trying to cover it up. Then he asked if he could watch them while I cleaned. I was a little uneasy with that at first but I didn't want the girls getting in my way. So I said sure.

"I kept a close eye on him at first. He took them in the kitchen and gave them a snack. Apple cider and cookies.

"But I eased up, seeing how happy the three of them were together. They started playing a card game and pretty soon his son Patrick joined them. They were having a grand ole time."

She chuckled. But then her face hardened and she looked at the frozen picture of our daddy on the TV screen.

"When it was time to go, I had the girls go and get their coats. And just before he paid me, this is what he said."

Tabby glanced at Buxton before continuing in a low voice. "'I'm sorry about your grandmother.' That's all he had a chance to say before the girls came back in. I couldn't sleep that night. What was he getting at?

"The next day I called him. I asked him what he meant by saying he was sorry about my grandmother. He acted like he hadn't said it. *The man has lost his mind,* that's what I thought. He was creeping me out. The next day I found a letter in my mailbox. No stamp. No address. Just my name written across the flap.

"Inside I found a handwritten letter from him. He apologized for not protecting Grandmamma. It went on and on. Almost three pages. Front and back. He talked about how he'd used Daddy. How he'd regretted turning his back on us the day Daddy burned down the trailer park."

"You're kidding me. 'Not protecting'? What did he mean by that?"

"It means someone else killed her."

"No it doesn't, Tab."

"What do you want from the man, Cee Cee? He's suffered. He's going to prison after all this stuff in the news is done with."

"You know about that?"

"Mama told me when she called earlier. For all we know he could be dead right now. Lying on a cold slab in the hospital. When I talked with Mama earlier, she said he was bad off. What more do you want from him, Cee Cee? Why are you trying to kill him?"

"I'm not trying to kill him."

"Well, then what?" She hunched her shoulders and slid off the bed. "Dead is dead. After somebody is dead. That's it." She grabbed the remote from the nightstand.

"I dunno. I'm just trying to sort something out in my head."

My thoughts went to Betty Douglas. I wasn't truly convinced that Abraham had nothing to do with Grandmamma's death. But what of Betty? The reporter in me still wanted to know. Wanted others to know and care.

Did any of this have to do with our wayward brother? It frustrated me that Tabby didn't seem to care.

I rubbed the sore muscles at the base of my neck and sat on the bed. "Do you remember a woman named Betty Douglas?"

Tabby was busy with the remote. "Huh? Betty Douglas? Umm. Why won't this thing work? Batteries must be dead. Betty? Betty? Betty? Oh, here we go."

She'd found the correct button. The picture of Dad had come to life again. John Carter's voice, though, filled the room.

"So, what upset you most about your daughter being with a white man?"

My heart sank.

"Do we have to watch this?"

"Shhh. He was getting to a good part. Apologizing. About you and Steven. You do remember Steven?"

"Tabitha, please!"

My ringing cell phone cut my protests short.

"Okay. I'll wait until you're done."

She muted the TV and hopped back on the bed. Out of the corner of my eye, I saw my father's movements; but thankfully, I couldn't hear his voice.

Buxton frowned like a stern parent. He extended his hand.

"One call please," I begged.

Crossing his arms, he nodded.

"Hello," I spoke into my phone, trying my best to block out Quincy Johnson.

"Hey, Celine," Bob said. "What's up?"

"Nothing much. Just being held against my will here in Pettigrew. I know Coulton is having a fit."

"Well, um . . . "

Traffic noise obscured his voice. I spoke louder.

"Can you hear me? What did you find out about our little investigation?"

"You sitting down?"

I was standing near the window with my back to the room. A glance over my shoulder told me that Tabby was still on the bed and Buxton was still standing over the threshold.

"What is it?"

"It's not what you thought, Celine."

"Bob, just tell me for goodness' sake."

"What is Abraham Benson's full name?"

His full name?

"I dunno. You tell me."

He let out a sigh.

"You know how I was missing things with John Carter Manning. The name thing and stuff."

"Bob! What is it?"

He sighed again.

"Karl Abraham Benson married Beatrice Anne Douglas on May 21, 1984 in WRAL-TV Gardens."

Barely breathing, I sank to the bed.

Married?

"Celine, did you hear what I said?"

I clicked the phone off and held my head in my hands. Without another word, Buxton took my phone and resumed his post.

"You okay, Cee Cee?" Tabby asked.

There wasn't any husband that Abraham killed. Nothing that would lead me to a decent story. Just a few straws of information I was grasping at. At that moment they had all been blown away.

"Wait a minute," I said. My mind went to Isaac. "How old is he?"

"You're talking to yourself," Tabby said, resetting the DVD.

"Isaac is twenty-three. That's what the news report said. That meant he was born in 1984. But what month?" I ticked off fingers on my hand as I counted nine months from May of '84.

If she was pregnant when they married . . .

"Stop it, Celine." I sprang to my feet and let out a little scream.

What did it matter if they married after or before Isaac was conceived? It was their decision. Not mine.

"Cee Cee?" Tabby's hand warmed my shoulder. "What's going on?"

"I've been a fool."

"What is it this time?"

I faced her, frowning and fighting tears. "Tab, please stop."

She pulled me into her arms and pressed her cheek against mine. "I'm sorry, Cee Cee. I don't know all of what's going on but I'm here for you. Everything's gonna be okay. For sure. For sure."

Tabitha didn't know my situation. In the past decade we'd done little more than exchange Christmas cards. She didn't know about the painful lump in my breast. Or the reasons behind my lie about my background. She didn't know about the feelings I had for John Carter. I barely knew where my head (and heart) was concerning that man.

In that moment I didn't need for her to know. I just needed to be held. And that is all she did.

Chapter 24

"I LOVE YOU."

Tabby gave my shoulders a squeeze and kissed my cheek before getting into the backseat of the sheriff deputy's car. With the door closed, she pressed her palm against the window and mouthed the three magic words again.

"I love you too, Tab. For sure," I said and blew her a kiss. Special Agent Buxton motioned me back onto the porch and the car pulled away.

We had connected, Tabby and I, like never before. She hadn't spoken more than three words as she held me in the bedroom. She hadn't told me how to solve all my problems like everyone else.

There were things that needed fixing in my life. Without a doubt. But I didn't need solutions. I needed a heartfelt love to tackle the mountains before me.

I needed someone to help pull me up and over. In those few moments before the deputy came, I knew that someone was my sister, Tabitha.

Buxton escorted me back into the house and locked the door behind us.

"Can I make you a sandwich or something?" I asked him.

"No, thank you. But feel free to get something for yourself. We'll be leaving soon."

He was smoothing a large map across the living room coffee table.

"Yes, I almost forgot. I'll only be a few minutes."

My happy mood took a dip. I was still a suspect in a murder investigation. But, I still had a job in Raleigh, as far as I knew.

I left him making notes in a small notebook and went into the kitchen. My half-eaten apple had turned brown. I tossed it into the trash and filled a glass with water.

"Mind if I take a shower?" I asked Buxton as I reentered the living room. "You know, freshen up a bit."

He barely lifted his head.

"No problem. There's a man stationed outside."

"You don't have to worry about me, Agent Buxton. I'm not going to try to escape. I'm concerned about my brother but—"

His fingers tightened around his pen. "Go shower, Ms. Johnson."

I went back to my room and sat on the edge of the bed for several minutes. What else could happen? I had no life. No future.

Buxton's knock on the door broke me from my trance.

"Ms. Johnson, looks like you'll be spending the night here. Special Agent Hunt will be keeping you company. I'm required elsewhere."

Sweat glistened on his creased forehead. The twinkle in his eye rivaled the sparkle of his earrings. Were they on Brother's trail?

I lowered my eyes and studied my phone some more.

"Ms. Johnson, did you hear me?"

"Yes. I heard you. You're leaving and Agent Hunt is going

to stay with me. Slap me around with a wet noodle, no doubt." Something clicked in my brain and my eyes snapped wide open. "Wait a minute. *Agent* Hunt?"

"Yes." He stepped aside. "Ms. Johnson, meet Special Agent Ulysses Hunt."

A tall, well-dressed man, in his sixties judging by the graying temples, with a coffee-with-cream complexion, stepped into the room. I shook his extended hand.

"Pleased to meet you, Celine Johnson."

"And you. I've seen you testify."

"Oh yes, the hate crimes hearings with Abraham Benson. Yes, I suppose I've had my share of airtime these days. Maybe I should go into broadcasting like you."

Not all that it's cracked up to be, I wanted to say. But I gave my best TV smile instead.

A smile creased his face in nice lines. His soothing gray eyes softened my resolve.

"It seems that the camera has lied," he said, tipping his head to one side.

"Sir," Buxton interrupted. "I'll be leaving now."

"Very good, son. Be careful."

"Thank you, sir." Buxton nodded and left.

The senior agent turned his attention back to me. "Might I get you a cup of coffee or tea?"

"No, sir. I'll be fine."

"Call me Ulysses, please."

I smiled.

"Do you have a cell phone? Might I have it?"

"I surrendered it to Agent Buxton earlier."

Hunt nodded.

"Tell you what, I'll give you some time to yourself. How about that?"

"Sir . . . I mean, Ulysses, what did you mean about the camera lying?"

"Oh." He chuckled. "You are more beautiful in person than on TV."

I blushed.

"I hope you don't mind my saying so."

"No. Well, okay. Maybe a little."

He laughed. "Honesty is a good quality."

"I've found that it's one that's hard to maintain."

"So true, Celine. So true. Especially in my line of work." His smile faded. He lifted his chin for a moment and seemed to sniff the air. His eyes darted this way and that. To the window. The closet. The muted TV. And back at me. "I'm sorry. Old habit. Some pieces just fell into place in my old brain. If you'll excuse me, I need to make a call."

"Sure."

He tipped his head and left the room, closing the door behind himself. My phone had not buzzed since Bob's call. Would Coulton have the nerve to fire me over the phone? Well, now that my phone was in federal custody, Coulton would just have to leave a message.

From somewhere else in the house, I could hear classical music. I pulled the comforter over me and closed my eyes. Tension quickly left my body and, for the first time since arriving in Pettigrew, I felt at peace.

❋ ❋ ❋

Ulysses Hunt was still on the phone when I woke up. I heard his voice like a low rumble under the strains of violins and cellos coming from the radio. The room was dark and stuffy.

I glanced at the digital clock—7:12 p.m. Later than I thought. What was I really supposed to be doing now? I probably had no job. And no prospects. I had been planning to move on but this was not the way I wanted it to happen. I pulled myself out of the bedding and let my legs dangle over the edge of the bed.

"What do I do, Lord?"

In an attempt to settle my heart, I closed my eyes and tried to remember the words I'd heard the Lord speak to my heart the night before as I stood on the edge of the field.

My thoughts then had centered on John Carter and climbing the ladder to success. Now with my brother's life in ruins and possibly my own, I knew for a certainty that my pursuit of success had not been worth it.

"Lord, help me to listen. What do I do next? I need to hear from You."

I sat there for several minutes. The sounds of the night outside mingling with the voices of Ulysses Hunt and the radio.

"Lord, please. Speak."

Listen.

My eyes snapped open. The word had come at me like a fist to the rib cage.

"Yes, Lord, I'm trying to listen. Please speak."

My heart beat faster as I looked heavenward.

"Speak, Lord."

Listen.

There it was again. His voice. It was as clear as it had been so many years ago. Tears came to my eyes. I clapped my hands over my mouth like an astonished child at Christmas.

Yes, Lord, I'm listening.

I giggled and stood with my arms upraised. Hands flailing, I twirled. I hopped. I danced.

"Yes, Lord, I hear You," I whispered. "What is it? What do You want me to hear? I'm here. I'm listening. Speak, Lord. Speak to me."

Breathless and sweating, I stopped. My eyes fell on the blue screen of the TV.

Listen.

"Oh no."

My racing heart quickened its pace.

"No, Lord. I can't look at that DVD. No. No."

I caught my breath.

I can't do this, Lord.

I gripped the edge of the mattress and shook my head until the hat tumbled off my head.

"You're being childish, Celine. You know that, don't you? Yes, but why am I talking to myself?"

I stood and paced the room.

"It's just a video, girl. You can watch it. Pretend you're previewing something Bob taped. Yeah, I can do that."

The remote sat on the nightstand where Tabby had left it. I took a deep breath and clicked the on button.

The blue screen came to life with a blur of cornfields, like I'd seen from the car window many times. The young corn was a bright green against the neat black rows. A soft idyllic melody faded in, and the camera panned out to reveal the interior of a long black limo and my mother's profile. Through a cascade of black veils covering her face, I could see the tears staining her cheeks.

A lump rose in my throat and I fought the urge to turn the set off.

"I don't need this, Lord."

Listen.

I squeezed my eyes shut and covered my mouth against the sobs that threatened to rise from deep down.

John Carter's voice startled me. It sounded so alive and happy. I choked back tears.

"This is the story of Quincy Johnson Sr., a man who found himself by losing himself in Christ. It is his hope that you will follow his example into that rich, deep place with the Savior. This is not a happy story. It is more of the tale of a life unfinished. And for that reason, I thought it fitting to begin his story at the end. My name is John Carter Manning. I am honored to have called Mr. Johnson my friend and brother. I present this video journal as a gift to his family."

Words scrolled up the screen, chronicling my daddy's life.

My mind drifted back to two days ago when I sat facing Abraham in his office. The things he'd told me about my father had only deepened my hate of him. But sitting here watching an account of his sad, hate-filled life scroll by, I felt sorry for him. Had he produced anything good in his life?

The picture faded to the front gate of Central Prison, a maximum security prison not far from my house in Raleigh. John Carter's voice-over continued.

"Prison is a hard place. I think that goes without saying. Many men change in prison for the worst."

As he spoke, the camera led me through the gatehouse, down a long dark hallway, past empty cells, to a man with a Bible raised above his head. He was talking or maybe singing. His lips were moving and his eyes were closed. A thick salt-and-pepper beard covered the lower half of his face. Several men in the audience before him stood as well, Bibles held above their heads. I yearned to know what he was saying. John Carter's voice-over continued.

"I first met Quincy Johnson Sr. several years ago during

the filming of an educational video. This was my first impression of him," said John Carter.

No wait. This can't be . . .

I jumped off the bed. The remote fell to the floor. I grabbed the TV set with both hands. Was that man my father? The audio faded in.

"Jesus said to him, 'Today salvation has come to this house,'" he said in a voice I could not mistake. I gasped and stumbled back.

Shaking the Bible with fervor, he went on, "'Because this man, too, is a son of Abraham. For the Son of Man came to seek and to save what was lost.'"

Chapter 25

"I GREW UP in Pettigrew, North Carolina," said John Carter. "The small town where Quincy Johnson Sr. grew up. I knew the man to be a thief and a liar. So naturally, I was more than a little skeptical. I decided I'd do a little exploring. Chaplain Eaton was a valuable ally. My two-hour exploration of this bearded evangelist turned into two months of digging and growing."

"I grew up in St. Louis," said a middle-aged man with a long scar along his dark brown jaw.

A name appeared below his face: Dr. Sean Eaton, Central Prison Chaplain.

The man flashed a gold-studded grin and went on. "I tell my guys 'I'm from the Show Me State.' You have to show some signs before I put you in a position of authority. Brother Johnson was showing some major signs. Men were coming to Christ through his ministry.

"By ministry, I mean he was writing little stories. Tracts, you know. They had a strong salvation message. So I set about trying to get to know the brother. Trouble was it quickly became clear that the man didn't want to come along nicely, as they say.

"He's a renegade. So am I. Took us the better part of a year to win each other over. I love him like blood kin. To this day, though, I don't know how he came to the Lord. I've asked him and he ain't telling a soul."

Someone offscreen chuckled.

The camera panned out to reveal my father, in a gray work shirt, sitting beside the chaplain. They were both smiling. My father was shaking his head.

"That's one I'm taking to the grave," Daddy said.

There was no mistaking it. The bearded man in the prison-issue shirt was my father. The laugh. The voice. Both things I could never forget.

But how had he become this man I saw on the screen? There had to be a catch. This was my father after all—anti-Christian, former black militant, con man, murderer. It had to be an act.

He made tracts?

When had my father written anything? This chaplain had to be mistaken. It was an act for sure. His most masterful one.

The scene switched to a large, flat prison yard. John Carter's voice came across like a whisper above the jeers and calls from the surrounding men milling around the yard.

"During my first week at Central, this is where I spent most of my time. Having done the educational video just days prior, the men already had a level of comfort with me and my camera. They talked freely about Quincy."

The camera cut to a group of gray-shirted black men sitting in a semicircle. A wooden cross hung on the wall behind them. The caption at the bottom of the screen read: The names of these men have been changed to protect their families.

"So, Blake," said John Carter offscreen, "tell me about the first time you met Quincy Johnson."

John Carter zoomed in on a young man with a dragon tattoo on his neck. His assumed name and sentence faded in: Blake, serving a life sentence for rape and murder.

"It was like real freaky at first," the man said, smiling. "I would get these little storybooks. They'd be like little comics with pictures and words coming out of people's mouths, you know. Like in the funnies. 'Cept they won't funny."

His smile faded; he leaned forward and rested his elbows on his knees.

"It was like this cat knew just what I needed to hear. The drawings won't that good but it was the *question* that got me, you know."

Another man cut in. The camera angle changed to reveal a man with thick eyebrows. His slick head gleamed under the fluorescent lights.

The caption beneath his face: Art, serving fifty-five to life for murder.

"Yeah, when I saw that question, I remember thinking this was some kind of joke. What kind of Looney Tune was this joker?"

"The question? What do you mean by that, Art?" John Carter asked.

"Well, it's kinda crazy," Art said. "What if Jesus is black?"

John Carter cut in again, "A lot of folks have said that Jesus is black. What made this claim any different?"

Blake answered. "He didn't make it a race thing like most stuff I've read online. You know, look Jesus has African blood in Him. Naw, those little booklets was more like, look, black man, Jesus is strong and real and deep, just like I was before I got messed up with drugs and hate and mess. But with Jesus you can be that way again. And you can be that way all the time—but only through Him."

"Yeah, it was deep, man," someone said off camera.

"Yeah," Blake continued. "I don't know how scriptural they were. But they were deep. So deep that I couldn't shake it. He kept sending 'em to me.

"Pretty soon I found out that other cats were getting 'em. These little comic books were everywhere. It was like he was stalking me. We started calling this guy 'Black Jesus.' We were tracking down 'Black Jesus' for months."

A chuckle rippled through the group.

"Where did you find him?" John Carter asked.

"In the library," Art said.

The men laughed. The picture faded to walls lined with books. The camera panned along shelved books and came to rest on the profile of my father sitting in a wooden chair.

"So, why the library, Quincy?"

My father smiled. "This place was God's choice, John Carter. When I first came here and found out they'd assigned me to work here, I thought I'd died and gone to hell. Melissa, my wife, she thinks it's God's sense of humor."

"Why's that?"

"For all the grief I used to give her for her writing. I burned one of the books she was writing once. Used to keep me up with that durn typewriter."

I couldn't help but smile. Mama's typing at all hours had been a little annoying.

"But now?" John Carter continued.

"Now, I like it. It's peaceful. I got the idea of the tracts here. I'd see the guys out on the yard. The lifers, mostly. I targeted them because I figured they were my mission. You know."

"So, why a black Jesus?"

Daddy laughed.

"Why not? Does it offend you?"

John Carter cleared his throat. "Stop trying to switch the subject, Mr. Johnson."

"Quincy. Just Quincy."

"You know they call you 'Black Jesus'?"

"Yeah," Daddy said, stroking his beard. "Wish they didn't. I'm no Savior. This cancer in my body is gonna take me soon but I won't save nobody when I go. I'm just an ordinary man trying to do what I thought God wanted."

"And when did you come to this knowledge about God?"

"I'm gonna tell you about how I came to Christ. You'll be the first but since you're taping this here interview, I guess you won't be the last to know."

He lowered his head for a moment and scratched his forehead.

"On May 21, 1984, I attended a wedding not too far from here."

Every nerve in my body was on alert. Was my father saying he had attended Abraham and Betty's wedding?

"Whose wedding?"

"Well, if I told you I'd have to kill you."

They laughed. My heart fell to my stomach. It had to be Abraham's wedding.

Daddy continued. "The couple took Communion after their vows. The young minister who performed the ceremony gave a salvation message during Communion. That was the first I'd heard Christianity explained. For the first time it made sense. It wasn't a whole lot of rigmarole and nonsense. It was God sending His Son for me. And that Son was one bad cat.

"He was strong even in His weakest moment. And that challenged me. 'Cause up till that point I'd been deep into black consciousness. Black Panthers. Black militant. You know my story. So I struggled with that Jesus for years after that. He was the man I wanted to follow. But why did He have to be white?

"One summer day, shortly after my mother died—"

"In 1988?"

"Yeah, in 1988. I got into an argument with Melissa. I was drunk and tired. She'd kept me up all night typing on that durn book of hers. I got so mad that I decided I'd burn that book. She was getting too big for her britches, or so I thought. All this talk about being a writer and going back to school. So I got mad and got my gun. Forced her to give me the manuscript and I threw in all the vacation Bible school stuff that the kids had brought home. It had been bugging me too. Why was she putting all this nonsense into my children's heads?

"We were fighting real bad. The kids were outside. Melissa was yelling for the kids to run to safety, which made me even more mad. So mad that I started a fire in a barrel behind our trailer. I was gonna burn all that mess. No more writing books. No more ideas about going to college. No more Jesus in my house.

"So, there I've got her crying on the back step. The kids hiding in the woods, I guess. I'm waving my gun around, shouting, throwing stuff in the fire."

John Carter interrupted. "And you remember all this? As drunk as you were?"

"I wasn't too drunk. Some things are fuzzy though, especially after I'd thrown everything into the barrel and Melissa had run off into the woods. I remember going back into the trailer to finish my 40. After that things get real fuzzy. I went to prison for manslaughter."

"The fire killed one of your neighbors?"

"Yeah. But I don't remember the fire getting out of hand. I barely remember hearing the fire trucks."

Daddy frowned and shook his head.

"That really upsets me. I'd done a lot of bad things in my life before that but I'd never killed a man. But I think God had to bring me to that point to show me something."

"What was that?" John Carter asked.

"One of the things I threw in the fire that day was a plastic Jesus statue that my middle child, Carla Celine, had won at vacation Bible school. When the heat hit it, the face and hands turned black just like that."

Daddy snapped his fingers.

"And it was like a switch in my brain, reminding me of that preacher's message some five years earlier. How Jesus took my punishment. He endured hell so I wouldn't have to. And there that little statue of Jesus was, right there in that barrel, burning for me. I deserved to burn."

"Why do you say that, Quincy?"

"I'd done so much bad stuff. Illegal stuff. You see, working for Benson Ridge was no ordinary job. It felt like I was living a lie. All my talk about Black Power and I was doing nothing to empower my people. In fact, I was doing everything to tear them down."

Were there tears in my father's eyes? Frowning, I leaned in closer. The shuffling of chairs somewhere else in the house reminded me that I was not alone.

Not yet, Agent Hunt.

I heard voices at the front door. John Carter's pointed question on the TV pulled my attention back to the interview.

"What exactly do you mean? How were you tearing blacks down?"

A tear rolled down my father's cheek and mingled with the curly hairs of his beard. My hand went to my mouth.

"After I got out of prison for manslaughter, I was running

guns for the United Front. Sometimes I carried sensitive information for them too. Maps, letters, photos. Lots of stuff that I could have gone to jail for. On paper I worked for Benson Ridge. In real life I worked for the United Front.

"They controlled me by threatening to kill my friends or members of my family. At first I didn't take them serious. Then they killed Betty Douglas, a woman they thought I was having an affair with."

"Were you having an affair with her?"

"No. Never cheated on Melissa. But when they killed my mother a few months later, I knew I couldn't get out. No matter how much I wanted to. After seeing Jesus in that fire, I wanted to turn to Him. But how could I? I was a sham. A liar."

He covered his head with one hand, bowed his head, and with a handkerchief from his back pocket, he dried his face. The camera continued to roll as he composed himself.

John Carter cleared his throat and spoke with the tenderness of a child. "Would you like to stop?"

The gentleness in his voice gave me pause. Memories of our night on the porch flooded back. I blinked at tears.

"No. Just give me a minute."

The back of John Carter's head blocked the camera as he leaned forward. When he sat back, my father had composed himself.

"I just want to say one last thing before we go on to how I got the idea for the tracts." He paused to rub the handkerchief across his nose. "I want to apologize to my family. I let them down. I wasn't ever the husband or father I could have been. But I tried to change, especially after I went to prison that first time.

"I felt the Lord was calling me out of my involvement with

the Front and Abraham Benson but it was just so hard to get out. So much was tied to my family's safety. Since being in here a second time, the Lord has helped me forgive Abraham and the others. It's only been through His strength. His blackness, if you don't mind the expression. To my family, I beg for your forgiveness."

His brown eyes bore through me.

"And to my Carla Celine. I want you to know that I love you. I never meant you any harm. The whole thing with Steven Kepler. I'm sorry if it seemed like I did you wrong. I just didn't want you to end up like me.

"There's some good white folks in this world but Steven Kepler wasn't one of them. I wanted you to have a chance in life. You were so impressionable and you always seemed to live in a dream world, with all your stories and things. I wanted you to see that life was hard for a black person. I wish it wasn't so. Maybe one day it won't be."

He stopped and let out a heavy breath.

"Anything else, Quincy?"

"Yeah. I'm sorry for saying that I thought you were being foolish when you told me about your new cameraman. We argued about that when you came a few days ago. It wasn't anything about Steven. You left before I could explain. I wanted to tell you that I knew of a pretty good cameraman." Daddy pointed to a spot to the left of the camera. A broad smile on his face. "This here man. John Carter Manning from Pettigrew."

"That's not necessary, sir."

"It's true."

"Thank you."

"Anyway, that's all I have to say right now. I love you all. Melissa. You're my sweetheart. Always have been. Tabby.

Stay strong. Brother. Get out while you can. Make a clean break. You'll do fine, just keep your eyes on your *real* Father," he said, pointing up. "And Cee Cee. Everything I did was out of love. I hope you can find it in your heart to love me."

His eyes glistened with new tears. The camera faded to cornfields again. That lilting tune from the beginning mingled with my father's voice. He was reading Langston Hughes's "Crystal Stair."

With trembling hands, I clicked the power button on the television. I fell back across the bed and let the tears come.

My father's conversion, though unorthodox, had been genuine. He had brought hardened criminals to Christ. How could anyone discount that? Not even me.

And through it all, he had thought of me. His love had not been perfect but it had the power to reach me, even after death.

I covered my head with a pillow and wept.

Chapter 26

WITH MY HANDS folded, I knelt in the darkness beside the bed and said a prayer for Abraham Benson.

And then on the bed again, I wailed and writhed. My heart cried out for Brother. I prayed for his safety and sanity. I prayed for his wife, a woman I'd never met. And somehow, just before drifting off to sleep, I remember praying that the Lord would forgive me for holding on to the hate and fear for so long.

Then after waking, tired and hungry, I slipped from the bed and knelt in prayer again.

My mind raced and sadness clung to my heart. My frantic thoughts centered around Abraham, of all people. Was he out of danger? The word *closer* occupied my mind. I felt impressed to pray in that vein.

"Lord, bring Abraham closer. Closer to total healing. Closer to You. Closer to me. Amen."

Only a few hours earlier I had wanted to kill the man. Now, I wanted nothing more than to talk with him. He had to be alive. God had to bring him closer.

Closer, Lord.

My mind drifted to my wayward brother again, a man

who still wanted Abraham dead. What had my father said in the video?

Get out while you can. Make a clean break.

What had he meant by that?

And John Carter? Dare I even think about the man? He'd rejected me. It was time to move on.

A knock on the door interrupted my wonderings. I wiped my face with my palms and went to the door.

"Yes?"

"Celine, it's Ulysses. How are you doing?"

I'm tired of fighting for what I don't really want.

I opened the door and looked up into his open face. "Everything and nothing."

"You're not making sense, Celine."

"More than likely I'm unemployed and definitely in trouble with the law. How do you think I should react? Click my heels?"

He lowered his fine head and scowled at me like only a grandparent could.

"I'm sorry," I said. "That wasn't fair."

"It's okay. I know you're under a lot of stress. I'm here if you need to talk." He placed a hand on my shoulder.

How could I even begin to talk to anyone about the emotions churning inside me? Part of me wanted to click my heels. Part of me wanted to cry my eyes out. If only I had tears left.

"Just spoke with someone at the hospital where Abraham's being treated. He's been moved out of ICU."

"He's still alive." My heart leaped and my stomach rumbled. I glanced at the digital clock on the nightstand—9:12 p.m. That cheeseburger and fries were long gone.

I thought of John Carter. My throat tightened.

"And what about John Carter? Isaac said the doctors thought that he would walk. Any more news?"

"Mr. Manning? Why don't you talk to him yourself?" Smiling, Ulysses stepped back, pulling me into the hallway as he went.

I screamed and covered my mouth.

"John Carter!"

His head had been shaved. A bandage was taped across most of his forehead. He moved closer to me and flashed that movie-star smile.

"Celine, I'd like to apologize. If that's okay with you?"

Chapter 27

MY MOUTH GAPING, I stood and nodded. John Carter took another step forward and cleared his throat. But he stood there for several seconds looking at me before he spoke.

His scalp was a stark white against the tanned skin of his face. The blue sweats he wore were tight across his thighs and chest. A hospital bracelet still dangled from his left wrist. His right hand was swaddled in white gauze.

"I was a fool. You came to me in goodwill and I was rude. Beyond rude. I'm sorry for anything I said and did that hurt you."

The sadness in his eyes tore me apart.

"I'm sorry, John Carter."

"No, Celine—stop. Don't feel sorry for me. You didn't do this to me." He swept a hand toward the bandage and his shorn head. "It's not your fault. I offended you."

A knock on the door made us both turn. It was Agent Hunt.

"Excuse me. Could you both accompany me to the kitchen?"

I moved to follow. John Carter touched my arm.

"I am sorry," he said.

"I know and I forgive you."

Agent Hunt led us into a dimly lit kitchen. Agent Skelly was seated on a bar stool in the corner, eating an apple.

"Good evening, Ms. Johnson. Remember me?"

"Yes, sir. Good evening."

I sat in the chair that Agent Hunt indicated. He seated John Carter across the kitchen table. Groaning and holding his right side, he eased into the wooden chair.

Hunt stepped aside to have quiet words with Skelly.

"Are you okay?" I asked John Carter.

He played with the bandage on his right hand. "I can walk. I'm okay. Just a little sore."

"You fell from the window."

"More like pushed. You've been crying."

"Pushed?" I ignored his comment about my crying. "Brother?"

"No, it wasn't your brother. He wasn't upstairs. Why were you crying?"

I clenched my teeth and looked away.

"Did you watch the DVD?"

My eyes still averted, I nodded.

"You okay?"

I shrugged. "I guess you could say that I've been a fool too. About my dad, I mean."

He frowned and turned his head to one side. "He was a good man."

"I know that now."

"Okay, kids," Agent Hunt said, clapping his hands like a schoolteacher. "I know it's late but this needs to be done. The quicker we get started, the quicker we get done."

"Done with what?" I asked.

"Questioning. We've still got a man at large, two agents

dead, and two suspects." Hunt pulled a third kitchen chair around and straddled it, resting his forearms on the back. "I know you've talked with Special Agent Fesperman here already but you know us Feds; we like to duplicate our effort."

My stomach let out a loud growl. Agent Hunt looked at me with eyebrows raised high.

"My goodness. That was a loud one. Can't have that." Standing up, he took off his suit coat and rolled up his sleeves. In the dim light I noticed the outline of a gun in his shoulder holster. "Got any peanut allergies? Lactose intolerant?" He was soaping up at the sink.

"What?"

He faced me, drying his hands with a dish towel. "I'm not much of a cook. All I'm good at is PBJ and milk. Hopefully, they have some bread around here."

"You don't have to do that, sir."

"Naw, no problem. Go ahead and start, Skelly. I'll jump in when I'm ready."

As Hunt pulled together ingredients on the counter across the kitchen, Skelly tossed the apple core in the trash and sat in the empty kitchen chair, his eyes on me.

"Agent Hunt, what's up with the light in here?" Skelly asked, glancing up at the frosted globe fixture overhead.

Agent Hunt answered, "Can't find any bulbs."

Skelly wagged his head and turned his attention back to me. "Oh well. Now, Ms. Johnson, when we last spoke I had not had the benefit of corroborating your story with Mr. Manning's here. It seems there are a few inconsistencies."

My stomach growled again. I pressed a hand against my abdomen.

"I'm sorry."

"It's okay." He glanced at Agent Hunt and pulled a pad

and the pink pen from his pocket. "Now, I'm still working on my time line. See?"

"Skelly likes his time lines," Agent Hunt said, placing a plate in front of me with two crustless peanut butter and jelly triangles. He followed it with a glass of milk. It brought a smile to my face.

"Wow. Thank you. I haven't had the crusts cut off in years."

"Always did the trick for Isaac."

Isaac?

"I'm his granddad," he whispered in response to my questioning look. He winked at me and went about cleaning up after himself.

Agent Skelly sighed and continued. "Now, when we spoke at the hospital, you said you saw your brother this morning."

I nodded and bowed my head for a quick prayer for my food and my brother.

"Sorry," Skelly said. "Don't mean to rush you. So you saw him but you didn't talk to him. Is that what you said?"

I swallowed and responded. "I did call out to him when I saw him at the fire."

"In the dark?"

He was rubbing me the wrong way.

"Yes, in the dark. I told you he has a distinctive walk. I spoke to him but he didn't say anything."

"So he was walking?"

"Running. I meant running."

"Running? Hmmm." He glanced at his notebook. "Mr. Manning says he saw you talking with your brother."

My eyes met John Carter's.

"Did you talk with your brother this morning?"

I chewed and swallowed and took a drink of milk.

Tell the truth, Celine.

"Ms. Johnson, answer the question, please."

"I did talk with my brother this morning. Yes, we had a conversation, if that's what you're getting at. But Mr. Manning was not present. He had nothing to do with it at all."

"When did this conversation take place?"

I stared at the man. He lifted his freckled face and stared back. In that moment, he looked like the kind of man who would shoot someone in the back. Even an unarmed man like my brother.

Or maybe these were good men in bad situations. Maybe they didn't like their jobs. But it was a job. A "J. O. B." as Tabby had said. Maybe it was hard slapping folks around in darkened kitchens in the boondocks but it was a living.

They had children who wrote with pink pens and biracial grandchildren who had survived hell. They were normal, I told myself and that helped me calm down. I took a deep breath and went on.

"I was getting to that. When I went to make the 911 call at my mother's house, I saw him there."

"Before or after you made the call?"

What does it matter?

"After. We spoke briefly. Actually, it was more like an argument. I urged him to not do anything stupid concerning Abraham Benson."

"I see. That clears things up. And now, about the truck."

"The truck?"

"They're bent out of shape about my truck," John Carter said. "Your brother's using it."

Skelly gave John Carter a warning look. "Mr. Manning."

John Carter studied the plastic hospital bracelet on his wrist.

"Now, Ms. Johnson. When you spoke to your brother at your mother's house, did you give him the keys to Mr. Manning's truck?"

"I never gave him any keys."

"Your fingerprints are on the truck."

"When I got there, the truck door was open. I closed it. I didn't want the battery to run down."

"How considerate. So the keys must have been under the floor mat."

"I have no idea where the keys were. Ask the owner. I've never been in the truck. I'm telling you the truth, Agent Fesperson."

"It's *Fesperman*." He screwed up his lips and stood up. "This afternoon you saw your sister and your brother in this house."

"Yes."

"Did you speak with your brother?"

"Yes."

"About what?"

"Nothing really."

"Care to elaborate?"

"No."

"Celine," John Carter whispered.

"I'm sorry. He wasn't very talkative. The house had been left open. My sister, who had come to watch one of our mother's DVDs, had walked in on him. And I then walked in on both of them.

"When Agent Buxton entered, my sister and I were trying to convince Brother to turn himself in. He jumped from the window. We tried to grab him but he slipped away and ran into the woods. And I'm guessing since you're here asking me questions you have yet to find him."

282

No answer from Skelly. And no reaction from Hunt. I took that to be a yes. Skelly finally drew a breath and shifted in his chair as he consulted his notes.

"Johnson Industries. Does the name ring a bell, Ms. Johnson?"

I shook my head. "Should it?"

"The name of a company your father started. Willed to your brother when your father died. Could be the source of some bad blood between your brother and Mr. Benson."

"Skelly," Agent Hunt said in a warning tone.

Skelly put away his sparkly pen and pad and took his perch on the bar stool.

"General, I'm all done," he said.

Agent Hunt moved forward, rolling down and buttoning his cuffs. He stood behind John Carter and rested a hand on the chair back.

"John Carter? May I call you that?"

John Carter swallowed and sat up straighter. "Yes, sir."

"Tell me about your relationship with Abraham Benson. Would you call it good?"

"Yes."

"Tell me about your employment with Benson Ridge. When and why did it end?"

"I've been a farmhand. Abraham taught me to drive a tractor when I was fourteen. I worked for him on and off during high school, and then again from January to March of this year. I quit because I wanted to spend more time working on a play."

The infamous play.

"Abraham is a friend. He didn't like it when I quit but there was no bad blood between us. In fact, he paid me while I produced the play."

"You're a filmmaker."

"Yes, but I do occasionally write things for the stage."

"Do you own a gun?"

"Yes. A hunting rifle."

My eyes widened in alarm.

"Do you know where it is now?"

"Since you're asking me about it, I would suppose Quincy Johnson Jr. has it. It was under the seat of my truck."

Oh no. They're going to kill him.

"The registration is in the wallet you took from me."

Agent Hunt's phone buzzed. He grumbled and snatched it from the holder on his hip. Answering it sharply, he stalked from the room. Skelly hopped off the stool and tapped on the back door. A uniformed man opened it. They had us surrounded, it seemed.

Keeping one eye on his prisoners, Skelly joined the man having a smoke in the darkness of the back porch.

"I'm sorry about the gun," John Carter whispered. "It was behind the seat. Unloaded."

"You didn't know Brother would find it. What did you mean earlier about Brother?"

"I think he's in the same trap your father was in." John Carter glanced over his shoulder at the men on the back porch. He lowered his voice even more. "Being a runner for the Front."

My face fell. "How do you know this?"

"It's just a feeling. He needs a way out."

I nodded and noticed Skelly blowing smoke to one side. He was glaring at us and doing the mean cop thing up right.

"Is your hand okay?" I asked, loud enough to be heard.

He looked down at it, flexing it within the thick dressing. "Yeah. It'll mend. It's a good thing I'm left-handed."

When I looked up, his eyes were on me. He was smiling. "About what you said in the hospital . . . "

I blushed and toyed with the edge of the plate.

"I've been praying for you." He reached across the table with his good hand and rubbed a finger along the opposite side of the plate. "And for your broken heart."

I could hardly breathe. I wet my lips and felt foolish for doing it. Happy and confused all at once.

"That's enough talking, Mr. Manning," Skelly said as he reentered the kitchen.

He didn't need to say another word. Even in the semi-dark room, his eyes were saying volumes. Fear rose up in me like a blister.

He pushed the plate aside and touched my hand. I smiled and looked away. His fingers were warm and comforting. It felt good to be noticed, to be desired. So why did I feel like running away?

I needed to concentrate on Brother.

Just then Agent Hunt marched back into the room. John Carter pulled his hand back.

Hunt put on his suit coat and positioned himself behind my chair. "I have one more question." He looked down at me and then across to John Carter. "Skelly here has this thing about timetables. I have this thing about connections. Connections, also known as relationships, give a foundation for motivations. And motivation is what my work is all about. Motivations make the world go round. But let's not get too philosophical about this thing."

He paused and looked at me again. "Ms. Johnson. Your relationship with Mr. Manning. How would you describe it?"

My heart had stopped beating. All eyes were on me, I sensed, and my voice had left me.

"Would you call it affable?"

"Yes, affable," I stammered and wrung my hands.

"Amorous? Affectionate?"

Why was he drawing this out? It was driving me insane. I pulled my eyes away from the tabletop. John Carter was looking at me and smiling. I looked away.

"Yes." The word had left me like a shot.

"And how about you, Mr. Manning. Is this mutual?"

There was no hesitation in John Carter's response. "Yes, sir. I'm falling in love with Cee Cee Johnson."

Chapter 28

WITH A CHANGE of clothes over my arm, I slipped across the hall to the bathroom and showered.

The light caressing my bedroom walls had reminded me of Christmas morning—warm and cold at the same time. Silly, since it was the middle of April. But somehow I half expected to smell the heady scents of gingerbread and peppermint.

I had paused in the hallway, listening to the sounds of sleeping men, the chirp of a bird outside, the rush of a passing truck. I was glad to be alive. Strangely, a word had occupied my dreams.

Learn.

Was it another word from God? I hoped so. Lingering memories from my "God high" yesterday were still vivid in my mind as the warm water splashed on my body.

After my shower, I planned to fall headlong into the Gideon Bible I'd found after Hunt and Skelly had finished with me and John Carter.

There was no telling what plans they had for their captives today but it didn't matter. I planned to celebrate my new freedom.

Sure, I was jobless (most likely) and my little brother was

still at large, but there was an excitement inside me about both events. I knew nothing about Johnson Industries. It sounded harmless. Knowing that my father had started a business and passed it on to Brother was a good sign. There was hope of another chance, a fresh start in both situations.

Hope.

I dressed in the bathroom, tied a silk scarf over my unruly hair, and tiptoed to my room where the little green Bible lay in the middle of the bed, spine up. I'd left it open to Proverbs 3.

My dreams about learning had prompted me to relearn the Scriptures I'd committed to memory in college. College had been an explosive spiritual high for me as I pressed into God. It had also drawn me away from everything that led me back to Pettigrew and Quincy Johnson Sr.

Scripture memory, fasting, prayer, church, and community service—all things that had gone hand in hand with my studies. On the outside I was a devoted sister in Christ and a diligent student. In reality I was merely seeking a diversion. But the result had been wonderful. I had grown closer to God than I would have without my tremulous past.

But this morning I wanted more than a diversion, a side trip of God. I wanted Him like never before. Hearing His voice yesterday had reminded me of just how good He is. He loves me. And I sensed that He wanted to talk to me.

Me. Cee Cee Johnson.

Near giggling, I grabbed the small Bible and pulled the comforter from the bed. I sat on a pillow on the floor and swaddled myself in the comforter.

Did other people feel this way about God? Did John Carter? My mother and Tab? And Brother? Did he even profess Christianity? My heart went out to him.

Whispering, I read verses 5 and 6 of the third chapter from

288

Proverbs: "Trust in the Lord with all thine heart; and lean not unto thine own understanding. In all thy ways acknowledge him, and he shall direct thy paths."

I had memorized the verse more than a decade ago but I hadn't taken it truly to heart. My trust had not been on God's understanding. I hadn't trusted Him to direct my paths. I had so much to learn.

Lord, teach me.

I closed my eyes and let the words I'd just read tumble through my mind.

Trust in the Lord.

My mind went to the possibility of not having a job. What would happen to my house? My savings and investments?

All my heart.

And what of John Carter? How did I reconcile these affections, these desires for him with what I knew to be right and practical?

Lean not.

Frustrated, I opened my eyes.

"How can I do this, Lord?"

With my finger, I stabbed the page at verse 5. Tears stung my eyes.

It's too much for me.

I pulled my finger slowly from verse 1, down the columns, letting my nails crease the thin paper. The crinkle-hiss of the pages seemed to mock me. A tear dropped on my thumb and ran down my wrist.

With me alone, it was too much. But with God . . .

My eyes were drawn to the first verse. Someone had lightly underlined the words "keep my commandments." And then below that, in verse 3, the words "bind them about thy neck" were underlined.

Bind what around my neck?

I read the entire verse.

"Let not mercy and truth forsake thee: bind them about thy neck; write them upon the table of thine heart."

Mercy. Truth.

The words were like daggers through the very core of my being. I had lived a life of "dress up." But now I could no longer wear a mask. If I was to be truthful and show mercy, I'd have to learn to be a new person. LEARN.

Lord, I want to be merciful and truthful. But how?

Straining at the verses once more, I tried to make sense of them. I had memorized verses 5 and 6 in the *New International Version*. Why couldn't Gideon Bibles be NIV? This version seemed so convoluted.

Concentrate, Cee Cee, you can do this.

I read the verses again from the beginning. One word impressed me like never before.

Heart.

That was the key. My heart had to be the place where I kept His truth and His mercy. Not my head.

John Carter's words came back to me: *"I've been praying for you and for your broken heart."*

My heart.

I flushed at the thought of him praying for me: But then it hit me. I had never prayed for my broken heart. I had spent countless hours complaining about it and saying "woe is me" but I had never taken it back to its Maker.

I set the Bible down and threw off the covers. Leaning forward, I bowed my head and prayed.

"Yes, Lord. I know now that there is help for my heart. You can heal it. You can heal me. From the inside out. I ask for Your healing now. Heal me of hate. Heal me of lying. Help me truly put Your commandments in my heart. I want Your commands and not mine. They will guide me into peace and wisdom.

"Oh, Lord Jesus, I need understanding. Help me bury Your Word so firmly in my heart that I won't be able to do anything but trust You. There will be no room for distrust or anything that looks like fear. No more fear. I trust You, Lord. And I love You. Amen."

No exhilaration washed over me. I opened my eyes. But there was no heavenly stardust drifting down. No angelic hosts singing my praise.

I lifted my hands in silent thanks. But there were no angels' wings brushing my fingertips. Only a hope that God was pleased and He was at work in me.

And because of that I knew there was hope for my family —especially for my brother, Quincy Johnson Jr., and his hate-filled heart.

Chapter 29

THE SMELL of eggs and toast drew me out of my room. Voices drew me to the kitchen.

"Good morning," Agent Hunt said, arranging three sets of plates and glasses on the table. A blue-checkered apron was tied tightly around his dress pants. The handle of his gun gleamed in the holster strapped around his torso. "How did you sleep, Ms. Johnson?"

John Carter stood barefoot at the stove, a dish towel slung over his shoulder and a spatula in his hand. He wore a sleeveless green T-shirt, jeans, and a Dodgers ball cap. Smiling at me over his shoulder, he said, "Good morning, Cee Cee."

Cee Cee?

"Good morning. I slept well, thanks." I averted my eyes and hoped the pleasure I took in the way he said my name didn't show.

Morning light filtering in from the living room cast a dreamy haze in the kitchen. Steve Inskeep's voice competed with static on the little radio propped on the windowsill. I moved toward the table and smiled at Agent Hunt. "How can I help out?"

"How about you make some tea?" Agent Hunt said,

winking back. "Hope you don't mind. I couldn't find coffee or lightbulbs."

He pointed to three boxes lined up to the right of the stove.

"I don't mind."

"I'm not sure where the cups are but the water's still hot in the teapot. I'll take Earl Grey."

I nodded.

"Cups are over here," John Carter said. He nodded toward the cabinet to his left as he folded green peppers, onions, and cheese into a thick envelope of eggs.

For a moment, my eyes followed the blunt edge of his thumbnail, up the contours of his bare arm, to a sharp horizontal line on his upper arm where his skin turned whiter.

He's not Steven, Celine.

"I'll take Earl Grey too," John Carter said, breaking me from the bad memory.

I found four white mugs on the bottom shelf of the cabinet. Hooking three of them on my fingers, I moved to the sink to rinse them out.

"I would have come for you earlier," John Carter said, leaning over me to drop dirty utensils into the sink. The faint aroma of oranges and onions came with him. "But I heard you praying."

"Mmm hmm," I responded, inhaling his scent and trying to hide it.

My heart was beating faster than I wanted. I watched him rinse his left hand in the running water. I felt self-conscious about the head scarf. Why couldn't I have braided my hair or something?

"You okay?"

"Yeah. God is . . . " I glanced up into his face. He was

frowning. My voice faltered. "Good. God is good."

"All the time," he added. The frown melted as he looked into my eyes. His breathing deepened as his eyes moved across my face. I wet my lips and held my breath.

Okay, Lord, what now?

I heard John Carter's words again: *"I've been praying for you and for your broken heart."*

I was sure he could hear my heart beating even above the gurgle of water over the mugs in the sink.

"All right, kids," Agent Hunt announced, "let's eat."

While John Carter and I were making eyes over the sink, Hunt had finished setting the table. The food sat steaming on a platter at the center. Long white candles stood unlit on either side. John Carter and I drew near.

"Mind if I say grace?" Hunt asked. Standing behind his chair, he bowed his head and began just as the phone on his hip buzzed. He groaned and prayed all the same. "Dear heavenly Father, we begin this day together with praise for Your everlasting mercy and grace. Thank You for this new day."

His phone buzzed again. The phone in the living room started to ring. Agent Hunt let out a sigh and continued louder. "Thank You, dear Lord, for the food You've provided and the company You've blessed me with. Bless our endeavors today. In Christ's name. Amen."

I sat down and stole a glance at the man. He was as surprising as his grandson. This man was in hot pursuit of my only brother but there I was praying that the Lord would truly bless his endeavors to bring Brother to justice.

I wanted this thing with Brother to end well. If there was anyone I could trust to end it well, it was Agent Hunt. Yes, he was a man with a gun, but what he had was more powerful than any gun. I hoped Brother would see that.

The phones rang again. Pulling the cell phone from its clip on his belt, Agent Hunt excused himself and went into the living room.

"I'm sure this has got to be hard for you," John Carter said. His lean muscular arm was extended toward me, pouring orange juice in my glass.

We were seated in the chairs we had occupied the night before. So much had happened since last night. My public admission to attraction was one thing. Could I follow through and allow my heart to go further with him in private?

I cleared my throat and spoke. "Hard? That's an understatement. I want to be close to you but I don't know what to do when we are. My mind goes back to how you touched me when we were in the canal together during the tornado. Part of me liked it . . . a lot . . . but part of me wondered if I should have liked it at all."

He tipped his head to one side and stared at me. My face flushed with heat. "That's not what you were referring to, was it?" I shoved eggs onto my plate.

Smiling, he lit the candles. Light danced in his eyes, across his perfect teeth. "Nope. I was talking about knowing that Agent Hunt is tracking down your brother. But it's good to know you like being near me. I like . . . "

Agent Hunt burst into the room. "We've found your brother," he told me.

I gasped. "Is he okay?"

"Yes, yes. He's fine. As far as we can tell. Agents have located him. They haven't apprehended him yet."

Hunt moved to his seat and rested his forearms on the table. "Last night, he sent us a message."

"When?"

"Shortly before we talked with you. He said he was will-

296

ing to let us bring him in on the arson charge if we give him assurance that he won't be prosecuted for environmental violations at Johnson Industries."

"Wait a minute. I'm not trying to be difficult here, sir. But I truly know nothing about Johnson Industries. Let alone violations."

"Well, until last night neither did we. Skelly shouldn't have asked you about it last night. He's a new regional leader. A little rough around the edges yet. Too many years in the field." Hunt chuckled. "Anyway, Johnson Industries turns out to have been an agricultural chemicals facility three or four miles north of here. At least that's what it was on paper.

"On the ground, it appears to be an empty shed with several rusty oil drums inside. Improperly stored, according to Buxton and other agents on-site. I would not be surprised if there are some drums buried around it. Your brother is a junior executive for a shipping company in Elizabeth City."

Junior executive?

"He lives in Elizabeth City. Not sure what he does there. You say you have located him?"

"He's on the site now. Barricaded himself in the shed. He's fired some shots at my men."

I bit my lip.

They're gonna kill him.

"With my gun," John Carter said.

"Yes, I'm afraid so. Prayerfully, he's familiar enough with a rifle not to kill himself."

Lord, please protect my brother from himself.

"I'm sorry, Ms. Johnson. I shouldn't have said that. You and Mr. Manning are free to go or stay." He untied the apron and tossed it across the chair. He took his jacket off a hook behind the door and turned to go.

I stood up. "Wait. What will happen to him when . . . ?"

"We'll take him into custody for questioning. Just like you were. No rough stuff. That's not our style. We have some environmental types waiting in the wings right now. Once we've got Quincy Jr. out of there, they'll move in to assess the area.

"I won't lie to you, Celine. He's in big trouble. Setting a fire. Two agents dead as a result. We need to see what's on that site before we make any agreement with him. He's going to be fine if he keeps his head. Keep praying. Don't stray too far—we'll be in touch."

Before leaving, he gave my shoulder a squeeze, smiling like a grandfather would.

Chapter 30

"I'M NOT SURE what to do next, John Carter."

He didn't respond. We had been eating breakfast in silence, sitting across from each other with eyes only for the food on our plates.

Thoughts of my baby brother lying in a pool of blood took my appetite away. How could I think about my own needs or wants when Brother was in trouble?

While John Carter had stacked the dirty dishes in the sink, I checked my voice mail. Sure enough, my only message was from my boss, placing me on indefinite leave. I was on the front page of the *News & Observer*. Breaking news on WRAL. I didn't blame Coulton for letting me go. I would have fired me.

The warm breeze coming through the window drew us outside. We sat on the back step, warming our toes and drinking our tea.

"Special Agent Hunt is quite a guy."

"Did you hear what I said?"

"After he sent the other agent to get a change of clothes for me, he sliced up the green peppers, grated cheese, cracked eggs. Of course I guess his motivation was to not let the prisoner handle sharp implements. Even if I was only a one-handed prisoner."

John Carter chuckled and set his empty mug down behind me.

"My brother is throwing his life away and all you can talk about is Agent Hunt."

"Cee Cee," he said, easing his feet into a pair of men's bedroom slippers and standing up. "You worry too much. Didn't God see you through the storm? He spared your life then. He won't let you down now. He'll take care of your brother. Everything's going to be okay. You've got to trust Him. God is good."

I nodded. "All the time."

My head knew he was right. But my heart . . .

Love.

The word came like a punch in the arm. I drew a sharp breath. Gooseflesh stood up on my arms. The Lord had given me three words. Listen. Learn. And now, love.

Love, Lord?

I looked at John Carter. He was looking at me with his head to one side.

"You okay?"

Love.

There it was again. From God to my heart.

"What? Yeah . . . yeah . . . I'm fine."

Did God command His people to love? As soon as the thought entered my mind, I knew the answer. Of course, He commanded us to love one another. But was He telling me to love *this* man?

John Carter reached forward and touched the goose pimpled flesh on my elbow. I flinched and felt silly for it right away.

"I'm sorry. I shouldn't have pulled away. It's just that . . . I'm . . . "

"I'm not Steven Kepler, Celine."

"I know that up here." I tapped my head and then my chest. "But in my heart, my memories are still so fresh. Maybe because I've allowed them to replay so much. And being here in Pettigrew where it all happened. It's just so hard, John Carter."

"Another place then? Is that what you're saying? Because after what you said in the hospital and last night, I felt like you want us to go further. You know I do."

"I do. I do. I really do." My mind drifted to reactions of townspeople seeing me walking the streets with a white man. *Stop it, Celine.*

"I want to take the next step and see if 'us' can happen, John Carter. I want to stop taking the easy road."

"And the easy road would be . . . ?"

"To just go back to Raleigh and pretend I don't have feelings for you. It would be easy for me to do that. Relatively speaking. But it wouldn't be the happy road.

"You're a talented, hardworking, compassionate man that I enjoy being around. I would be a fool to run away now . . . just because you're white."

"A fool?"

I gave him a "don't go there" glare. He chuckled.

"I watched the DVD."

"You told me. Remember?"

Smiling, he watched me as I drained the last of my tea and set my cup aside.

"My father had a hard life. Harder than I ever imagined. In a million years I would never have known how my blackened Jesus changed his life—and mine. He lived his later life in pursuit of a black Jesus. I want that too.

"A Jesus who is strong enough to see me through anything. To see me through helping my family during this difficult time. To see me through being jobless. To see me into a relationship of a different sort."

"Different? Not sure I like the sound of that. How about a black relationship with a white man?"

"You're doing that foolish thing again."

"And you're doing that diva thing again."

"Don't you dare go there." I pointed my finger.

He whispered the word *diva*.

"I'm not kidding," he continued out loud. "How about a black relationship? Black as in strong. Deep. Meaningful. Lasting. Should I go on?"

I gulped and looked away. The words gave me pause. "Let's take it slow."

"Fair enough." He turned and looked out across the yard. Sun glistened on the uncut grass waving in the breeze. The leaves on the trees at the edge of the nearby cemetery flipped up, revealing their silver undersides.

"Celine, have you seen where they put your father to rest?"

Wide-eyed, I shook my head.

John Carter nodded toward the cemetery. "His grave is over there. Can I show it to you?"

I followed him through the long smooth grass of the yard into the neatly clipped grass of the small gathering of gravestones.

Beyond several mossy headstones marked with names like Ross and Douglas, I saw a large rectangular concrete slab standing to one side. John Carter paused and spoke to me in a whisper.

"You okay?"

I nodded and followed him to my father's graveside.

"You came to the funeral?" I asked him.

"Yeah. Your mother's talking about getting a marker headstone. Don't know why she keeps asking me what to put on it. I'm not family. You should talk to her, maybe."

"You did a very nice job on the DVD, by the way."

"Thank you. The FBI has three others. His last testimony, he called it. They'll be using them in the hate crimes hearings."

I nodded.

"I wish I'd been here. I wish I'd been a better daughter, especially after I found out he was sick. I was so selfish and hateful."

The words caught in my throat. Tears welled in my eyes.

"I wish . . . I wish I could tell him just how sorry I am."

"You can."

"What, you want me to talk to the grave? That's Hollywood, John Carter. I think you spent too much time in Cali."

I wiped my face with the back of my hand.

"Talk to me."

"Talk to you? That's crazy. What good will that do?"

He moved closer to me. "Try it. You'll be surprised."

Looking down on the hard slab resting on the earth, I swallowed hard, took a deep breath, and started. "Daddy, I'm sorry for being such a bad daughter."

There, I'd said it and all I felt was stupid, particularly with John Carter standing there staring at me. He moved closer still and took me by the shoulders. I started. He squeezed hard and spoke to me in a deeper voice like some character out of a gangsta flick. It felt childish and trite.

"Cee Cee, you know I did all I could for you. You know I tried to do my best. But it was hard. And I was confused and cornered."

I tried to pull away. I didn't like this little parlor game John Carter was playing. It was weird and he was hurting my arms. His grip tightened and he continued.

"I wanted better for you, Cee Cee. You were my favorite. My sweet Cee Cee. I didn't want you to get stuck in this town. When you got mixed up with Steven, I didn't know what else to do. I had to run you away from here. Can you ever forgive me? I'm sorry. How can I show you that I love you?"

Enraged, I lifted my fists and pounded at John Carter's chest. "But he didn't love me. Not in a way that I knew it. Love is what you feel. It's a connection deep inside."

Love.

My body was trembling. I covered my face and screamed. John Carter pulled closer and smoothed my hair. His breath warmed my cheek. He was talking softly but I couldn't hear it. Other words were reverberating in my heart.

Listen to learn to love.

In that moment, I understood that love had to be more than a feeling. It was a destination. A place to pursue. From listening to learning to loving. It is a *doing* word. There is feeling in loving. And there is a connection. But there is also a depth to it. Like a hole in the ground with a slab over the top.

If I choose to listen only a little, then I would only learn a little. And as a result, that hole, that love would be shallow. But if I choose to listen a lot, then the love, in turn, could be boundless.

Could I listen to my father? Could I learn from him? Could I love him?

Help me, Lord Jesus. Please be black enough, strong enough for me. Please.

Sobbing into John Carter's chest, I spoke to my father.

"Oh, Daddy, I know you tried. I'm sorry for holding on to the hate for so long. I forgive you."

John Carter spoke to me quietly once more. "That's good," he said and then he lowered his head and pressed his lips against my forehead.

Chapter 31

"I'M SORRY. I shouldn't have done that." John Carter had pushed away from me and stepped back.

"Kissed me or done that silly voice?"

"Kissed you."

I had enjoyed the sensation of his soft, warm lips on my face.

"It didn't bother me."

"Nope?"

"The word platonic does come to mind."

"Not what I was going for. And there was nothing wrong with the voice I used."

"I must look a mess."

He brushed the back of his hand against my wet cheek. "You were his favorite. One of the many things he told me that didn't make it to the DVD."

The sound of a ringing phone interrupted the calm. Suddenly it felt odd to be standing in the cemetery hoping for another kiss.

I dug the phone from my pocket.

"Hello."

"Cee Cee, you've got to get here fast."

It was my mother, out of breath and yelling.

"Mama, calm down. What's going on?"

"It's Brother. He's bleeding."

"Brother's been shot!"

I looked at John Carter.

"I'll get one of Abraham's trucks," he said and hurried toward the path I'd taken the night of the fire.

"Where are you?" I asked her.

Mama let out a long, strangled sound. There was yelling and a good deal of thudding. No doubt, she had dropped the phone.

"Mama!"

I ran for the house.

"Mama!"

"Celine?" said a man's voice that was strangely familiar.

"Who is this?"

I flung the kitchen door open and ran to my bedroom.

"Isaac Hunt."

"What's going on?"

I pulled one of my suitcases from the closet and emptied it on the bed.

"She's fainted."

I froze.

"Who? My mother?"

"Yes, but she's being taken care of."

"And my brother?"

"Your brother? I'm not sure. There was a man here, I think, and he ran away." I heard more commotion in the background. Shouting and running.

"What's going on?"

"I'm not sure. I just got here. Abraham's doing a lot better. No small miracle. He's been moved here to the critical care unit."

I held my breath. My little prayer had been answered. I smiled and looked heavenward.

Thank You, Lord.

"Celine? Are you okay?"

I sat on the bed and let my breathing even out.

"Yes, I'm fine, Isaac. Where are you?"

"Finleigh General. Do you know where it is?"

"Yes. John Carter is coming around with a truck. We'll be there soon. Bye."

I threw a change of clothes in my bag while I dialed Tabby's number. Her machine picked up.

"Hey, Tab. Brother's in the hospital. I'm not sure what's going on. Mama just called me all frantic. I'm on my way to Finleigh General."

The front door banged open. In a blink, John Carter stood in the bedroom.

"Bye. I've got to go." I left my number and hung up.

"Celine, you okay?"

"I need to get my things, don't I?" I sat on the bed and held my head in my hands. "Mama fell out. Brother's probably dead."

"Let's go."

"John Carter, what if he's dead? They've shot him. He's not a good shot. Not a good runner. Just a scared kid. What if he's dead?"

"Cee Cee." He knelt beside me and cupped my face in his hands. "Let's go, honey."

With my hand firmly in his, he snatched up my purse from the dresser and pulled me to the truck.

Honey?

Chapter 32

JOHN CARTER had settled in a quiet mood with his left hand on the wheel and his bandaged right hand in his lap. Countryside flew by at lightning speed. Hog farms. Pine tree plantations. Chicken farms. A trillion ears of corn. Just one big blur.

"How can you be so calm?" I asked him.

"What did you say to me in the storm?"

"What?"

"In the tornado when I . . . when I held you. You said something."

My heart beat faster. I had tucked those memories away and placed them in the envelope marked "what fast girls think."

"I don't remember. I was saying parts of the Twenty-third Psalm in my head. Maybe I said some of it out loud. I don't know."

I looked at him. The green T-shirt stretched tight across his muscled back. The ball cap pulled low over his eyes. He looked like a boy. An All-American. Football playing. Tractor-driving. White-girl-dating boy.

A good ole boy.

What did he see in me? I needed to know. I swallowed the fear that rose like vomit in my throat.

"John Carter?"

"Yeah?"

We were nearing the city limits. He slowed to the speed limit of forty-five miles per hour.

"Can I ask you something?"

"Sure."

"What . . . um . . . Do you think I should look for a job locally?"

Chicken!

With raised eyebrows and hunched shoulders, he said, "If you want. It's up to you, Cee Cee."

He signaled left and slowed down as he entered the turning lane. The hospital entry was just ahead.

"That's not what you really wanted to ask me, was it?"

"No."

"Thanks for your honesty. Promise me you'll ask me the real question later?"

I took a deep breath. "I promise."

John Carter nodded and pulled around a police car to stop close to the ER door. "I'll meet you inside."

I opened the door and slid out. "I'm sorry for . . . "

"Go, Cee Cee. We can talk later."

"Ms. Johnson?" Someone called me from behind. I turned to face a policewoman. "Are you Celine Johnson?"

"Yes."

"And you, sir, please place the truck in park and get out."

John Carter complied.

"What's going on?" I asked.

She took me by the elbow and guided me into an empty emergency waiting room. "This way, please."

312

"Officer, wait a minute. Is this about my brother? Where is he? Is he okay? What's this about?"

She looked me in the eye and didn't respond until John Carter drew near. A male officer appeared, out of nowhere it seemed, and patted him down.

"He's good," the policeman said. He nodded toward me. Approaching footsteps halted the protest I was preparing to launch.

"She's here. Good." It was Agent Hunt, holstering his gun as he took long strides toward us. His face and shirt front were smeared with blood.

"Special Agent Hunt," I said. "What's going on? Where's my brother?"

He placed a warm hand on my shoulder. "He's fine. But he's taken Abraham hostage."

"What!"

"While he had us in a standoff in Pettigrew, your mother called him. Unwittingly tipping him off about Abraham being moved here. He says he won't talk to anyone but family. But your mother . . . well, she's too worked up right now. Could you speak with him?"

Our last real conversation had ended with him taunting me, calling me a sellout. Would he listen to me? God only knew.

Please, Lord, go before me.

"Yes, sir. I'll try to talk with him. My mother called me too. Said something about blood. Is my brother hurt?"

"Hurt? Quite the Houdini, your baby brother. No, the young man faked a gunshot wound to the foot. We rushed him here. Then he cut me with a paper clip he had stashed inside his mouth, stole a gun, and holed up in Abraham's room. Wish he was on the right side of the law. Kid's got skills." He smirked and walked away. I slipped my hand into John Carter's and followed.

Agent Hunt led us down a long shiny hallway and through several sets of double doors. At the last set, four policemen and Special Agent Buxton stood with guns drawn, their eyes fixed on the doors marked Critical Care Unit.

"Mr. Manning can't come with you," Agent Hunt said.

John Carter gave my hand a squeeze and let go.

"God is with you, Cee Cee," he whispered.

Fear churned in my stomach. My legs tingled with pins and needles. "I can't do this, John Carter."

"You can't. But He can. Do you trust Him? He's black enough."

He squeezed my shoulder and smiled. Seeing his loving face strengthened me and gave me an idea.

"Agent Hunt, can I take my purse in?"

"I'm afraid not."

"How about my tape recorder? I want to conduct an interview."

He screwed up his lips for a few seconds then nodded. "Okay. I'll be right in there with you. Nothing funny, Ms. Johnson."

"Don't worry, I'm not as skilled as my brother. I only know how to smile and ask questions for a living."

Chapter 33

I HAD SLIPPED the scarf from my hair, rolled it on my thigh and retied it like a headband around my nappy locks. After turning up the collar of my shirt and smearing on a little lip gloss, I surrendered my purse to the female officer and followed Special Agent Hunt through the double doors.

"Quincy," Agent Hunt called out.

There were six doors opening to a lobby area. A nurses station, minus nurses, stood at the center of the lobby. Five of the six doors stood wide-open. The sixth door was only slightly opened.

My heart sank.

Why, Brother?

I fingered the buttons on my recorder and searched my memory for verses. Psalm 23 came to the fore.

Yea, though I walk through the valley . . .

"I've got your sister here with me, Quincy."

Today, I am Celine Johnson. Reporter.

"Stay here," Agent Hunt whispered and walked a few steps away from me.

Mercy. Truth.

I looked down to make sure the tape was cued.

Listen. Learn. Love.

Hunt dabbed at his face with a handkerchief. "Quincy. Talk to me."

"Where's my mother?"

Brother's tone was coarse. I started to have second thoughts.

"Carla Celine is here," Hunt tried again.

"I don't wanna talk to Oprah."

That's good. I didn't come to talk to you, Brother.

"Quincy," started Hunt. "You can't get what you want unless you let Mr. Benson go. Don't make this worse for yourself, son."

"I ain't your son."

Agent Hunt motioned me forward. "Say something to him."

"He can see me." I saw the crack in the door widen.

"He needs to hear your voice."

"I didn't come to talk to him."

Agent Hunt flashed me a confused look. I cleared my throat and walked toward the door. I felt him close behind.

"I'd like to conduct an interview, Brother."

He grunted. "Figures."

"Is Abraham still alive?" I asked through the door.

"Course. I ain't killed nobody, Cee Cee. I just want some assurance they ain't bringing Johnson Industries into this."

Meanwhile, you're giving them so much more to charge you with.

"May I come in? Five minutes."

This would be the quickest interview I'd ever conducted. I scanned the mental notes I'd stashed at the beginning of the week. So much had happened since that night in Abraham's office. I scratched my notes. Seat-of-the-pants was my only option.

My legs quaked with a new feeling. Pure excitement.

"Brother?"

There was the sound of a chair being moved.

"Yeah, come in."

Agent Hunt held the door for me. Holding my tape recorder in plain sight, I took two steps in before I stopped.

Brother still wore the yellow shirt I'd seen him wearing at the Ross house. It was still streaked with blood as was his right pant leg and shoe. His face was twisted in a snarl as he waved a handgun.

Had he really shot himself in the foot? Where was John Carter's gun? My heart broke for my baby brother and the man he held prisoner. Could I truly help bring this situation to a good end?

Bandages covered Abraham's arms from shoulder to fingertips. Under the tightly tucked blanket, his left leg seemed more bulky. A cast, perhaps. Tubes from his nose snaked across his chest and connected to a machine next to the bed. His face was marred with cuts and bruises but his blue eyes were no less sharp.

Lord, help. Please.

I greeted my brother with a nod. Brother snorted his disapproval and turned his attention to Agent Hunt behind me.

"That's far enough, Agent Hunt. Put your gun on the floor and kick it toward me. Cee Cee, you and your tape recorder can come here."

A silver bracelet on his right wrist caught the light. To my knowledge he was never one to wear jewelry. Except for the small band of gold on his left hand, nothing else on his body glittered. I was compelled to take a closer look at the bracelet.

He pointed to a chair in front of him. I allowed Agent Hunt's gun to come to a stop before I starting walking again.

I pushed my shoulders back and looked again at the bandaged man in the bed.

"I'd like to finish our interview, Mr. Benson. If you're up to it."

"Interview!" Brother growled. "You've got to be kidding me. I want some assurances about Johnson Industries. I want him to tell the truth about . . . "

Cutting my brother short, I said, "I like to finish what I start." I gave him my best TV smile before leaning in toward the bed to place my hand on Abraham's arm. My breath caught at the amount of heat I felt leaving his body.

I'm so sorry, Abraham.

Fighting the urge to burst into tears, I placed my hand in my lap. Abraham Benson was not the monster that I thought he was. He was human. He could bleed. He could die. He had loved and lost. He had a heart and it beat for God. If only I'd seen it earlier.

"That's fine, Carla Celine," Abraham said.

I smiled again. His body had been weakened but his voice was just as strong. I sat in the chair Brother had indicated and glanced back at the bracelet on his wrist. A medic alert bracelet. Just as I thought.

Had Mama told me anything about Brother being ill? I couldn't remember. But wait . . . yesterday in the bedroom with Brother and Tabby. She had asked him about medication.

There was hope. I had my angle. I nodded and clicked the record button and stated my full name and the date. Then I extended the recorder toward the bed.

"Please state your full name, sir."

"Abraham Benson."

"Is that your full name, sir?"

He cleared his throat and said, "Karl Abraham Benson."

"Karl. Similar to my first name. How about that? Thank you, Mr. Benson. Now, let's start with a little background, shall we? You have three sons. Tell me about them."

Abraham wet his lips and stared at me. I glanced across the room at Agent Hunt. By the puzzled look on his face, I figured I was on the right track.

"Mr. Benson, did you understand the question? Your three sons. Let's see, the youngest will be ten soon. His name is Patrick Benson. He's the child from your union with Olivia Ross Benson. And then your oldest child, Isaac Hunt, is also Special Agent Hunt's grandson. By legal adoption."

I paused and nodded to the shocked FBI agent at the door.

"Isaac was born to your union with Beatrice Douglas Benson. A marriage that you hid for their protection from your family. But we can get to that later."

Abraham's breathing had quickened. His eyes were stretched wide. I heard movement behind me but I slid to the edge of the seat and continued.

"Sons are very special. I'm sure you agree with me. One day I hope to have one or two myself." I chuckled. "Even though I'm not married and I don't have any kids, I consider myself a mother of sorts.

"There are a handful of little ones in my church who call me Mom. Sometimes I buy them clothes and take them to McDonalds. A few times I've even paid for medicine or taken them to the doctor. They're not my children by birth or even adoption but . . . "

I hunched my shoulders and paused for effect.

"You've done that sort of thing for one particular young man, haven't you, Mr. Benson?"

Abraham lowered his eyes. "Yes, I have."

"Would you consider this young man your son?"

"Not with the way he's acting right now."

"Does he know about what you did for him?"

"I don't know. I never asked him."

"It doesn't appear that he does."

He clenched his jaw. "I suppose it doesn't."

"Perhaps someone should tell him. How could we expect him to know unless he's been told? Surely he can't expect to show gratitude if he doesn't know."

"I'm not looking for gratitude, Carla Celine."

"Cee Cee," Brother said. "What's going on?"

"Well, Mr. Benson, tell me what you are expecting? Respect? A bond? How was any of that to happen if he didn't know? He's a smart young man, even got a little Houdini in him, so I hear; but he doesn't read minds.

"You've paid for his medical treatment. You've helped him get a job he's not qualified for. What else? I think he should know. I think you should tell him the truth."

Abraham took a deep breath and cleared his throat. Slowly, he lifted his eyes to a spot over my head. "Quincy Jr. . . . . "

"What's going on here? What kind of trick is this, Cee Cee?"

"You wanted the truth, didn't you? Be quiet and listen to the man."

Listen. Learn. Love.

I turned back to Abraham. He went on. "I'm sorry for being so secretive. Your father and mother thought it was better this way."

"What are you saying?" Brother asked.

Abraham went on. "You can ask your mother who paid for the trips to the Duke doctors and the medicine for your bleeding disorder. I'm not sure what you're getting after with Johnson Industries, but we can talk."

What bleeding disorder?

I stood and looked at Brother. Confusion knotted his face. Nervous energy churned in my stomach.

Listen. Learn. Love.

"So, you know about my disease?" Brother asked Abraham.

"What disease?" I whispered and quickly regretted it. Brother flashed me an icy look.

"I know more than you think," Abraham continued.

"Like what?" Brother asked, waving the gun in a circle.

"Like the Benson men who have been harassing you. Threatening to kill your wife. You've got her hidden away. It's good that you're trying to protect her but let General Hunt here help you. They can protect her and you. They can make this mess stop, son. You don't have to keep doing what they're telling you to do. There's a way out."

Abraham stared at Brother for a few moments before looking at me and continuing. Brother was wagging his head. Indecision twisting his features.

"Your father wrote you and your sisters letters but they were destroyed in the fire. He loved you and wanted you to be provided for. So, give General Hunt here the gun and we can sit down and talk about it. The FBI will still have to take you in, but I hold nothing against you. You are truly like a son to me."

With a deep sigh, Brother lowered the gun. I slipped it from his hand and hugged his shoulder.

"You did the right thing, Brother," I whispered. Was he near tears? I wanted to hold him like I did when he was small and hurt. Just hold him and kiss the pain away. But those days were gone.

Swallowing my tears, I stepped around him and handed

the gun to Agent Hunt. He had come closer to pick up his own gun from the floor.

"And you didn't do too shabby yourself, Celine," Hunt whispered as I passed by him. "I'll see you outside. Can I borrow that tape recorder?"

Smiling with relief, I nodded and slipped the recorder into his hand. I was free now, and in a way, so was my brother.

Epilogue

∽⃝∽

"I'M NOT READY for a long-term relationship," John Carter said. His dark curls waved in the early fall breeze. He wore a white polo and smelled slightly of sweat and a sweet musk. Our little pigtailed shadow, Isabel, had attached herself to his back. Giggling, he squatted on all fours with a brown-skinned girl for a hump.

She crossed her dark eyes at me and I laughed.

"Why are you saying that to a child," I asked, smoothing the grass from her hair. She and John Carter had been playing leapfrog while I packed up our little picnic. "She's not going to understand."

"I was trying it out. See how it felt to give someone the brush-off."

"I didn't give you the brush-off. I said I was not ready for a long-distance relationship. I was trying to sell my house, remember?"

He arched his thick brows and nodded. Isabel gave his neck a squeeze and kissed his cheek. "Finally, a female gives me a *little* sugar."

I rolled my eyes.

"Bye bye, John Carter."

"Bye, my sweet."

He watched the little girl skip away before turning to me. "You sold your house in May. It's September. Lord knows what you've been doing since then. Got some big chocolate brother on the side?"

"John Carter!"

"Catty says you've been back since the beginning of the month."

"You had started teaching."

"Man, if I knew that teaching would scare you away . . ." He stood up and brushed the grass from his jeans. "I'm trying to make sense of things. That's all. You tell me one thing in your e-mail and another in person."

I winced and gathered trash and half-eaten food into a bag. In the distance I saw Isabel playing ball with her godfather, Isaac, on the concrete pad that was once the floor of the old red barn.

The entire yard had been razed. Thick grass now grew where the cinders of the main house had stood. The hush of dried cornstalks mingled with the rustle of pecan trees overhead.

Across the fields, my mother was visiting with Abraham and Catty, now living in the Ross house. Abraham was recovering nicely, though he used a cane now. I was staying with my mother and learning to love my family all over again, especially my brother. He was in prison now but free in Christ. We had spent long hours on the phone getting to know one another better over the past few months. Funny how things had come around for Brother and me.

But as for me and this white man?

Listen. Learn. Love.

John Carter turned his back to me and stuffed his hands

in his pockets. "I don't know what to think or do, Cee Cee. I don't want to rush things with you. I told you that. I understand about your history in this town but . . ."

"I want to ask you that question now."

"Question?"

I stood up and looked into his beautiful eyes. "The real question I started to ask you that day we rushed to Finleigh General. Can we walk and talk?"

He nodded and helped gather up our basket and blanket.

"Don't know if you've noticed but I worry a lot."

He let out a dry chuckle and led the way across the cornfield to the Ross house.

"I worry that you don't really love me." I didn't turn to see his stare. "That this attraction is merely some brief infatuation. Don't take this wrong. But I worry that it's like what I call the 'all black babies are cute' reaction I've seen with some white women. That black baby's gonna grow up into a black kid one day. And he might not like you, and you might not like him anymore. Cute wears off. And then what?"

He let out a long sigh and kept walking. We walked for several minutes in silence. The Ross cemetery with my father's new headstone was in sight when John Carter finally spoke.

"You're not cute, Celine." He took the blanket from me and placed it on a split rail fence that ran along part of the Ross property. I set the picnic basket on the ground near my feet. Voices in the distance drew my eyes temporarily away from his gaze.

My mother saw us and waved from where she stood with Isaac, Catty, and Abraham on the Ross house's new back porch and ramp. I waved back.

John Carter touched my chin and pulled my face up to his. I swallowed a squeal.

"You're beautiful, Celine. The first time I saw you on TV, years before I met your dad, something stirred inside me. I was attracted to you even then. I pushed it aside 'cause I thought, *man, that's Cee Cee Johnson. Wasn't she wrapped up in that mess with Steven Kepler? Besides, she's black and I'm not.*

"But the light I saw in you. Despite all that I know you've been through. The presence you had on TV. The way you flash those eyes and turn those lips up into that smile. Even so, my attraction to you is not just on the outside." His breathing deepened and he wet his lips.

"But after holding you during the storm, I knew that I'd never be able to let you go. I wanted you to be a part of my life. Maybe you would choose to walk away from me but that storm wasn't going to take you away from me."

He smoothed a hand over my hair. I gulped.

"I love you. The way you smell. The way you laugh. The way you move. The way you are just you. Brown or black or purple. I would love you no matter what. Thank you for sharing about your cancer scare. I know that was big for you. Opening up and sharing. I want to share my world with you. I want us to travel together. I want us to do your father's play together, like you e-mailed me about.

"It's gonna be a tough time—you and me in this town. But I thought we'd settled that. Jesus is black enough. Right?"

Barely breathing, I nodded.

He moved his right hand to the small of my back and took a firm hold of my chin. His warm breath flooded over my mouth.

"Can I kiss you?" he asked.

I licked my lips and nodded again.

Smiling, he released me. "I'll keep that in mind."

"What?" I screamed, stumbling back against the basket on the ground. He gathered the blanket from the fence and continued toward the house. "Hey, what was that all about?"

It didn't matter at that moment that all eyes were on me. I jogged past him and stood in his path.

"Don't ever do that to me again, John Carter Manning."

He looked to the group on the porch a stone's throw away. Then he looked down on me with his head tipped to one side. "Now this is more like it, Diva."

And without another word, he kissed me long and soft on the lips. My mother let out a little shriek. From the noises coming from the porch, she had most likely collapsed. And if it weren't for the firm hand at the small of my back, I too would have fallen out.

Acknowledgments

TO MY LORD and Light, thank You for choosing me and using me. It is only through You that I can listen, learn, and love.

Many thanks to my friends and family for their support and prayers. To my critique partners—Pam Meyers, Tammy Barley, Anne Greene, Tyora Moody—you're the best. Kisses and hugs.

Thank you to Cynthia Ballenger and the hardworking crew at Moody Publishers and Lift Every Voice.

To my agent, Les Stobbe, thanks for believing in me and my writing. I really appreciate your input and support.

If you enjoyed this book, you will also enjoy

The Making of Isaac Hunt

ISBN 978-0-8024-6269-5

Find it now at your favorite local or online bookstore.

www.MoodyPublishers.com

Loving Cee Cee Johnson
Discussion Questions

NOTE: This discussion guide is ideal for use by a mixed-race Christian group. If at all possible, meet regularly over a meal or dessert. Commit to meet and commit to participate. The questions posed in the guide are meant as a springboard. If other things in the chapters resonate with you, go with that discussion.

Be flexible. Be prayerful. Be honest.

Listen. Learn. Love.

Prologue   Cee Cee's father destroyed something that she treasured. Has someone ever done that to you? How did you react?

Chapter 1   Cee Cee is an intelligent, professional woman. Why do you think she is running from her health problem?

Chapter 2   Why does Cee Cee get really uptight about John Carter's involvement with her family?

Chapter 3   Cee Cee was more than a little nervous when she thought she was on a date with Bob, her white cameraman. Have you ever been on a date with someone of another race? How do you feel when you see a biracial couple in public?

Chapter 4   Cee Cee has lied about her hometown. Why do you think she must face the consequences of having let the lie live on for so long?

Chapter 5   Who has helped you through the tough times in your life?

Chapter 6   When Cee Cee discovers the connection between her black activist father and the former staunch racist Abraham Benson, she's floored. What are your thoughts about that relationship?

Chapter 7   Cee Cee is impressed with Isaac Hunt. In her words, she "would have called him a black man on a dark night." What do you think she means by that?

Chapter 8   The family secrets that are revealed during Cee Cee's interview with Abraham Benson are disturbing. What should she do with what she now knows?

Chapter 9   Cee Cee tells Abraham she hates him. Is Abraham's reaction believable? Why? Why not?

Chapter 10   Isaac talks about the price of justice in reference to doing the right thing even at great personal loss. What does he mean by that?

Chapter 11   Cee Cee and John Carter's first meeting is less than ideal. How did her description of his eyes strike you?

Chapter 12   John Carter saves Cee Cee's life. Why does that upset her so?

Chapter 13   Catty and Cee Cee talk about racially motivated hate. Is Catty's way of thinking childish or right on-target?

Chapter 14   Cee Cee's confession to Isaac frees her. Abraham's confession to her does not. Why not?

Chapter 15   John Carter corners Cee Cee with a question that she doesn't want to answer. What's disturbing her most about this handsome white man?

Chapter 16   John Carter pursues Cee Cee further by expressing feelings for her. She thinks he's gone too far. What do you think?

Chapter 17   Cee Cee is determined to make Abraham pay for his abuse of power by finding evidence of his misdeeds. Will her efforts pay off? Why? Why not?

Chapter 18   How could Cee Cee have handled things differently when she went to Benson Ridge Farms the night of the fire?

Chapter 19   The truth about her brother and her feelings for John Carter slap Cee Cee in the face. It's almost more than she can take. What should she do?

Chapter 20   What do you think of Isaac's theory of the hate-filled heart?

Chapter 21   During her ride with Special Agent Buxton back to Pettigrew, Cee Cee seeks validation. Why is his approval important to her?

Chapter 22   Cee Cee's reunion with her brother and sister was less than ideal. What did she want most for her brother?

Chapter 23   Cee Cee's sister, Tabby, thinks Abraham Benson is innocent. What do you think?

Chapter 24   What challenges did Cee Cee face after seeing her father in another light?

Chapter 25   How has Cee Cee's life been affected by the conversion her father, Quincy Johnson Sr., experienced?

Chapter 26   How do you think Cee Cee felt at John Carter's surprise appearance?

Chapter 27   For a brief moment, Cee Cee felt hatred for Special Agent "Skelly." How did she resolve those feelings?

Chapter 28   The Lord leads Cee Cee to study Proverbs 3. Read the entire chapter out loud. Do you reach the same conclusions that Cee Cee does? Or different ones? If so, what are they?

The Negro National Anthem

Lift every voice and sing
Till earth and heaven ring,
Ring with the harmonies of Liberty;
Let our rejoicing rise
High as the listening skies,
Let it resound loud as the rolling sea.
Sing a song full of the faith that the dark past has taught us,
Sing a song full of the hope that the present has brought us,
Facing the rising sun of our new day begun
Let us march on till victory is won.

So begins the Black National Anthem, written by James Weldon Johnson in 1900. Lift Every Voice is the name of the joint imprint of The Institute for Black Family Development and Moody Publishers.

Our vision is to advance the cause of Christ through publishing African-American Christians who educate, edify, and disciple Christians in the church community through quality books written for African-Americans.

Since 1988, the Institute for Black Family Development, a 501(c)(3) nonprofit Christian organization, has been providing training and technical assistance for churches and Christian organizations. The Institute for Black Family Development's goal is to become a premier trainer in leadership development, management, and strategic planning for pastors, ministers, volunteers, executives, and key staff members of churches and Christian organizations. To learn more about The Institute for Black Family Development, write us at:

The Institute for Black Family Development
15151 Faust
Detroit, MI 48223

We hope you enjoy this book from Moody Publishers. Our goal is to provide high-quality, thought-provoking books and products that connect truth to your real needs and challenges. For more information on other books and products written and produced from a biblical perspective, go to www.moodypublishers.com or write to:

Moody Publishers/LEV
820 N. LaSalle Boulevard
Chicago, IL 60610
www.moodypublishers.com